ECHOES OF US

TEEGAN LOY

Dreamspinner Press

Published by
Dreamspinner Press
5032 Capital Circle SW
Suite 2, PMB# 279
Tallahassee, FL 32305-7886
USA
http://www.dreamspinnerpress.com/

This is a work of fiction. Names, characters, places, and incidents either are the product of author imagination or are used fictitiously, and any resemblance to actual persons, living or dead, business establishments, events, or locales is entirely coincidental.

Echoes of Us
© 2013 Teegan Loy.

Cover Art
© 2013 Christy Caughie.
Cover content is for illustrative purposes only and any person depicted on the cover is a model.

ISBN: 978-1-62798-299-3
Digital ISBN: 978-1-62798-298-6

Printed in the United States of America
First Edition
November 2013

To my way-cool brother, who probably thinks I'm insane but loves me anyway.

ACKNOWLEDGMENTS

I want to say thank you to my wonderful beta reader Nancy for helping me make this a better story. A special thanks to Laura for answering my music questions. And many thanks and a thousand smiles to all my C & B peeps. You all know the secrets behind this book and who inspired it.

CHAPTER ONE

Most people think falling in love is a wonderful thing. It isn't. It fucking ruins everything.

"I'VE CHANGED my mind," I said as the town came into view. "Let's go home."

All I got out of my best friend was a headshake punctuated by a roll of her bright blue eyes.

"You don't understand. I can't handle my family or this stupid town," I whined and pulled the car over to the side of the road, right next to the sign giving everyone a hearty welcome to Mayville, population 1,945 respectable citizens. I wondered if that number included my brother, who had recently moved back home because his life was in crisis again. Translation of a life crisis for Lucas was he just broke up with another girl.

"Rylan, how bad can it be?" Maggie asked.

A strange noise came from my throat, and my mouth fell wide open. She didn't understand. We were walking into a shark tank with fresh bait dangling from our necks. We were different, and different didn't fly in this town. People were more comfortable with cookie-cutter images of themselves. Neither of us fit into their idea of a perfect world.

Maggie sighed and straightened her short skirt. Her bracelets rustled when she raised her hand to run her fingers through her long dirty-blonde hair, with ends colored blue like her nail polish. She wore multiple earrings in both ears, and the only way her tattoos wouldn't show was if she was bundled in a snowsuit. I didn't think I could convince her snowsuits were in style here, not with the sun out and the temperature hovering around a near perfect seventy-five degrees.

The thought made me cringe. I didn't want Maggie to hide who she was. No one should have to pretend. I'd done it the whole time I'd lived in this town.

My blond hair had always been too long, and I didn't have enough muscles on my slender frame. My brother constantly made fun of me, telling me that sometimes I was more feminine than my sister. I slid my bracelets off my wrist and stuffed them into the glove box. There was no need to add extra fuel to the fire.

"What are you doing?" Maggie asked.

"I don't know. Possibly having a panic attack," I said. "I don't know why I'm here. I don't fit, and it drives them crazy. I have no idea why my mom even wanted me to come home?"

"You're her kid," Maggie said. "It's a big day. It's her fiftieth birthday."

"I bet she sometimes wishes—"

"Don't say it," Maggie interrupted and scowled at me. "Come on, Rylan, let's go to the party. I promise I won't leave your side."

I sighed and banged my head against the steering wheel. "Fine," I said, flooring the gas pedal and sending gravel spraying everywhere as I pulled back onto the road. I felt like I was driving to my execution.

The Blake family house was on the outskirts of the small town. It used to be in the country, but the town had grown enough to catch up to our land. My dad said he wasn't going to let urban sprawl swallow up his farm. Maybe that's why I ran to Chicago the moment I graduated from high school. My parents didn't like the city, and Chicago was one of the largest cities in the United States. It was a good way to keep them out of my life.

The gravel under the tires crunched when I turned into the driveway.

"Holy shit, are you kidding?" Maggie shouted. She rolled down the window and hung halfway out like a puppy enjoying the wind. "This is a farm?"

"My mom may love the rural life, but she likes nice things, and she has good taste. It's a renovated barn."

Questions poured out of Maggie as I pulled the car up to the house. I think I had to tell her four times we didn't have any animals. My dad was a grain farmer; we'd never had cows or sheep or chickens.

"Every farm has animals," she argued.

"Fine, we raise cats, and I'm sure there's a dog somewhere," I said.

Maggie smiled triumphantly. "I knew there were animals."

As soon as I put the car in park, she jumped out, opened the back door, and dug for her bag. I stayed in the car, watching my foot twitch against the gas pedal until I noticed my mom standing on the porch waving at me.

"Christ," I muttered.

"Rylan, hello," my mom shouted.

My mom was either possessed or she'd hit the cocktails already. I reluctantly pocketed my keys and got out of the car, forcing a smile to my lips.

"Hi, Mom," I answered. "Happy birthday."

She glided down the steps and embraced me, awkwardly patting my back before she let go. I felt her fingers tangle in my hair where it touched my collar. I'm sure she was horrified.

Maggie popped out of the back seat and grinned. Mom's face didn't change, except for a small twitch that turned the corners of her mouth down for a few seconds when she spotted Maggie. She recovered quickly. Only a trained eye would notice the sour taste that filled her mouth when she scanned Maggie.

"Mom, this is Maggie Mae Stewart," I said. The less information I released on Maggie, the safer it would be for her. I wasn't going to label her as my roommate or my best friend. No one had to know what Maggie was to me.

"Hello, dear. Welcome to our home," she said and gave Maggie a hug. "Please call me Kimberly."

"Thank you so much for having me," Maggie said, beaming back at her. "This place is phenomenal. Rylan said you had a hand in the creation of this magnificent home."

My mother's face brightened. "Yes, would you like a tour?"

"I'd love one," Maggie said.

She was good. I don't know why I ever worried about Maggie. Her major was public relations, and she knew how to work people. My mother would never know what hit her. Once she graduated, Maggie was going to be a star in the world of PR.

"Rylan, go help your brother. He's in the back," Mom said as she dragged Maggie away, talking a mile a minute about all the work it took to change a smelly barn into a home. It may be lovely to look at, but it had been stifling to live here. It was going to be a long week.

The house wasn't much different from the last time I was home. A few updated pieces of furniture and a couple of new pictures on the walls. I noticed my face did not grace the Blake hallowed walls of fame. I did see a tiny photograph on the mantel of my dad and me when I was nine years old. We had just come back from the field where he'd let me drive the combine. It was probably the last time he had been proud of me.

A trip down memory lane was the last thing I needed right now. I sighed and hauled our bags up to what used to be my childhood room. The room had been changed to a reading room and a place for my mother to store her art supplies. She rarely painted or drew anymore, but she liked to pretend she was still an artist.

There was no sign I had ever occupied this room. It was even a different color. My mom had probably cracked open a bucket of paint the moment I headed for Chicago. The dark purple I'd painted the walls had irritated the shit out of her. For one year, she wouldn't come near my room, and she let me keep the door closed at all times. It was a great success on my part.

The walls were now a lovely neutral taupe. A daybed and two stiff chairs had replaced my bed. There was a blow-up mattress leaning against the wall with a pile of sheets and blankets stacked on the chair. I grimaced when I thought about sleeping on the floor, but the daybed didn't look much better. At least she hadn't relegated me to the shed.

"Rylan," my brother shouted from downstairs. "Mom said you were supposed to help me."

Some things never changed.

"Get your scrawny ass down here!" Lucas shouted, louder this time. Lucas's idea of me helping him was barking out orders, while I did all the work.

"Fuck," I mumbled.

My brother waited impatiently for me at the foot of the stairs. I held my breath, anticipating some comment about my hair being too long or my earring or some other less than clever thing about my physical attributes.

"Hey," Lucas said.

I gave him another minute, but he said nothing to me. Lucas looked the same except for the bags under his eyes. His brown hair was trimmed neatly, just like my mom liked it. The khakis he wore were the same color as my bedroom wall and his golf shirt was a lovely shade of stone with tiny red stripes.

"Um, hey," I said back.

"I need to go pick up the ice. Could you finish setting up the bar?" Lucas asked.

"Where's Dad?"

"Went with Kelli to get the cupcakes," Lucas said. "I have to go now or Mom is going to shit her pants."

He disappeared before I could say another word. Everyone was acting strange. No one had said one derogatory word to me. Dad and Kelli would have to pick up the slack or I was going to start checking ID's.

I walked through the house and went out back. The largest blue tent I had ever seen was set up in the backyard. A small circus could put on a performance in it. It made me wonder how many people were coming to this birthday party. The bar was off to the side by the stage. I vaguely remembered Kelli telling me they were hiring some band that was popular in the area.

Lucas had a good start on the bar, so it didn't take long for me to get everything in place. Sneaking a few sips before the party was well within my rights, even if I wasn't quite twenty-one.

"There you are," Maggie said.

"Here I am," I said. "You look okay."

"I'm fine. Your mom is nice." Maggie sat down on the grass and messed with her knee socks. "She asked a lot of questions about us."

"What did you say?"

"Nothing. I deflected the questions by asking about the house and her birthday and your brother and sister." She picked up the glass and the vodka bottle sitting by my foot and sniffed it. "You seem a little more relaxed."

"I took the edge off," I said.

She leaned against my legs and poured a shot before handing me the bottle to put back on the shelf.

"Rylan!"

"That would be my brother, Lucas," I said, refilling the glass.

"Relax," Maggie said, and leaned forward to kiss me on the cheek at the same moment my brother walked around the bar. He whistled, and I wanted to punch him for being such a jerk.

"Introduce me, baby brother," Lucas said.

"Maggie Mae Stewart," Maggie said. She rose and held out her hand.

"Really?" Lucas asked.

Maggie laughed. "Why would I lie about my name? And yes, before you ask, I'm named after the song."

Lucas and Maggie continued chatting while I hauled most of the bags of ice to the bar and dumped them into the giant galvanized washtubs. Lucas may have carried one bag. Maggie added the beer, pop, and water bottles to the tubs. I did a final sweep of the bar and figured it would pass my mother's scrutiny. Lucas cleared away the empty boxes, and we admired our work for a few minutes.

"Lunch," my mother shouted from the porch.

Lucas was gone in a flash, dragging Maggie with him. I cringed when I saw my dad and sister waiting for me on the porch.

"Hi," I said. "The place looks great."

My sister rolled her eyes, and my dad yawned. It was the end of planting season, and I was sure he'd spent countless hours getting the crop in the ground.

"Did you get all the fields seeded?" I asked my dad.

"Yes. It was a godsend that your brother came home and helped me. I probably couldn't have done it without him."

The unspoken words screamed at me, and I tried not to feel guilty for leaving the farm. Farming was fine for some people, but it wasn't for me. It never had been, and that was just another sore spot between my dad and me.

"That's great, Dad," I said. We stared at each other for a few uncomfortable moments. I waited for the criticism, but the second my dad started to say something about my unkempt hair, my sister shut him down.

"Dad," Kelli said firmly. "You promised Mom."

He clamped his mouth shut and left me standing on the porch with Kelli. She had the same dark circles under her eyes as Lucas and my dad.

"How are you?" Kelli asked.

"Okay," I said carefully, trying not to frown at her. This was strange, because we usually didn't do the small talk. We usually didn't talk at all. The last time I'd seen her had been six months ago when my mother insisted we all meet at the halfway point. It had been a disaster. I'd lasted exactly two days before I hightailed it back to Chicago.

"How are you?"

"I'm...." She paused and closed her eyes. "I'm fine."

The door opened, and Maggie came out carrying a tray with two plates stacked with sandwiches and two glasses of lemonade.

"Hi," she said to Kelli. "I'm Maggie Mae Stewart. You must be Kelli."

I nabbed my plate from Maggie and scurried away. Everyone was acting really weird, which meant I needed to spike my drink if I was going to make it through the evening

Lunch didn't last long enough, and I spent the rest of the afternoon dodging strange questions and following my mom around as she barked orders to everyone.

When the people started arriving, my mom shifted into hostess and tour guide. I was almost positive everyone at the party had seen the house before.

The band showed up several minutes late, and my mom almost went into cardiac arrest. Maggie diffused the situation by asking about a woman who just arrived wearing a huge flowered hat and directing me to get my mother another cocktail.

"She's interesting," my brother whispered, pointing at Maggie. "Shocked the shit out of the folks. I think they thought your roommate would be a guy, and she's definitely not a guy."

"Don't start with me, Lucas," I said.

"I'm just making an observation," Lucas said, holding up his hands in a mock surrender. He grabbed a drink and wandered away. I shook my head and went back to the bar to refresh my lemonade.

"Can I get a beer?"

The voice sounded like nails dragging down a chalkboard, and I considered crawling away before he could see me. Lucas's best friend was a total ass and had tortured me at every opportunity he could find.

"Get it yourself," I snarled when I stood up.

"Ah, the prodigal son returns." Seth sneered.

"Fuck off," I said, staring at him. Seth looked old, much older than he should. His out-of-date dress shirt was stretched tight across a stomach that hung over the waistband of his sagging jeans. His hair was noticeably thinner, and I couldn't resist running my fingers through my thick blond hair and making sure Seth saw me do it.

It was hard to believe this was the guy who once beat the shit out of me because I got my ear pierced when I turned fifteen. My brother and his friends had worked harvest for my dad when they'd noticed it. Seth decided it wasn't right for me to wear an earring. Said it looked gay, and gay boys weren't allowed in this town. I had just started to think about my sexuality, but I'd never breathed a word about it to anyone. It freaked the shit out of me to think someone could tell I might like guys by things I wore.

Seth and Andrew had tackled me and ripped the earring out of my ear. They then proceeded to beat the crap out of me, while my brother watched, doing nothing.

"Come on, sweetheart, open the bottle for me," Seth taunted, swinging his beer in front of my face.

Before I could respond, Maggie stepped in and grabbed his bottle, then twisted the cap off and flicked it back in his face. "Here you go, sweetie. Wouldn't want you to fuck up your nails," she said.

Seth stared at her, and she growled at him, sticking her tongue out so he could see the metal stud that rested in the center of her tongue. He backed away, stumbling over his feet, and I collapsed on the ground, laughing.

"I can't leave you alone for one second," she said.

"Thanks. He's a fucking jerk. Can I remind you how much I hate this place?"

"Come on, babe, the party is in full swing. It'll be easier to blend in if you at least try to have some fun," Maggie said.

"Okay, let's go check out the band. They don't sound half-bad," I said and burst out laughing again. There was no way we would ever blend in with this crowd, and I would proudly tell anyone I didn't ever want to blend in here.

The evening progressed painfully slowly, but with Maggie's help I managed to keep my lemonade nice and tart. I was almost numb enough to ignore everybody until two girls from my high school graduating class walked by and started whispering and pointing at Maggie.

She rolled her eyes and said something about their lack of style. They tried to say something shitty about Maggie's hair. It didn't work. I think one started to cry when Maggie told her she dressed like an extra from a bad '80s music video.

"A splash of neon is a statement, but you look like a blinking sale sign hanging over a discount store," Maggie said.

I snorted lemonade out my nose and clutched at my sides, laughing as the girls ran away. I was so thankful for her witty sarcasm I allowed her to drag me out onto the dance floor. The band was playing songs I'd never heard before, but Maggie was having a good time jumping around like an idiot. People stared at us, but most were buzzed enough to not really care.

The tempo of the music sped up, and Maggie spun me around so quickly I banged into someone. I turned around to apologize, and came face to face with someone I hadn't seen since I was a senior in high school. I seriously could have survived the rest of my life without seeing this guy again.

"Rylan?" he said. "It's me, Jesse."

Images of a dark-haired boy flew around my head and made me dizzy. Jesse stepped toward me, holding out his hand. I stumbled back into Maggie because there was no way I was going to let this guy touch me. I twisted away before Jesse could grab my wrist and hightailed it off the dance floor with Maggie jogging behind.

"Slow down," Maggie said. "What's wrong?"

"The ghosts are out in full force tonight," I muttered. I'd never told Maggie the story about Jesse and how he broke my heart, and I certainly wasn't going to do it tonight. "I need another drink."

There were questions on the tip of her tongue, but something in my face told her not to ask me anything now. "Okay, I'll go get you something." She eyed me. "I'll be right back."

"It's fine," I said. When Maggie walked away, I slid back into the dark of the evening. Kelli snuck up behind me and put her arms around my waist. I almost clocked her.

"Jeez, you're wound up," Kelli said.

"Why is Jesse Channing here?"

"He married Sierra Johnson, and Mom is good friends with Sierra's mom," Kelli said. "I think the whole town is here anyway. It was slated as the social event of the decade, you know. Is something wrong, Rylan?" She sounded concerned.

"No," I answered quickly. I didn't want her asking any questions about Jesse, so I covered by pointing out other people and asking questions about them. Kelli hung out with me until she saw one of her classmates. She waved at the girl and bounded away. I sank to the ground and leaned against a tree. Coming here had been a huge mistake.

Maggie finally showed up with more lemonade, which I gulped down before she could explain what took her so long.

"Better?"

"No," I said, scowling at her.

"Demons?" she said.

"They're everywhere," I muttered.

Later in the evening, after we'd toasted my mother and eaten cake, people finally started to go home. Jesse approached me again, but I flipped him off, and Maggie puffed up like a mama cat and told him to get the hell away from us. He looked incredibly sad, and for one small moment, I actually felt bad, but he made his choice and it had almost destroyed me. I owed him nothing.

The band played its last song and packed their gear. Soon it was just a few stragglers hanging around. It didn't take long for my dad to clear the rest of the people out. Maggie deserted me and went inside with Kelli to get ready for bed.

I headed toward the house, hoping to sneak inside, but my mom spotted me and waved me over. I glanced into the dark of the evening and considered making a run for the shed, but I was too tired and didn't feel like sleeping with the cats. I slid into a chair and stared at her. My dad sat down next to her and grinned.

"That was a great party, huh, Kimmy." He put his arm around her. He must have been feeling no pain. My dad wasn't a guy who hugged anything on a regular basis.

"Yes, Davis, it was. Thank you, and thank you for coming, Rylan."

She made it sound like I was some random guest. I didn't know how to respond.

"So, boy, how long have you been dating Maggie?" His speech was slightly slurred.

"I'm not dating Maggie," I said.

"Why not?" my dad asked.

"She's my roommate, not my bedmate."

"Rylan," my mom snapped.

"What?" I said innocently.

"She seems like a nice girl," my mom said. "She has a strange sense of fashion, though. And all those tattoos. Those things are permanent."

Maybe it was the liquor, or the snide comments from my mom about Maggie that made me snap. "I'll be sure to let her know," I said sarcastically.

"No woman is going to date you when you're living with another girl," my dad said.

"Fine by me," I snorted.

"What's that mean?" My dad set his beer on the table and stood up. He still created an imposing figure, but I wasn't a kid anymore. I wasn't going to shrink away this time. Plus I had the added bonus of being slightly drunk. It fueled my bravery.

"What do you think it means, Dad?" I asked, standing up and putting my hands on the table to face him.

"Don't get smart with me, boy," my father snapped.

"Davis, Rylan. Stop it," my mom said sharply. "I'm sure Rylan didn't mean anything."

"Really, Mom? I'm pretty sure I did mean something," I said.

"Don't talk to your mother using that tone," my father snarled.

"Fuck," I whispered under my breath.

"I could cut you off," he threatened. "School costs a hell of a lot of money and you can't even find the time to call your mother. Maybe if you came home for a visit."

I started to speak but my dad started yelling again.

"And another thing, why are you living with that strange girl? I think—"

I slammed my hand on the table. "I don't give a shit what you think, Dad. I know you guys don't like me. I can deal with that, but Maggie is my best friend, so leave her out of this."

My dad spluttered, and my mother looked horrified. It would have been easy to walk away from this argument, but I'd had enough. I wanted to sink the final nail into my coffin and be done with them.

"There's never going to be a girl. Ever. I'm not interested in girls." I dropped my empty glass on the table and headed toward the door to collect my things and get the fuck out. No way I was staying in this fucking house. Maggie and Kelli stood in the doorway, wide-eyed and frozen.

"Rylan!" my dad roared. "Don't you walk away from me. We are not done with this conversation."

I sighed and took a deep breath before I turned to face him. "Do you really want to continue, Dad? Would you like me to spell it out for you in plain and simple terms?"

"Rylan," Maggie whispered in a warning tone.

Years of pent-up feelings rose to the surface and exploded out of me. My parents made me feel like it was my fault for being different, like I did it just to hurt them. I always felt like I needed to apologize every time I came down the stairs.

"I'm gay, Dad. You know, I like guys. Girls need not apply and all that shit," I sneered.

For a few minutes, no one said a word until the lightbulb in my dad's head went on like a beacon and the entire countryside quieted. At first, I thought he was going to lunge across the table and punch me in the face, but a small touch on his shoulder from my mom stopped him. At the last second, he excused himself, slammed his fist into the doorframe, and stomped into the house swearing loudly.

My mom frowned, straightened the tablecloth, then lit into me for upsetting my dad. I had to turn my back on her and count to ten to avoid telling her to fuck off.

She didn't let up, so I grabbed my discarded cup, jumped off the porch, and headed toward the bar to refill my glass. Unfortunately, all the bottles were empty. The only thing left was a warm beer sitting at the bottom of the washtub. I cracked it open and started to drink, but my mom ripped it out of my hand and dumped the contents on the ground.

Rage and hurt filled me. I wanted to scream and cry at the same time. I hung my head, avoiding my mother's stare until she burst into tears and started babbling about how this couldn't be right, that I had to be mistaken, that it was just a phase.

"It's not a phase, Mom," I said. "I'm gay. I know what I like."

She actually cringed and backed away from me like I was contagious. But it didn't stop her from continuing to argue with me until Maggie stepped in between us and whispered something to my mother. The sobs stopped and she walked back to the house, leaving us standing in the middle of the yard. I thought about asking Maggie what she'd told my mom, but I didn't really care what words she used. At least the crying had ended.

"We're leaving," I said in a shaky voice.

"You can't leave," Kelli said. "Both you and Maggie have been drinking."

I sighed and sat down on the ground, then pulled my knees to my chest. Kelli and Maggie joined me and put their arms around my shoulders.

"I'm tired. We've been up since two in the morning," Maggie said.

"Just go upstairs and sleep it off. I'll wake you before Mom and Dad get up," Kelli said.

"Why are you being nice?" I asked.

"Rylan, you're my baby brother." I looked at Kelli like she was completely insane.

"That never meant anything before."

She hugged me tighter. "I was jealous of you. Always have been."

"Of me? Why?" I asked.

"Because you've always gone after what you wanted, dressed and acted like you didn't give a shit about what anyone thought. You're talented and special, and you're not afraid of anything."

"I'm afraid of everything," I choked.

"He is," Maggie confirmed. "Once, I was sitting in the living room and Rylan screamed so loud I thought someone was murdering him. Even our next-door neighbor heard him. She came rushing over to our house wielding a golf club like it was a machete, and she's eighty years old. We found Rylan perched on top of his desk shouting about a giant weasel that ran across his floor. Mrs. Morgan burst out laughing and got down on her hands and knees, talking softly to something she called Harry. A few seconds later, a cute little ferret poked his nose out from under Rylan's bed. It was one of our neighbor's missing pets. Mrs. Morgan picked him up and left, laughing."

"I didn't know it was a ferret."

"You grew up on a farm," Maggie fired back.

"Mom doesn't allow any critters in the house. There's not even spiders in the farmhouse."

Kelli burst out laughing. "He's right."

The tension shattered and we all started to laugh. When I finally caught my breath, I frowned.

"I'm sorry, Kelli. I didn't mean for this to happen."

"I know," she said quietly and patted my cheek. "And really, it shouldn't matter who you want to be with. Go get some sleep."

The sound of my parents arguing filled the house as we crept up the stairs to my room. Kelli promised to wake us early, which in farm language meant before the crack of dawn. She shut the door, and I buried my face in my hands, feeling the guilt wash over me. It was my mom's birthday, and now she and Dad were arguing because I'd outed myself.

"Stop feeling guilty, Rylan," Maggie said. She pulled the covers back on the daybed and signaled for me to get in. I wasn't going to object to sharing a bed. She crawled in behind me and spooned with me.

It seemed like only ten minutes before Kelli was whispering in my ear, telling me it was time to get up. No matter how poorly I felt, I wasn't going to stick around. I poked Maggie and she groaned, but she didn't complain. We had a long drive, and I wanted to get the hell out of here without another confrontation.

"Take care, Rylan," Kelli said. "You can call me anytime."

"It goes both ways, Kel," I said. I'd said things like this before, but this time I actually meant it.

Kelli smiled and hugged me. I sighed and picked up the bags, then followed behind Kelli and Maggie, who were chatting like long-lost friends.

There wasn't any noise in the house, which was a little odd. Whenever my dad drank, he snored like a chainsaw. I kept my hopes up for a clean getaway.

The front door creaked and we all froze, staring down the hall at my parents' bedroom door. Nothing happened, and I was able to relax a fraction when we made it out to the car. Maggie crawled into the front seat as I shoved our bags into the backseat. My spirits lifted higher when I started the car and jammed it into reverse, but it was short-lived when I spotted my mom coming out of the house.

"Shit," I said. I considered stepping on the gas and racing out like I hadn't seen her, but I decided against it. I put the car in park and waited. This was her show. Maybe she was just coming out to wave as we drove away. But she walked all the way out to the car and tapped on my window. I rolled it down, and she leaned in, lightly touching me on the shoulder.

"Be happy, Rylan," she said, smiling sadly. "I really don't understand any of this, but...." She looked away and dabbed at her eyes.

There wasn't anything I could say to lighten the moment. It felt like a final good-bye. I was heading into my senior year of college, and it was time for me to make my own way in the world, to create a spot that was just for me. This small, gossipy town was neither what I wanted nor where I needed to be ever again. If no one could accept me for who I was, then I didn't need to be around.

"I'm doing the best I can, and your father will come around," she said.

Sadness surrounded her, and I had to blink several times to stop the tears. It pissed me off that my family could make me feel like an unsure little boy. I knew who I was and what I liked, but with a few words and a pointed look, they could turn me into a spineless, whimpering child who questioned his choices.

The urge to retaliate, to stick up for my choices, was intense, but I wasn't up for another argument that would only result in more hurt feelings. My nerves were raw, and I'd probably say something terrible.

I settled on returning her sad smile. I doubted my father would ever get over finding out his son preferred the company of men. I wondered if someone would tell Lucas what went down the night before. Deep down, I was pretty sure Lucas already knew about me, but Lucas liked to live in the happy clouds. He believed if no one ever spoke the words out loud, then it couldn't be true.

Kelli had been the big surprise. I never thought I'd find her in my corner. She had always ignored me. I figured it had something to do with me being the baby of the family and her being stuck in the middle.

"I'll call you when we get back or something," I mumbled. We both knew I wouldn't place that call. She was almost to the front steps when I muttered good-bye. She looked like she'd aged a few years, and once again, I felt like it was my fault.

As I backed the car out of the driveway, I spotted my father standing next to her on the front porch, staring at me. The harshness of his glare made me feel like the car might burst into flames at any moment.

"Fuck," I said.

A warm hand slid across my shoulder. "Not your fault, Rylan," Maggie said.

I'd almost forgotten she was in the car.

"Sure feels like it," I mumbled. "I'm sorry."

"The good news is it's out now and you don't have to worry about it anymore," Maggie said. She swept her hair away from her eyes and stared at me.

I snorted. "Right, no worries."

Maggie squeezed my shoulder. "That's not what I meant and you know it. Don't get mad at me. If you knew they were going to freak about this, why didn't you just lie about us. I would have gone along with anything you told them."

"I wasn't planning on telling them anything. I don't see why there has to be an issue with who I want to sleep with. It's not like I brought a guy home and fucked him on the kitchen table. I don't even have a boyfriend."

She snorted. "You never have a proper boyfriend, but you're right, it shouldn't matter who you want to fuck." She leaned over and kissed my ear. "It'll work out. Just be happy you live so far away and don't have to deal with this on a daily basis."

"Don't think I'll ever be welcome back there again," I muttered. The sad thing was I didn't really care if I ever came back. Next time would be worse. There would be stares and questions, because that was how things were in this town. You could whisper your secrets to a tree, and somehow the town would find out. By the time we got back to Chicago, the entire world would know my business.

I gnashed my teeth and gripped the steering wheel.

"Let it go, Rylan. It's out now, and you can't control their reactions," Maggie said, then turned up the radio.

For Maggie to say something like that was jaw-dropping. She was always the one who wanted answers to every question. She wanted to talk things out, analyze the situation and fix things, no matter how long it took. She never let me off the hook when something big happened in my life, and this counted as a huge moment.

I always told her she should have majored in psychology and not public relations. She told me there wasn't much difference.

Maybe this was her gift to me. She always knew when to push me or when to pull back. This was definitely a time to step back, because I was worn out. Of course, she could be waiting for us to get a few miles out of town before she nailed me with the questions. Instead of driving myself crazy, I settled on staring at the road and letting the music playing over the radio take over everything.

Music was always my refuge. It could heal anything. Music was there when everything else was going to hell and life threatened to consume me. It was there when things were good or bad or boring or a fucking roller-coaster ride. Music never judged me. It settled me and kept me grounded.

IT WAS two hours into the drive before Maggie finally opened her mouth. I held my breath, waiting to be interrogated about my feelings for my family and what I was going to do next, but she started talking about our new roommate.

"So, I don't know a lot about him except his name is Jade and he's in his last year. I think he's majoring in art, or was it architecture, or accounting?"

She continued to list several other majors with absolutely nothing in common with the other.

"Jeff said he's nice and quiet, but he likes to let loose on the weekend, or nights when he doesn't have to study. He loves music, so you guys have that in common."

"Most people like some sort of music, so that doesn't mean anything," I said.

Maggie ignored my comment. "Jeff didn't say much about his personal life at the moment, but when they lived in the dorms, he was very popular with the ladies."

I rolled my eyes. "Maggie, I don't care who he sleeps with. I'm taking a break from any sort of physical interaction with people."

My comment made her giggle into her hand. "That's the only sort of interaction you ever have with people."

"Are you including yourself in this category?"

"You know what I mean, Rylan. You only interact physically. You never get involved emotionally."

"Why are we having this conversation? I'm not going to talk about this right now. I don't do relationships. Every time I try, my heart gets torn to shreds. It's not worth it. Besides, we don't even know the guy. The only thing I do know is I'm not getting involved with my roommate."

She stared at me and raised her eyebrows.

"Shut up, Maggie. I'm not getting involved with my roommate." I paused and added a dramatic "Again."

"But what if he's so hot you can't help yourself?" she asked.

"No," I said firmly. "Absolutely not. I'm not looking to get involved with anyone. It complicates everything. Maybe he likes boobs and it will be you getting involved with our roommate."

She whacked me on the head with my notebook.

"Hey," I shouted. "Do you want me to drive into the ditch?"

"Have you been writing?" Maggie asked as she flipped through the pages of the notebook. The pages were filled with disjointed sentences, random words, and scribbles. "I guess this means no." She traced a few of the doodles with her finger and frowned at me.

"I haven't had much time," I muttered.

School had been crazy for both of us. Finals had been difficult, and then right after the semester ended we headed to Maggie's hometown for a quick visit, followed by this disaster of a trip. It didn't leave much time for creativity.

"You used to write some of the best depressing shit when your life was in disarray."

I growled at her, deciding not to offer a comment. I really didn't know what to say because it was true. I was good at writing sad shit.

"You're getting that look," Maggie said.

"I don't have a look," I said.

Her laughter filled up the small space of the car. I wanted to push her out and leave her on the side of the road for animals to ravage, but then I wouldn't have anyone. Maggie always listened to my complaints when things were crappy. Her shoulder was always available if I needed to sob about everything that was awful. She was with me when times were good, and she was here when I felt like life was burying me alive in shit. I would have to keep her.

"You have many looks," Maggie said smugly.

I furrowed my brow and concentrated, trying to flush all the emotions out of my entire body. It only made Maggie laugh harder. I needed to work on my stoic face.

"Okay, fine," I huffed. "What look?"

"That look you get when you're thinking nothing is ever going to work out for you again, like you're never going to be happy, like everything that is wrong in the entire world is your fault."

"Must be some look," I said. I snuck a peek into the rearview mirror. My face looked like it always did. I had no idea how Maggie could read my emotions like an open book. "You know I'm not good with change."

She rubbed my knee. "I know, but I'm still here and not planning on going anywhere. And we're going back to our own little house, only Jeff won't be there anymore, and Rylan, you know that's a good thing."

Hearing her say all that made me feel a tiny bit calmer. She was right about Jeff. The whole thing had been a fucking disaster when feelings became involved. Not mine, because I didn't do feelings anymore. Okay, maybe feelings had crept into my heart a tiny little bit. But I shooed them away before they turned into something serious.

Jeff got a little upset when I didn't return the spoken sentiment. What was I supposed to do? Jeff graduated, and I had another year to go. It wasn't like I was going to tag along with the guy. It was supposed to be a casual thing, but Jeff had to go and say the three most dreaded words in the universe.

"Can I put one of your CDs in?" Maggie asked. She grinned at me and batted her eyelashes, begging me with a long litany of please, please, please.

"I didn't bring any with."

"I did." She waved a CD case in my face.

"Okay fine," I finally agreed. "But only so you'll shut up."

Maggie beamed at me and quickly jammed the CD into the slot before I changed my mind. There weren't a lot of people I let listen to my music.

"Oh, lighten up and enjoy," Maggie said as she sang along.

I tried to put the critic in my head to sleep, but I always managed to hear things that made me cringe. "Jeesh, I should have…."

"Shut up, Rylan," Maggie said. She reached across the car to place her hand over my mouth. I licked her palm and she shouted at me. We spent the next hour singing and arguing. She told me how wonderful my music was, and I pointed out all the mistakes in the recording and some awkward lyrics.

Relief flooded my body when the final track ended and Maggie flipped over to the radio. She leaned her seat back, turned her head, and stared at me with her pretty eyes. Even though I didn't date the ladies, I knew a beautiful girl when I saw one, and Maggie fit that bill. She had an easy beauty, not the overwhelming type that scared people away. People flocked to her, men and women. She was never arrogant or diva-like.

"We should make a pact."

"What sort of pact?" I asked.

"We only have one more year of undergrad, and I think we should loosen up a little and have some fun. Time is running out on us. Soon we will have to be adults and get real jobs so we can complain about how much we hate them."

"What is this fun thing you speak of?"

"Well, for one thing, you should play your music in public?"

"Um, that sounds like it only involves me, and it definitely doesn't sound like fun at all," I snorted. "I'd probably die of embarrassment, or people would throw things at me that would hit me in the head. You'd have to take me to the hospital to get stitches, and you know how I feel about going to the doctor. My only option is to say no."

"Just think about it, okay," Maggie said. "You're really very good, and I'll be your own personal fangirl. Mrs. Morgan would probably join me, so there you go, two fans already."

"New subject," I said.

We spent the next few hours speculating about our new roommate again. Maggie offered to text Jeff to ask him a few more questions, but I shook my head. I wasn't going to get involved with this guy in any way, shape, or form. Which in layman's terms meant I didn't give a shit if he had a cute ass, sculpted abs, or nice hair. He could be mean, hairy, and toothless for all I cared. It was all the same. Maggie took up enough room in my life. I didn't need anyone else.

"Stop it," she said.

"What now?"

"You're telling yourself you don't need anyone but me," she said.

I pursed my lips and felt my eyebrows knit together. "No... fine. Fuck, how do you do that?"

"I know all your moods, my darling," she said.

I grunted. "Maybe we should get married. It would make my folks happy."

She pretended to swoon, fanning her face with her hand and clutching at her chest like she was having a heart attack. "It's the proposal I've been waiting for all my life. Did you practice in front of a mirror, because it was perfect." She punched my arm. "I love you, but I also want sex in my life."

"I suppose that would be a problem. Unless I bought you a dildo or some other sex toys."

"Aren't you sweet, but I prefer a warm body some of the times," she said. "We'll find our happiness. I promise."

I thought about laughing in her face, because she knew I didn't believe in a happily ever after. In my world, happiness lasted until the afterglow of orgasm turned into a sticky, sweat-filled moment when what I needed was a shower, not cuddling.

It took a few harsh nips to the inside of my cheek to keep from snickering. If I laughed, I would be subjected to one of her pep talks about love. At that moment, I wanted to wallow in self-pity and be miserable for a few more days. I deserved to be grumpy. It had been a shitty month. To save my sanity, I conjured a lovely fake smile and showed my beautiful white teeth to her. It probably didn't fool her, but she didn't sling any happiness clichés in my face, so I was safe for now.

Maggie changed the subject again, talking about her summer schedule and her plan to have more fun. I didn't remember agreeing to the plan or pact or whatever the hell she called it. It was going to be a long summer.

The road stretched on forever. We switched places so Maggie could drive for a while and I could take a nap. When I woke up, the scenery had started to change from desolate to a few scattered towns dotting the landscape. I got in the driver's seat again, and slowly the land filled up with more and more houses until finally we were in the city. I felt like I could breathe again. It would be nice to slide back into the anonymity of the big city.

The relaxed feeling didn't last long when I tried to pull into the driveway of our house. A car stuffed with junk blocked my spot, and I immediately hoped our new roommate was mean, hairy, and toothless.

CHAPTER TWO

"IS THAT him?" I asked.

"Probably, I don't think some random person just parked in our driveway," Maggie said. She didn't seem all that concerned.

"How did he know we'd be home early?" I asked.

"I sent him a text before we left this morning," she said. She jumped out of the car and waved at the vehicle currently occupying my parking space.

"Wait," I shouted at her, but she was already standing by the other car.

The car door opened, and my brain suddenly short-circuited. It started when I spotted the tips of the guy's sun-kissed brown hair poking out from beneath a baseball cap.

Damn, this didn't look good.

He climbed out of the car, smiled brightly, and flashed a full set of white teeth. He definitely wasn't toothless, and he was as far away from ugly as one guy could possibly get. My final two hopes were that he was a complete prick, or he could be straight as an arrow. Then I wouldn't have to think about him at all.

I quickly rolled my window down so I could eavesdrop. Maggie introduced herself, and he immediately asked the standard question about Maggie's name.

"Yes, my name really is Maggie Mae Stewart," she said. "And yeah, I'm named after the song. My parents are incredibly weird. My brother's name is Cobain after Kurt Cobain. We just call him Coby."

Usually, she added an eye roll for good measure, but with this guy she smiled and blushed. He whispered something and Maggie giggled like a smitten schoolgirl. He didn't seem mean, either. I was doomed.

Maggie waved at me, signaling for me to get out of the car. I was scared to move. Nothing was working correctly, so I ducked down and pretended to search for something under the seat. I was pretty sure I'd actually forgotten how to walk.

When I peeked over the dash, hoping to see nothing but the car, I was treated to the sight of him casually leaning against the car, chatting with Maggie. She looked as starstruck as I felt. The cap he had been wearing had fallen off, exposing messy brown hair streaked with blond strands. Dark sunglasses still hid his eyes, but his pouty lips were in full view.

His T-shirt was low cut and exposed his collarbones and the hollow of his throat. There were two chains hanging around his neck that disappeared under his T-shirt. I wanted to crawl under that shirt and gaze at them.

He had several bracelets on his left arm and a tattoo peeked out from the bottom of the shirtsleeve on his right arm. I felt physically ill as I stared at the low-hanging jeans that covered long, lean legs. My new roommate was beautiful, and I couldn't take my eyes off him.

He pushed off the car and pulled himself to his full height. I guessed he was over six feet, because Maggie was around five-eight and he was taller than her. I watched as he wrapped Maggie in his arms and hugged her tightly against his chest. I banged my head on the rearview mirror and swore. The sight of his lightly tanned bicep wrapped around Maggie made me drool with jealousy.

"No," I said sharply and pounded my hands on the steering wheel. I was not going to develop the hots for this guy. It was best to ignore his beauty and just think of him as a person helping with the rent. I still clung to the idea that he was a complete jerk. But then, why was Maggie giggling with him? She could spot an asshole from a mile away.

A shoe bouncing off the hood of my car startled me. It was Maggie's not so subtle way of telling me to get my ass out of the car and meet our new roomie. If I put it off any longer, she would come and physically drag me out of the car, which might not be a bad idea because I still wasn't sure I could walk.

I tried to smooth out my wrinkled shirt but stopped when I remembered I wasn't trying to impress anyone. I'd been trapped in a car for hours with very little sleep, and no one should expect me to look good. I did run my fingers through my hair for that casual messed up style.

"Hi," I said weakly as I left the safety of the car. I was pretty sure no one heard me, but I was still trying to get my brain working again.

Maggie saw me and beamed, then bounced across the yard to take my hand. "Oh my God. Oh, oh my God," Maggie stuttered. She was practically vibrating. "He's so… well, judge for yourself."

"Hi," he said, meeting us halfway. "I'm Jade Marin, your new roommate."

His raspy, deep voice slithered down my spine, setting my nerves on fire. It was hard to concentrate, but I managed to choke out my name. "Rylan Blake," I said.

From afar, Jade had been beautiful; up close, he was scorching fucking hot.

Jade held out his hand for me to shake, so what was I supposed to do? I couldn't snub my new roommate because he was a tiny bit attractive. I steeled myself and shook his hand.

It would have been nice to be able to claim I felt nothing when our palms met, that my stomach didn't do a nosedive into my shoes, or my skin didn't feel like it was too tight and much too warm. It would be a big fat lie to say my dick didn't stir and my imagination stayed in a safe place. Right now, I wanted to rush into the house and lock my bedroom door so I could jack off to thoughts of Jade's hands on my body. Either that or jump Jade in the front yard, which would get our neighbor, Mrs. Morgan, totally excited.

"You okay?" Jade asked.

"Oh, um, um," I stammered, as I snatched my hand back and shoved it in my pocket. "Long drive. Family driving me crazy, and now I need to unload the car."

Jade smiled again and I forgot how to breathe. The walking thing wasn't working out too well, either. I stumbled back to my car to find my suitcase and crawl inside the bag. Maybe I could live in my car. It was comfortable, and I would be warm enough since it was close to summer. The only problem would be the bathroom, but I could use that whenever Jade wasn't around.

"You're not living in your car," Maggie said.

I grunted. "How do you do that?"

She shrugged and grabbed some stuff out of the trunk. All I could do was load up and follow her into the house, muttering about some sort of divine punishment just because I didn't believe in love. I would argue until I was blue in the face, because if you'd seen my dating record, love didn't fucking exist in my life.

I figured I had one more day to be the moody emo guy until Maggie would insist I cheer up or she would peel my skin off. She had such a delightful vocabulary when it came to threatening me.

Jade met me on the steps and grabbed the backpack off my shoulder, then headed straight for my room. He dumped the stuff on my bed and turned around.

"I hate to ask, but do you think you can help me unload my car?"

"Oh, sure," I said before my brain could catch up. I wasn't supposed to be talking to my new roommate. He was a business transaction, nothing more. My brain informed me it was good business to keep the customer happy, so if that meant turning into a pack mule that was what I was going to do. Maggie would be so impressed I actually remembered something from my business class.

"I can't believe I got this lucky," Jade said as he handed a box to me. "I needed a place to stay and out of the blue, Jeff tells me he'd moved out and you guys were in need of a roommate. He's getting married or some shit."

"What?" I gasped. "Married?"

"Yeah, his girlfriend is knocked up, so they decided to get hitched," Jade said.

The world pressed down on my lungs, squeezing the air out and not allowing me to take a breath. I was going to pass out. Jade grabbed the box out of my hands just as I slid down the side of the car.

"Rylan!" Maggie shouted from the steps of the house. "Rylan?"

She jumped off the steps and rushed over to me. She knelt in front of me and cupped my face. "Rylan? What's wrong?"

I grabbed her wrists and pulled her face against mine. "Did you know about Jeff?"

"Shit," she said and pulled me to my feet. "Jade, I need a minute with Rylan. Can you excuse us?"

"Oh yeah, sure," Jade said and headed into the house with a pile of his stuff.

"Did you fucking know?" I repeated. I sounded a bit hysterical, but this was huge. Jeff was marrying his pregnant girlfriend. The prick had been fucking me, begging me to run away with him, and at the same time he had been screwing some girl. This was exactly why relationships were a terrible thing. People fucked each other over regularly. My head hurt, and I wasn't exactly sure why this bugged me so much. I never loved the guy, but it still felt like a major betrayal.

"I found out a few days before we left on this trip, but I knew you were superstressed about going to your parents' house, so I was holding off telling you," Maggie whispered. "I'm so sorry."

"Things just keep getting better, but it illustrates why it's best for me not to get emotionally invested in anyone," I spat. "I'm going for a run."

She made a halfhearted attempt to stop me as I headed into the house to change, telling me it was getting dark, but I wasn't going to listen. The exercise would help clear my head and get some endorphins flowing. It might stop me from hunting down Jeff and spilling his secrets in front of his future wife. The woman had no idea what she was getting into.

When I raced out of the house, Maggie and Jade were sitting on the grass surrounded by a bunch of boxes. They both stared at me as I took off down the road. I'd take bets that Maggie was trying to assure our new roommate that I wasn't a total nut.

During the beginning of the run, I made excuses for my reaction to the news about Jeff. It wasn't love for me, but I did like the guy, so hearing he was fucking someone else when he claimed to be in love with me, stung. When I hit the third mile, my brain had devised multiple ways to murder Jeff. By the time I'd reached mile number four, I'd killed the asshole thirty-seven times. The fifth mile passed, and I decided I wasn't going to kill the jerk. I had no desire to spend the rest of my life in prison. As the sixth mile started, I had convinced myself that Jeff was the one going to virtual prison and I felt sorry for the girl who was about to marry a fucking liar. During the seventh mile, I decided everybody could fuck off.

Maggie was right. It was time to have some fun. Brooding about my parents and everyone else was nonproductive. I had no control over what other people said or did. By the eighth mile, I wanted to call Maggie and beg her to come pick me up. My muscles were in a major uproar over this workout, especially since I hadn't been doing much running the past week. The ninth mile almost killed me. I finally made it to our lawn and collapsed in a sweaty heap at Maggie's feet.

"Feeling better?" she asked hesitantly.

"Marginally. A shower would improve my mood greatly."

"Mine too," Maggie said, holding her nose. "You stink."

"How about I take a shower and make dinner for all of us," I said.

"Really?"

I swiped a wet strand of hair out of my eyes. "Yes. I'm taking your advice. I can't live like this anymore. I need to have some fun. These last few days have drained me."

Her smile lit up the entire yard, and she squealed so loud, Mrs. Morgan opened her front door. Maggie waved and Mrs. Morgan shook her head.

"I'm going inside now," I said. Maggie moved to hug me, but when sweat dripped on her shoe, she backed away, leaving me to grope the air.

She was still talking a mile a minute when I opened the front door and almost ran into Jade.

"Hey, I'm making dinner after I shower. Would you like to join us?"

Jade smiled widely. "Yeah, that would be great. I'm sorry if I said something to upset you."

"You didn't," I lied. Our eyes locked, and I felt a flash of something deep in my gut. It made me squirm and back into the wall. I quickly schooled my features and lifted my shirt to wipe the sweat off my face, pretending not to hear the sharp intake of breath from Jade. It was probably my imagination anyway. I was still on an endorphin high from my run.

Once in the bathroom, I tried not to think of those brown eyes and pretty lips. I desperately wanted to touch my dick, but I wasn't going to go there. I'd just met the guy, barely talked to him. A cold shower was the best thing for me right now, and I welcomed the frigid water.

It was absolutely nuts to be thinking about him. He might be delicious, but I had to live with him for the next year, and I had solid evidence that fucking around with your roommate was a terrible idea.

"Friends," I told my reflection. "Pretty sure he's straight anyway, and even if he isn't, you aren't going to use him as a sex toy." I shook my finger at my reflection, but all I got for my trouble was a dick twitch. Thinking about Jade as a sex toy was not a very smart thing.

I tossed my towel at the mirror and styled my hair, making it look messy on purpose. When I opened the door, I could hear Maggie and Jade in Jeff's old bedroom. They were laughing and hammering something into the wall.

My stomach reminded me I was starving and I was the one who volunteered to cook dinner.

After several cupboard inspections, all I managed to find was an open package of noodles and one jar of spaghetti sauce. I couldn't remember the last time Maggie and I had made a trip to the grocery store. There was nothing else to do but order pizza, and since I didn't know what Jade liked, I settled on ordering one pepperoni and one cheese.

"I don't smell any food cooking," Maggie hollered.

"Nothing to cook. We need to hit the grocery store, so I ordered pizza."

"Did someone say pizza?" Jade asked. He strolled into the kitchen looking like a god artists should worship by creating marble statues and paintings to hang in the Louvre. If I kept this up, I might have to check myself into the nuthouse.

"There's nothing in the house to eat," I repeated to Jade.

"You guys should make a list and I can run to the grocery store after we eat. You're both exhausted, and I'm a little wired. I think I drank eight cups of coffee waiting in the driveway," Jade said.

"We're keeping him, Rylan. He's the sweetest," Maggie said. She yanked open a drawer, pulled out a piece of paper and pen, and started scribbling as she went through all the cupboards and fridge.

Maggie suddenly stopped writing and eyed Jade. "Hey, you're not one of those guys who would freak out if I put tampons on the list, are you?"

"Two sisters," Jade fired back. "Are you one of those girls who would pitch a fit if I asked you to buy condoms?"

"Favorite brand?" Maggie asked and giggled.

Jade grinned. "How about lube?"

"What flavor?"

Jade laughed and winked at Maggie. They continued their banter, but I was still stuck on the buying of condoms and lube part of the conversation.

"I think things are going to work out just fine," Maggie said. She bumped me with her hip, and my brain kicked into gear again. This arrangement was going to kill me. I should add lube to the list because I was going to be doing a lot of self-pleasuring. I'd only known this guy for an hour and my entire body was betraying me.

The doorbell chimed and made me jump.

"That must be the pizza," Maggie said and raced out of the kitchen, leaving me alone with Jade.

"She's a bit high-strung," Jade said.

"You get used to it," I said.

Jade pulled out a chair and sat down. He glanced at the list Maggie had filled out before he shoved it toward me. "Anything you want to add?"

I took a deep breath and threw myself into the lion's den. "Are you familiar with this area?"

"Not really," Jade said.

"I could show you the best grocery store," I said. I knew I could just give him directions, but apparently I was throwing my earlier decision to treat this guy as a business transaction out the window. Besides, I was curious about him.

"Yeah, that would be great. I've never lived on this side of town, so I don't know where anything is located," Jade said.

"Pizza," Maggie announced. She dropped the boxes on the table and tossed the napkins to Jade and me, smiling as she slid into her seat.

The next twenty minutes were spent sharing small talk in between bites of hot pizza. A couple of moans and several "oh, my God, this is the best pizza ever," and Maggie tossed the boxes into the recycling bin and excused herself to go take a shower.

Jade searched out his keys while I went to tell Maggie we were leaving and to find out if she had any more additions for the list. The shower was already running, but we were never shy around each other. I pushed open the door and walked into the steam-filled room.

"Hey," I shouted over the sound of the water. "We're heading to the grocery store. Do you need anything else?"

The shower curtain moved, and Maggie poked her soapy head out and stared at me like I'd grown a third eye. "You hate grocery shopping."

"Yes, but we need stuff," I said. My face flushed, and I was extremely happy the room was filled with steam. I could just claim it was hot in here.

"Rylan," Maggie warned.

"I'm not going to do anything stupid. He's our roommate. I can play nice." I added a frown and then blinked innocently at her.

She groaned and told me to add toothpaste to list. I scurried out before she could say anything else.

A horn honked and I guessed Jade was already in the car. I shoved the list into my pocket, grabbed my wallet, and ran outside. Our neighbor was leaning against the car, chatting with Jade. Mrs. Morgan was a nice but crazy lady who liked to wolf whistle at me when I was in my jogging shorts. I should have known she would be drawn to Jade.

"Hi, Mrs. Morgan. I see you met our new roommate," I called out.

"Good choice. Much better than the last one," she said and waved as she headed back to her house. Mrs. Morgan never liked Jeff. Her word for him had been "shifty," which I guess had been right on the money. I wondered what word she picked for Jade.

"She gave me cash and a grocery list," Jade said when I climbed into the car.

"She doesn't drive and her son is a complete jerk. She somehow always knows when one of us is heading to the store."

Jade laughed and started the car. Music filled the small space, but Jade changed it before I could tell who was singing.

"So, which way?"

"Way? Oh, right, to the store."

I forgot about the music and shifted into tour-guide mode, pointing out different things as we drove to the store. Jade laughed when I told him the story about Maggie getting lost on the walk home from the bar after she turned twenty-one. It had taken me thirty minutes before I found her sitting on some kid's swing set, singing loudly and off-key. Thankfully no one was home and the neighbors didn't call the cops.

Traffic was light, so it didn't take long to get to the store. Maggie usually drove the cart and barked out orders to me, but Jade let me take control of the cart. He picked up a basket for Mrs. Morgan's stuff. I dug our crumpled list out of my pocket and handed it to him. The cart was enough responsibility for me.

The trip through the grocery store was entertaining, and Jade didn't make fun of me when I shoved a box of my favorite chocolate cereal in the cart. I usually had to sneak that stuff into the cart and bury it so Maggie wouldn't see it. When she eventually spotted the cereal, she would lecture me about the lack of nutritional value and the high sugar content. Jade grinned and added two more boxes to the cart.

"It's my favorite too," he said, smiling smugly.

"Maggie is going to think I ruined you," I said.

Jade chuckled. "I was already ruined."

The way he dragged out the sentence made me forget what I was doing. I ran into a display of crackers and knocked several boxes to the floor. I was pretty sure Jade winked at me when he bent over to pick up the boxes. I did not check out his ass.

It went on like that for the rest of the trip through the grocery store. Jade always had an answer or comment that seemed like he was implying something else. Of course, I was known to have a very active imagination, especially when it came to sexual innuendos.

By the time we stood in the checkout lane, I was beyond turned-on and totally exhausted. It was an odd combination.

"You look like you're dead on your feet," Jade said. I moved forward to help him unload the cart, but he stopped me. "I think I can manage."

"Thanks," I muttered. "It's been a really long day."

Jade wouldn't let me pitch in for the groceries, telling me he was incredibly happy to have a place to live. We could figure out how we would divide everything later.

I never knew shopping could be so much fun. With Maggie, there was always a plan. The list was sacred; you never deviated from the list. But with Jade, it was a free-for-all, and we actually got some good food, which we would have to hide.

Mrs. Morgan thanked us several times for doing her grocery shopping. She insisted we keep the change, but Jade left the money, along with the receipt, on the bench by her front door.

Our house was quiet when we got back. It was going to be an interesting task putting the groceries away. I had no idea where anything went. Maggie had a place assigned for everything but damned if I knew where she kept things. When I cooked, she laid out the ingredients, or I just opened all of the cupboards until I found what I needed.

"Maggie is going to freak when she can't find anything tomorrow. We'll probably have to rearrange it."

"My sister is exactly like Maggie," Jade said.

"Oh right, you have two sisters."

"Brooke is older than me and a total neat freak. Hailey is the free spirit, but she's only sixteen, so that could change. How about you?" Jade asked.

"One of each. Lucas is the oldest and then it's Kelli," I answered.

"So you're the baby?" Jade teased. "Spoiled rotten I suppose."

"Hardly. I'm the total black sheep of the family. They may have even thrown me out after last night." I abruptly stopped and cleared my throat. I didn't want to get into my family drama with Jade. No one wanted to hear your ugly secrets on the first day you meet.

"Families can be difficult," Jade said as he shoved two bags of chips into a cupboard filled with pots and pans. I chuckled because Maggie was going to have a stroke when she saw the mess. It would take her hours to return the kitchen to her specifications.

When the last bag was emptied, I yawned. "I have to crash. Is there anything else you need?"

Jade rubbed the back of his neck and smiled. "Nope, I'm good."

"Well, okay, then," I stuttered and looked at him. Our eyes met, and I felt something stir deep in my soul. My stomach fluttered, and a heated flash headed for my groin.

"I had a great time tonight," Jade whispered.

"Me too. Night," I said quickly and rushed down the hall to my room. I slammed the door and let out a long breath.

"What the hell was that?"

My stomach fluttered again when I thought about Jade's brown eyes. This was bad or crazy or a little of both. I could try to convince myself the pizza had been tainted and caused my stomach to dive into my ankles. But the problem with that theory was it was completely false. The pizza was fine. I was the crazy one.

Jade caused the reaction, and because of him, I had a huge problem, and I was going to have to spend the next ten minutes thinking about horrible things or take my dick in hand and work it out.

The five minutes I spent conjuring awful images was a total waste of time, because everything morphed into Jade. I gave up and stripped off my clothes, quickly climbed into my bed, and grabbed the lube before I pulled the covers over my head.

Just as I wrapped my lube-covered hand around my aching cock, my phone buzzed. I glanced at the screen and saw Kelli's name pop up. In the past three years since I'd left home, Kelli had called me seven times, and never with good news. It killed my erection immediately, so I wiped my hand on my discarded T-shirt.

"Hello?"

"Rylan, this is Kelli," she said.

"I know who it is."

"I just wanted to make sure you got home and, you know, that everything was okay." She stumbled over the words and sighed when she finally finished the sentence.

"We made it back with no problems."

The line went silent, and I wondered if she had hung up on me. "Rylan, I'm sorry about Mom and Dad."

"Don't apologize for them."

"Okay," she said quietly. "Then I'm sorry for treating you like you didn't exist. I should have been there for you."

"It's in the past, Kelli," I said.

"I'm here for you now, okay," she said. I heard her take a deep breath. "I'll support you and any choices you make. After you left, I had it out with Mom and Dad. It wasn't pretty."

This was the first time since we were little kids that Kelli had stuck up for me.

"Does Lucas know what happened?"

"Yeah, Dad was totally freaked-out this morning, and Lucas kept bugging him until he exploded and said, 'your brother has decided he likes guys.' You would have loved Lucas's reaction. The words rolled around in his head and then his eyes got really wide. He spilled his coffee, and Dad swore at him. Mom came in and told them to clean up and that talking about this mess was not proper breakfast conversation."

"Nice," I said. Mentioning my name anywhere in the house was probably off-limits. From this day forward, I would be referred to as *the mess*.

We talked for close to an hour. She asked me all sorts of questions about school and Maggie, but she stayed away from my social life.

"It's okay to ask me about my personal life. I know you must be curious."

"I'm not going to pry into your life, Rylan, but I really would like to come to Chicago and hang out with you and Maggie…." She paused. "If you'd have me."

"Really? You want to come stay with me?"

"Yes."

"Well," I said. "Maggie and I start school in a few days. We don't finish until early August, but you can come anytime you want. I'm only taking one class."

She squealed into the phone, and I had to hold it away from my ear. "Do you mean it, Rylan?"

I stared at my phone for a few seconds, shocked my sister was actually excited to come see me.

"Yeah, I wouldn't ask if I didn't want you here," I said and yawned into the phone. Once I started yawning, I couldn't stop. Kelli apologized for keeping me up so late and said good-bye. It was one of the strangest and best conversations I'd ever had with my sister.

There were more yawns. My body was exhausted, but my mind was on fire. The ugly fight with my parents replayed until I wanted to rip my brain out of my head. When I chased those images away, the idea of Kelli coming to visit started a new round of thinking. The worst thoughts were the visions of Jade that would sneak into my head, making my dick come to life again.

I finally folded and gave in to my physical needs. This time I was going to do the fantasy justice. If I was going to be a pervert, I might as well do things right. I found my headphones and started my sexy playlist. I turned off the lamp so the only light was from the moon shining through my window.

I found the lube, popped the cap, and coated my fingers with the cool liquid. I didn't need to work up to the moment. My cock was hard again, dying for release.

My imagination kicked into overdrive when I tightened my grip on my cock. I stroked harder, faster, as my mind wondered what it would feel like to have Jade's weight crushing down on my chest, his naked skin against mine. I started to moan, but snapped my mouth shut. The last thing I needed was Maggie or Jade to interrupt because I was making strange noises.

My hand slid easily up and down my erection as the lube mixed with my precum that dripped from the tip of my cock. It felt good, so good. I sped up my stroking, and soon I felt the fire burning hotter in my belly as I neared completion.

"Jade," I grunted in a broken whisper as I filled my hand with cum.

I rolled over, grabbed my T-shirt, and cleaned up, pretending I didn't feel weird about jerking off thinking about my new roommate. At least I was finally relaxed enough to fall asleep.

CHAPTER THREE

NOT LONG after I'd fallen asleep, I heard noises outside my room and wondered what the hell Maggie was doing. Sometimes she'd sleepwalk when overtired.

"Shit," I mumbled into my pillow. The thought of getting out of bed was not appealing, but it was Maggie, and I didn't want to find her standing in the front yard wearing nothing but her underwear. Plus, we hadn't warned Jade of her strange habit of roaming the halls at night.

I slid on a pair of shorts and slowly cracked the door open. One time I had made a ton of noise, and when I opened the door, it crashed into the wall. Maggie punched me in the face, hitting me in that one spot above your eye that swells up in two seconds. She ranted for about ten minutes about vampires and werewolves, and then calmly went back to her room, leaving me standing in the hallway covering my swollen eye. In the morning, she had asked me what I'd done to my face. I didn't even know how to answer her.

This time it wasn't Maggie in the hall. It was Jade, and he was texting and frowning harder with each text. He finally swore and let his head bang against the wall, dropping his phone to the floor. Maybe he was a sleepwalker, too, but he looked wide-awake.

"Jade," I whispered, opening my door wider.

"Oh shit, I'm sorry," he said quickly. "I didn't mean to wake you."

"I thought you were Maggie. She sometimes takes a walk through dreamland. Punched me in the eye one night. You are awake, right?" I said, taking a step back.

He sucked in a quick breath. "Unfortunately."

"You want to talk about it?" I couldn't believe I was offering a sympathetic ear. That was Maggie's forte, not mine.

"You don't want to hear my stupid problems." He hung his head and his hair fell forward, covering his face. I wanted to tuck it behind his ears and get him to smile.

"I'm sorry for waking you," Jade apologized again.

"Jade, we all have fucking problems. It's not a big deal. You don't have to talk about anything. We can hang out in my room and listen to some music," I said. "Music always calms me down."

He nodded and followed me into my room, then flopped on my bed and sighed. It was a bit unnerving to think I had jacked off to thoughts of him a few short hours ago, lying in almost the exact spot as he was now.

His phone played a sweet jingle, and he grimaced and pushed the ignore button before the music replayed.

"Fuck," he sighed and buried his face in my pillow. My gaze drifted down his body, following the lines of lithe muscles I could see through the thin fabric of his T-shirt.

"You okay?" I asked.

He groaned and rolled over. His T-shirt bunched up, exposing a flat stomach with nicely defined muscles. He tugged his shirt down, hiding the sparse line of hair that disappeared under the waistband of his underwear. I tried to hide my disappointment by putting on my concerned face. I probably just looked like a lunatic.

"My crazy ex-girlfriend is threatening to throw my shit out in the parking lot if I don't come get it right this second."

"I could come with you," I volunteered. What the hell was I thinking? Apparently, seeing a tiny slice of skin affected my judgment. I was fucking exhausted. A little more than twenty-four hours ago I'd had a major blowout with my parents, and it was close to four in the morning.

"You don't have to do that," Jade said. His phone rang again, and he stared at me, biting his lip until I gave him an encouraging nod. He answered the call.

"Daria, I'll be there in forty minutes," Jade said sharply and hung up the phone. "Last chance to back out."

"No, I'm cool, but I should probably put on some pants and a shirt."

Jade chuckled. "Yeah, me too."

I would have been okay if he stayed in the thin sweatpants he was wearing, but he left to change. As I found some clothes, I realized a gigantic weight had been lifted off my shoulders. The guy was straight, crushing my dreams of having a sex toy, but it took the pressure off me. He could star in my dreams, but in the real world, we could be friends, and I was okay with that.

"You ready?" Jade asked when he appeared at my door.

"Yeah, I better send Maggie a text so if she wakes up, she won't think we ran away or something."

Jade laughed and we took off into the night. He was quiet for the first ten minutes.

"I suppose I should explain."

"No need," I said. "It's none of my business."

"Rylan, I dragged you out in the middle of the night to come with me. The least I can do is tell you what's going on with me."

"I can't deny I'm curious, but I said I would come with you. I didn't attach any strings."

"Thanks," he said. "But maybe talking about it will relieve some of the guilt I'm feeling about this whole mess."

"I get that," I said.

He took a huge breath and eased up on the steering wheel. It looked like he had been trying to crush it. "Daria was the first person I met when I came to school here. She was sweet and took me under her wing. I was a little lost in the big city, so it was nice to have someone who knew what they were doing."

"Maggie was the first person I met," I said.

"Did you and Maggie ever date?"

"Er, no, never," I said. I wasn't ready to share my sexual orientation yet. He didn't seem like he would be freaked out by it, but I didn't want to take that chance and have him dump me out of the car in the middle of the night.

He sighed and ran his fingers through his hair. "I wish we had kept our relationship platonic, but she pushed and pushed until I caved."

It didn't sound like he was all that into her.

"She finished school last year, and a lot of her friends have started to get married and have children. All of a sudden, Daria figured we needed to get married. Fuck that shit," Jade said sharply. "I'm only twenty-one. I'm not ready for the whole family thing."

I chuckled, and he smiled at me.

"You know what the worst thing was?" Jade said.

"There's something worse?" I asked.

"Oh yeah. I think she was trying to get pregnant on purpose," he said. "To force me into marrying her."

At least I never had to worry about that shit. As far as I knew, dudes couldn't get pregnant.

"She's not pregnant, right?" I asked.

"No, I stayed the fuck away from her after I caught her dumping her birth control pills in the toilet," Jade said. "It pissed her off."

"It would piss me off too," I said.

"What?"

"The not having sex part," I clarified.

"Oh," he said. "Right."

He didn't sound convinced, but maybe they had a terrible sex life. It wasn't like I was going to ask him to explain. I could care less what he and Daria got up to in the bedroom. I heard enough of hetero sexcapades from Maggie when she was knee-deep in a relationship.

"When we broke up, I felt like a massive weight lifted off my chest. She was stifling," Jade said.

I didn't know what to say. He didn't seem like he needed comforting. In fact, it didn't feel like he actually liked the girl. It was safer to change the subject. "How do you know Jeff?" I asked. It was a risky question, because I had no idea if Jeff's friends knew anything about me.

"His girlfriend and my ex are good friends. I don't know him all that well, but he seems like a good guy. Although, when he told me he was getting married, he didn't seem all that excited."

I was glad he didn't ask my opinion of Jeff.

He flipped the blinker and turned into a parking lot. At the far end, I could see a dark-haired woman sitting on the steps, surrounded by boxes and several garbage bags. She frowned when I got out of the car. Jade ignored her and didn't bother to introduce us. I had no desire to meet her anyway.

"Can I talk to you for a second?" she asked Jade when we were loading the last of the boxes into his car.

"Why?" Jade asked. "It's over. What could we possibly have to discuss?"

His voice was cold and it made me shudder, even though it wasn't directed at me.

Daria's eyes widened and filled with tears that soon streamed down her face. She sniffed and gave him a pathetic look that would have forced me to talk to her. I was a total wimp when people cried.

"Not going to work, Daria," Jade said. "Have a nice life."

He jumped into the car, revved the engine, and we took off before she could wipe the snot that dripped from her nose. She flipped us off and stomped back into the apartment building. Jade didn't even look back at her, but he seemed to visibly relax once we were about two blocks away.

"Thanks for coming with me," Jade said. "It's great to get my stuff back. Of course, it could be busted up, but it's still my stuff. I really didn't think she'd give it back to me."

"You're welcome," I answered and yawned widely. It was hard to hide how tired I was.

Jade turned the radio up, and I leaned back in the seat, closing my eyes. Before I knew it, Jade was shaking me, telling me we were home.

"Sorry," I muttered.

"I know you're tired," he said. "We don't have to unload this stuff right now. It can wait until morning."

"It is morning," I mumbled. "Might as well take a couple boxes when we go inside."

He nodded and we loaded our arms and made our way inside as quietly as possible. I set the boxes I carried in the corner of his room. The bed was in a different place, and he had clothes strewn around the room. The desk and the dresser had switched places. I collapsed on the bed and watched Jade carefully open a few of the boxes and dig through them until he pulled out a pile of CD's and a few notebooks.

He was murmuring happily about being reunited with his stuff. The last thing I remember was feeling the bed dip and hearing pages of a notebook being turned, until the sun shining in my eyes woke me up. For a moment, I thought it was Jeff snuggling into my side, but when my eyes finally focused, it was Jade's hair that was tickling my nose.

I rubbed my eyes and saw Maggie leaning in the doorway, holding back a smile, and shaking her head.

Jade moved closer to me. My eyes almost popped out of my head when I felt his hand brush against my thigh. Maggie chewed on her lip and snorted. I was incredibly thankful I was still wearing jeans.

He groaned, opened his eyes, and stared at me with big brown eyes. If I was a guy who fell in love, it could have happened right there. He blinked, grinning at me.

"You passed out in my bed," Jade said.

"Yeah, sorry about that," I mumbled and sat up, making sure I kept the blankets pooled around my waist. There was no need to show off my morning wood to anyone. Maggie was now snickering into her hand.

"Good morning, boys," Maggie said and disappeared before I could throw anything at her.

Jade rolled out of bed and headed into the bathroom. He was so quick I didn't get a good look at his naked back. The idea that he had been shirtless, sleeping next to me, was stimulating. Something I didn't need to think about if I wanted to get rid of my erection, which was painfully pressing against the zipper of my jeans.

Since Jade was in the bathroom and Maggie was in the kitchen, I took the opportunity to jump out of bed and race to my room. I dressed in workout clothes, deciding I needed to take a run.

Maggie was busy cursing us for hiding the food. Her voice was muffled, so I peeked around the corner. Half her body was inside one of the cupboards, and two bags of chips sat by her knees. Her cleaning supplies were on the chair. It was time for me to disappear unless I wanted to find myself wearing yellow rubber gloves and hauling around a spray bottle of something that made things sparkle and smell sterile. I backed up and banged into something solid.

"Are you going for a run?" Jade asked.

"Shhh," I whispered, pointing at Maggie, who was now mumbling about how could anyone not know that cereal did not belong in the drawer with the bread.

Jade nodded, and we both tiptoed to the front door.

"I heard you," Maggie yelled.

"We're going for a run," I shouted and shoved Jade out the door before Maggie could holler at us to get in the kitchen and help her. "Sorry about that, but she's on the warpath. We messed up her kitchen."

"It's okay," Jade said. "I was going to ask if you wanted to go for a run."

It was then I noticed he was wearing running shorts and tennis shoes.

"Good morning, boys," Mrs. Morgan shouted. "I see I get two for one this morning."

I nodded at her, and Jade laughed. "She's funny."

"Never a dull moment with Mrs. Morgan around. She really likes it when I wash the car. Sets up a lawn chair and sips on a drink."

His gaze swept down my body. "Maybe I'll join her next time," he murmured, or at least that's what I thought he said.

Usually I ran with headphones on, but today I listened to Jade talk. We had a lot in common. We both ditched our hometowns and families the minute we graduated from high school, and moved to the big city.

"My mom was never a very caring person," Jade said, choosing his words carefully.

"My mom doesn't like me," I said.

"Why would you say that?" Jade asked, slowing to a walk. "Mind if we walk the rest of the way home? I'm a little out of shape."

"Uh, she, well…." I stumbled over a few words and ended up laughing, because he was far from out of shape.

He shoved me and told me to shut up. We teased each other, bumping shoulders as we walked, forgetting about our family discussion. I didn't really want to get into my personal life.

Mrs. Morgan was still messing around in her garden when we got back to the house. She waved and winked at me. I shook my head and rolled my eyes.

Jade headed for the shower, but I stopped in the kitchen to get some water. Maggie's ass was still sticking out one of the cupboards, so I gave her a quick slap.

"Ouch!" she shrieked and banged her head on the cupboard. "Were you guys drunk when you put the groceries away?"

"No. I was exhausted, though."

She dismissed my comment with an exaggerated eye roll. "So, what do you think? He's really nice, isn't he?"

It would have been easy to lie, but why bother. She could read me like an open book. "Yeah, he is," I agreed.

"You look much better," Maggie said. She handed me a bottle of water.

"I actually slept well last night." She snickered and I shook my head. "He's straight, Maggie."

"Right, I always sleep snuggled up to someone I barely know."

"You snuggle with me."

"Because it's you."

"You did it on the first night we met. You didn't have a clue I wasn't straight," I reminded her.

Her cheeks stained red. "I was hoping you were straight."

I poked her in the ribs, and she laughed. "I went with him last night to pick up the rest of his things from his ex-girlfriend's place. Notice the girl part."

"Well, it sure didn't look like it when I was watching you two sleep this morning." She poked at her phone and shoved the screen in front of my face. Jade's face was buried in my neck, and my nose was buried in his hair.

"Erase that," I said.

"No!" she shrieked again and snatched the phone out of my hand.

"Maggie," I warned.

"Rylan," she said and stuck her tongue out at me.

"Um, hey," Jade said. "What are you guys doing?"

Maggie shoved the phone in her pocket and tossed a dirty cleaning rag at Jade's head. He snagged it out of the air and frowned at her.

"Don't worry," Maggie said. "I'm done cleaning. I was telling Rylan he should do my laundry since I had to clean up the mess in the kitchen."

Jade shrugged. "I can do that. Get your stuff together and show me where you keep the washing machine."

"Oh my God, we are so keeping you," Maggie said and pinched Jade's cheek. She skipped out of the room, singing about the best roommate ever.

"Are you nuts?" I asked.

"Doing laundry doesn't bother me," Jade said. "In fact, it's therapeutic."

I walked out of the room, returned with a basket of dirty clothes, and dropped them at his feet.

"Only doing my part to make you feel at home." I smirked at him, and he threw a dirty towel in my face. He raced out of the kitchen with me in hot pursuit. I caught him around the waist and tackled him on the couch. I thought I had the upper hand, but he flipped me over and we tumbled to the floor, laughing and trying to better each other. Jade was surprisingly strong, and I could feel his muscles flexing when I grabbed his biceps. I couldn't control my body's reaction.

The feeling intensified when he pushed his hips forward. It was too much, and I needed to get him off me before he felt something he shouldn't feel. I started to panic, so I did the thing Maggie totally hated. I licked his wrist. He yelped and rolled off me.

"Rylan cheated, didn't he," Maggie said, shaking her head.

"Yeah, he licked me," Jade said, staring at his wrist.

"He does it to me all the time," she said, offering her hand to Jade. He leaped to his feet and grabbed the basket out of her hand, leaving me on the floor and Maggie staring after him.

I sat up and raised my knee, hoping to hide my half-hard dick. "I needed to get him off me. Fuck, he's probably pissed at me, but...."

Maggie ruffled my hair. "It's okay, Rylan. He's fucking hot, and if he was ever on top of me like that...." She raised her eyebrows and bit her lip. I chased the image out of my head.

"Stop it," I said weakly.

"Good idea," she said and pulled me to my feet.

"I should finish unpacking."

She nodded and let me go without an argument. Shit, Jade probably thought I was a raging lunatic, but what the fuck would he have thought if he felt the growing bulge in my pants? Straight boys usually didn't like to feel another man's junk rubbing against their thigh.

Even though I hadn't been up long, the recent activities had worn me out. Instead of putting things away, I shoved my partially unpacked suitcase on the floor and climbed into bed.

When I woke up, I was disoriented and didn't exactly know where I was. There was a pile of clean clothes folded neatly on my chair. Jade must have really done my laundry, because Maggie was shit at folding. I crept out of my room, finding the house eerily quiet. There was a note in the kitchen propped up against a clean bowl, spoon, and a box of my favorite cereal, telling me they had headed over to the campus.

Halfway through my second bowl of cereal, my phone rang and Maggie's smiling face showed on my screen. I kept eating and let it go to voice mail. After the third call, I picked it up. Maggie shouted at me for not answering, calling me rude.

"I was eating," I shouted into my phone. "What do you want?"

She didn't want anything except to tell me she and Jade were picking up some books for her class and some art supplies for Jade. Apparently, he was an art major, or maybe it was graphic design. I needed to ask him myself.

"Can you check if my writing class has a book assigned?"

She agreed, and I gave her my class information. Before she hung up, she informed me I owed them both dinner. They would be home around five thirty and I was to have food on the table.

Although it was nice to have the house to myself, I was also a tiny bit jealous Maggie was spending the day with Jade. The good thing was she might find out some more information about the guy.

After I finished my cereal, I decided to unpack and put all my clean clothes away. I stared at my journals for a few minutes, but I really didn't have time to lose myself in writing; plus, the writing thing had sucked lately. I stacked the books on my desk and headed for the shower.

With that out of the way, I went to the kitchen and found chicken breasts sitting in the fridge with a detailed note attached to them. Maggie had provided the menu for tonight's meal and the location of all the ingredients.

Dinner was almost finished when I heard car doors slamming, followed by loud laughter and the rustling of plastic bags.

"I'm starving," Maggie shouted.

"Dinner awaits," I yelled back.

She bounded into the kitchen, grinning when she saw the table was set and her salad was waiting. The oven timer binged, and I opened the door, filling the kitchen with the smell of seasoned chicken breasts.

"Holy shit," Jade said. "What smells so good?"

"Dinner," I said proudly. I set the hot food on the table and watched Jade.

"Wow, Rylan, this looks awesome. Thank you," he said.

I found a bowl and took the baked potatoes out of the oven, then grabbed the sour cream and butter before I brought everything to the table. Jade's eyes widened.

"I will do your laundry forever," he said, spearing a chicken breast and scooping out a large serving of green beans.

"You're on," I said.

After Jade and Maggie cleaned up the kitchen, we piled on the couch and spent the rest of the evening watching some vampire show

Maggie swooned over. Jade laughed and teased her about drooling over dead guys. I kept my mouth shut, because I liked the show. Especially the hot vampire brothers, but Jade didn't need to know that, so I laughed along with him and teased Maggie until she pinched me and kicked Jade in the shin.

The entire evening, I was acutely aware of Jade's knee pressing into my thigh and his ankle hooked around mine. Eventually Jade's eyes drooped, and he excused himself, stumbling off to bed. Maggie was next, and I sighed, trudging to my room.

I wasn't sure how long I stared at the ceiling, wishing for sleep to take me away so I wouldn't think about Jade. The harder I tried not to think about him, the more his face filled my head. I needed to talk to Maggie. She would put me in line and help me get a grip on these horrible feelings bubbling up inside me. And by getting a grip, I mean squish the life out of the feelings.

I opened my bedroom door and saw Jade stalking down the hall, clutching a guitar. Instead of calling out his name like a normal person, I watched him. He paced around the living room before he slid open the back door and went out on the deck.

I waited in the shadows until he jumped off the deck and did a few laps around the yard. Mrs. Morgan's light came on, and she stepped outside and stared into the darkness. Jade was on the far side of the yard, so I carefully slid open our patio door.

"Is that you, Jade?" I heard Mrs. Morgan ask.

"Uh, yeah. I didn't mean to scare you."

"You didn't. I'm a night owl and, well, a day owl too, I guess. I don't sleep much anymore," she said to Jade.

She met him at the fence and stared at the guitar in his hand. I slipped outside, trying to stay hidden in the dark of the night. I could barely hear what they were saying, so I took a chance and crawled across the deck, hiding behind a lawn chair.

"I was trying to find a place to play without waking everyone up. I should have asked Maggie and Rylan before they crashed," Jade said.

"You're welcome to play at my house," Mrs. Morgan said.

Jade chuckled. "Really? Aren't you scared I'm going to hurt you or something?"

"Are you?" Mrs. Morgan asked.

"No, but you don't even know me," Jade said. "Most people wouldn't invite a stranger into their home."

"You've already been in my home. I'm a good judge of character, and I know enough about you, Jade," Mrs. Morgan said. "You did my grocery shopping and left my change on the bench when I told you to keep it. You're a college student, and I know money must be tight."

Jade shrugged, and I watched as he stared at the small woman standing in front of him. Her wavy short hair was almost entirely white. Her face wore the passage of time, but she was still beautiful, and her green eyes sparkled when Jade smiled at her.

"That would be great. I just need to unwind and music helps me. Things have been a little intense the past two weeks, and I haven't had a chance to play much," Jade said.

"Change can do that to a person," Mrs. Morgan said.

He nodded in agreement and followed her into the house. I jumped off the deck and crept across our lawn, acting like a proper stalker. Mrs. Morgan pulled the screen door shut. I lost sight of them when they walked into the kitchen, but the light turned on in the room where her baby grand piano was located. I casually strolled to the side of her house, thankful the window was cracked.

"Do you play?" I heard Jade ask Mrs. Morgan.

"Yes, but we'll save that for another day. I want to hear you play," she said. I readily agreed with her. She was a wonderful pianist, but I was interested in Jade. I leaned against her fence and sank to the grass.

When I played for her, she would sit in one of the wingback chairs. If I played the piano, my back would be to her, but if I played the guitar, I sat on the piano bench and faced her.

Jade plucked the strings, making sure the guitar was in tune before he started to play. When he strummed the first chords of the song "Can't Help Falling in Love With You," I could almost hear Mrs. Morgan sigh, or maybe it was me.

The moment he started to sing, I lost my breath. His voice captivated me, pulled me into the lyrics, and made my heart pound like crazy against my ribs. I'd heard the song a million times by a lot of different artists, but his version made me want to believe in the existence of love. I wanted him to love me. The thought scared me, shocked me, and made me feel totally psychotic. Like the song said, only fools rush in and fall in love.

Several songs later, Jade quieted the strings. I almost leaped to my feet to beg him for one more song.

"Sing one more," Mrs. Morgan pleaded. I wanted to kiss her.

He sang a song called "Stars." I think I swooned.

When it was over, I felt like I was floating across the sky.

"Thank you, Mrs. Morgan, for letting me hang out with you," Jade said.

I'm pretty sure I could hear her smiling. "Thank you for letting me listen. And please, call me Beth. You have a very lovely voice."

The piano bench scraped against the floor, and I knew Jade had stood up. I jumped from my hiding space and raced for my door, then quickly got inside.

"What are you doing?" Maggie asked.

"Holy shit!" I shouted, clutching my chest. "Are you trying to scare me to death?"

Maggie had the fridge door open and was looking at me over her shoulder. "I'm not the one creeping around in the middle of the night."

"I wasn't creeping."

"Mmmhmm," Maggie said. "So, where's Jade, then?"

The sound of his footsteps walking up the steps to the deck set off my panic alarm. "He's coming," I said, then grabbed her arm and yanked her down the hall and into my bedroom.

"Rylan, let go of me," she said. She tried to wrench her arm free, but I wrapped her in my arms to quiet her. "Were you spying on Jade?"

"No," I said. She gave me a strange look, and I caved. "Okay, yes. Shhhhhh."

We both stilled when we heard noise in the hallway. His bedroom door closed, and I let her go and sank down to the floor.

"Are you certifiably crazy?" she asked.

I buried my face in my hands. "Yes."

"What's going on?"

"Can I plead the Fifth this time? It's a new semester, so it's a clean slate."

Maggie and I had this thing where every semester, we had three plead the Fifth cards we could use when we didn't want to tell the other something. I always seemed to use mine before the second week was over. She stockpiled hers. But that was only because she told me everything, even things I didn't want to know.

She pursed her lips, thinking about it for a few moments before she decided to let me off the hook.

"Okay, but you're down to only one plead the Fifth card left for this semester."

"Why?" I protested.

"You pled the Fifth with the Jeff thing and the Jesse thing."

"I did not," I whined. How did she remember all this shit?

"Rylan," she said, putting her hands on her hips. "You're lucky I'm combining them. I could tell you that you're out of Fifth cards for the semester, and I have a feeling you're going to need them."

I huffed and folded my arms over my chest, scowling at her.

"And you're cooking dinner again tomorrow night," she added.

"Fine," I answered. She could have asked me for a week of dinners, and I would have agreed. I wasn't ready to spill my stalking secrets yet.

CHAPTER FOUR

NO ONE was around when I rolled out of bed the next day. It was a little disappointing to run without Jade, but after my stalking incident last night, I needed a little alone time to clear my head.

They still weren't home when I got back from my run. The house remained empty after my shower and after breakfast. I frowned and checked my phone for the millionth time, but there was no message from either Maggie or Jade. It was a bit silly to think that Jade would check in with me. He'd never asked me for my phone number.

I finally decided it was stupid to worry about those two. If I really wanted to know where Maggie was, I could call her. I did peek into Maggie's room just to make sure she wasn't hiding, but her room was empty and neat as a fucking magazine layout.

Jade's door was closed, and I stood in the hall, arguing with myself. I had no right to snoop, even though I was dying to look. To ease my nosiness, I locked myself in my room and turned on some music.

I was lying on my bed twiddling my thumbs when something I hadn't felt in a long time sparked inside my head. At first, I was afraid to move, because it could be a false alarm, but after several more seconds, I gave up and jumped out of bed. I held my breath as I snagged a notebook and a pen, doing a belly flop back on my bed.

The blank page nearly blinded me, but slowly I started scribbling words. The words turned into sentences, and they didn't stop until I was looking at the lyrics to an entire song filling the once blank page. It had been two months since I'd written anything, and now words were flowing like someone had turned the water faucet on full blast.

Three songs later, I heard the front door open.

"I don't smell any food," Maggie yelled.

"Oh shit," I groaned and rolled off my bed. Maggie was already standing in my doorway with her arms crossed. "I'm sorry."

"Were you writing?" she asked.

"Yeah, I lost track of the time," I said, holding my notebook open so she could see there were actual words and not only doodles on the pages. She snagged it out of my hands and flipped the pages as she read.

"Holy shit, Rylan. These are awesome," she said. She tackled me on the bed, pressing her body into mine and pinning my arms over my head. "I'm so happy for you."

The door banged open. "Oh, sorry," Jade said and quickly shut the door.

Maggie burst out laughing and shouted, "Jade, get back here!"

A red-faced Jade opened the door a crack. "I didn't mean to… well, you said we were having dinner, and I heard you laughing, and, oh shit, I'm going to leave you two alone."

Maggie rolled off me and laughed. "I'm not sleeping with Rylan."

The door opened wider. "Sleep wasn't what I was thinking," Jade muttered.

This time I laughed and smacked Maggie on the ass. "She's not my type." I wanted to add that no girl was my type, but Maggie shouted that she was hungry and all of us raced to the kitchen.

She pretended to complain and feigned dying of hunger, but she quickly forgave me when I whipped up omelets for everyone. She even let us eat in the living room in front of the TV. I was acutely aware of Jade sitting next to me, because for some reason, his knee rested against mine the entire time we were eating.

We played rock, paper, scissors to see who had to do the dishes. Maggie lost, so she took our plates and disappeared into the kitchen, grumbling loudly. Of course, when Jade turned his head, she winked at me, so I think she lost on purpose. The girl was clearly nuts.

Jade leaned back and patted his stomach. "That was great. You're good at that cooking thing."

"Thanks," I said. "And thanks for doing my laundry. You're good at that folding stuff."

Jade snorted. "Oh, I forgot to give this to you yesterday. There's no book for your class, but Maggie picked up some notebooks and these pens she said you liked."

Jade picked up a bag sitting by his feet and pulled out a pack of my favorite pens. I moaned when he handed me the package.

"Do you have a pen fetish or something?"

I laughed. "No... well, maybe. These are the best in the world."

"Are you a writer? I heard you telling Maggie you'd been writing this afternoon."

For some reason, my face flushed. I didn't think I'd ever said the words out loud before. "Um, I suppose I am a writer. I mess around with song lyrics. Sometimes, I try to write short stories. That's why I'm taking summer school. It's a creative writing class where I'll be forced to write different things."

"You write lyrics," Jade said, sitting up. "I mess around with music, but the words I write always sound so lame. Could I see some of your songs? I mean, only if you want to show me. No pressure."

"Only if you promise not to laugh," I said.

"I'll be right back," Jade said. He jumped off the couch and ran down the hall. I was trying not to bounce off the couch with excitement because I might get to hear him sing again.

Jade returned with his guitar. Watching him sit down next to me with that guitar made me break out in a sweat. When he ran his fingers down the neck of the guitar, all I could think about was what his calloused fingers would feel like against my bare skin. I shuddered.

"Do you sing too?" Jade asked, plucking at the strings.

"What? Oh, I mean a little," I said. "Not very well."

"He's lying, Jade," Maggie shouted from the kitchen. "He's good and his lyrics are awesome."

"Shut up!" I shouted back, because I didn't know what else to say.

Jade stroked the strings again and started strumming. He stopped after a few chords and tuned a string before he resumed playing.

"See if you recognize this one," he said, picking out some notes. Maggie appeared in the doorway and stared at him. We both knew the song.

When he opened his mouth and launched into "Maggie May," I almost slid off the couch, and Maggie looked like she was having a spontaneous orgasm on the spot. Hearing him sing had been good last night, but I had been outside, not sitting right next to him. Now I heard all the nuances of his voice, and it was like heaven. I was transfixed, frozen with wonder as he sang the words and coaxed the notes from his guitar.

"Take the next verse, Rylan," Jade challenged. When I didn't move, he nudged me with his knee.

"What?"

"Sing, Rylan. Sing the next verse," he repeated. I wasn't sure if I could make my voice work. He grinned when I started to sing. His foot tapped out the beat, and when he joined me in the final chorus, the real Maggie Mae turned into a fangirl and screamed.

"Holy shit, you guys sound great together. Rylan, you need to teach Jade one of your songs. Please. Please," she begged. She got down on her knees and crawled across the floor, like a woman dying of thirst.

"God damn," Jade said. "We did sound good together."

"You should get your keyboard," Maggie said.

"You play keyboard?" Jade asked.

"A little," I said. "I took a few years of piano lessons until my dad made me quit."

"Why would he make you quit?"

Shit. I wasn't about to reveal the truth to him. My brother had told my dad people were making fun of me for playing the piano. Lucas told my dad he didn't want me to get beat up, so my dad decided it was best that I stop playing. Really, Lucas thought I was getting out of work because of the lessons.

After my dad made me quit, my music teacher at school let me practice during one of my free periods.

"Not enough time. When I got older, I had to help with the planting and the harvesting and all the other fun shit that comes with living on a working farm." I shrugged. "I started playing again when I met Maggie. She gave me a keyboard."

"I'll get the keyboard if you show Jade the lyrics you wrote this afternoon," Maggie said.

Sweat beaded up on my forehead, and I shifted uncomfortably. Jade placed his hand on my forearm. A wave of calmness flowed through me.

"You don't have to show me," Jade said quietly.

"No, it's okay," I said. "I just...."

"Rylan, I won't laugh at you," he said.

Maggie cleared her throat. She was holding the notebook, giving me an encouraging look. I nodded, and she handed the book to Jade. I suddenly had the urge to bolt out of the room, but Jade shuffled closer to me. We were now touching from our shoulders to the tips of our shoes.

My leg vibrated as I watched his eyes shift from side to side as he read what I'd written a few short hours ago. He read for a few minutes and then picked up his guitar and strummed different chords before he settled on one and started singing my lyrics.

Out of the corner of my eye, I saw Maggie fumbling with her phone, but Jade's singing pulled me away from her. He stopped playing and I wanted to protest, but he changed a few notes and started again. This time he kept going, and the words meshed with the melody.

When he sang the last word and strummed the final chord, I was awestruck and unable to form a single coherent word. Maggie slid down the wall and sat on the floor with her mouth wide open.

Jade squirmed nervously next to me.

"Say something," he said.

"How did you do that?" I asked.

"It was your lyrics," he said. "I've never had a song come so easily before."

"You want to try another?" I asked.

"Really?"

"Are you kidding? You are unbelievably talented, and your voice is perfect," I gushed.

Jade's face was bright red, and I couldn't resist squeezing his elbow. He hooked his ankle with mine, which sent my stomach plummeting into my shoes again.

He fiddled with his guitar some more. I could hear Maggie rummaging around my bedroom. She came back carrying a pile of notebooks she'd fished out from under my bed. The living room was soon cluttered with open notebooks.

After a ton of prodding, Jade brought some of his journals out and let me read his lyrics. He begged me to make changes, telling me he wouldn't be upset if I changed everything. It wasn't that hard to clean up his words and make the lyrics flow better. I understood what he was trying to say with his songs.

At around two in the morning, Maggie reluctantly took the guitar away from Jade. We had class in a few hours, and sleepwalking through the first day of summer session was probably not the best idea.

We both protested, but Maggie frowned and shut the living room lights off. Jade groaned, resting his head on my shoulder.

"I can't move," he said.

"Me neither," I agreed. When Maggie left the room, he leaned against me, the warmth of his body seeping into my side and making me sleepy.

"You're a great writer, Rylan," Jade murmured. He grabbed the blanket off the back of the couch and tossed it over both of us. "You're also a great pillow."

I'm not sure if he said anything else, because the next moment, Maggie was shaking both of us and shouting about being late for the first day of class.

There was a lot of scrambling and swearing before we all piled into the car. We made it to the train station with about two minutes to spare. The Red Line waited for no man, woman, or child.

When we slid into our seats, all I could think about was how great last night had been. The songs played over and over in my head. Hearing my lyrics combined with his music and my words falling from his lips affected me more than I wanted to admit.

It was the first time in a very long time I had really shared an important part of myself with another person besides Maggie, and it scared me out of my wits. Jade smiled at me, and an insane giddy feeling spread through my body.

THE DAYS passed in a whirl, and we all fell into a comfortable rhythm. Jade and I ran or biked in the morning. When we got back, we showered, separately of course, and had breakfast with Maggie, listening to her bitch about her horrible history professor. She had put off getting her upper level humanities courses and was paying for it now.

My writing class was going quite well. I didn't think I'd enjoy constructing entire stories, but once I got past the initial fear of failure, the words flowed easily. Today we were going to attempt to write a sex scene using thoughts and feelings instead of painting graphic pictures with words. I was going to fail miserably. Feelings were banned in my bedroom, and remembering the few times I'd let feelings get in the way would not make for a very romantic, pretty picture.

"Come on, Rylan," Maggie grumbled. "I don't want to be late. I'm having enough trouble in this stupid class."

"Maybe we should skip today," I said. "We could go shopping."

Tempting Maggie with shopping was mean, but I was desperate to skip this assignment.

"You hate shopping," she said, narrowing her eyes at me.

"Maybe I would like to spend some quality time with you."

"Shopping is not quality time, because you make it through one store and then start whining. Spill," she said.

I groaned. "Today's assignment is writing a sex scene using feelings instead of graphic description."

"Did the professor tell you it had to be sticky sweet?"

I frowned and flipped through my notes. "No, but...."

"There's your answer," she said. She grabbed me by my belt loop and dragged me to the car.

About an hour later, the tap, tap, tap of people typing surrounded me while I stared at a blank screen.

I had asked the question and the professor agreed with Maggie. "You are absolutely correct, Rylan. Not all relationships are based on love. But I don't want you to write a sex scene involving a prostitute. If there aren't any feelings, I want to know why."

"I don't know if I can do this," I mumbled.

"Rylan, you are a wonderful writer. You can do anything you put your mind to. I'm not asking for an autobiographical account of your love life. It's just a story. It can be fiction."

"I'll give it a shot," I said. I still wasn't happy about this assignment.

People always say write what you know, but screw that; I wasn't about to write about all my failed relationships.

I thought about basing the story on one of Maggie's relationships. She once dated this guy who was boring everywhere except in the bedroom. Maggie had strung him along for a few weeks, but eventually, she ditched him. Her body mourned the loss for two weeks.

I thought about Jade and his girlfriend. I didn't know the exact details, but I witnessed the end of their relationship. My imagination could fill in the gaps.

It was a disturbing piece to write. I could have written about the beginning of the relationship where the sex was new and exciting, but I settled on describing the end of their relationship when having sex became more of a duty.

The story centered on the last night they were together as a couple. There were no fireworks to end the relationship. It fizzled out and after two years of dating, the end came down to a few cold words before the main character loaded his possessions in his car and drove away.

When I completed the assignment, I thought about Jade and his ex again. You'd think after two years of dating he'd at least have moments of regret, but Jade never even mentioned Daria. Relationships scared the hell out of me. Did this happen to everyone? You think you're head over heels and then one day, the flame just goes out? I would never let any of my liaisons go that far.

The professor stopped us before we all scattered. "There's a life drawing class in a few hours I would like you all to attend. If you can't make it to that one, I have a list of different times. Observe and write."

After my writing class, I needed a drink, but it was too early in the day to justify a shot of tequila. I settled on a giant vat of mocha latte. Jade sent me a text, and I told him I was still on campus, waiting to attend a life drawing class. He told me he was going and I could use some of his tools if I wanted to participate, or I could sit in the back of the room and write.

I'd been to a few life drawing classes last summer, and it was always the same. The guys would come rushing in all bright-eyed and flushed in the face. If you were a straight guy, you learned to jack off before sitting in on one of the sessions. Apparently, there were a lot of hot girls willing to strip naked and pose for the sake of art.

When we showed up for the class, it was already packed, and the professor ushered us to the front of the room and the last two chairs. Wonderful. I was going to get an eyeful of tits and pussy.

Jade handed me a tablet and several pencils.

"Thanks," I muttered and set up my easel, keeping my head down. The sound of a chair scraping across the wood of the platform alerted me to the presence of the model. The professor suggested various poses and the model dropped her towel.

Jade cleared his throat, so I looked over at him. He stared wide-eyed at the model. She must be totally hot, because his face was bright red, and I noticed tiny beads of sweat trickling down his neck.

I sighed at the typical male response to a naked woman, then raised my head to see what sort of body made Jade hot. Big tits? Skinny or curvy? Long hair or short hair? Blonde or brunette?

I lost my breath. Instead of a naked woman, my gaze fell on light-green eyes, dark hair splayed on broad shoulders, and a hard, flat chest with a smattering of hair that led to a cock.

"Fuck," Jade breathed out. I returned my attention to him and watched as he lowered his eyes and took a few shallow breaths before placing the pencil on the paper. His hand shook and a dark line squiggled down his paper.

Jade frowned and steadied his hand. I wanted to watch him draw but my gaze kept shifting to the naked guy in front of me.

I wasn't sure how I made it through the next hour. By the time the professor handed the guy his robe, I had a major headache. I think it was because most of my blood flow was located in my fucking dick. Staring at Jade and a naked guy sent my imagination reeling.

"I'll be right back," Jade said. He rushed out of the room before I could say anything. I packed up his stuff and stood outside waiting for him. A flash of jealousy flared when I saw Jade come out of the bathroom followed by the model.

The model frowned when he saw me wave at Jade. I shrugged and gave the guy a quick shake of my head, trying to tell him he was barking up the wrong tree. Besides, if there were any chance Jade was gay, I would be the one barking.

"Sorry about that," Jade said, taking his portfolio out of my hands.

"Sorry for what?"

"You looked uncomfortable."

"No, I was okay."

Jade ran his hands through his hair. "I... I...," he stammered, and I sighed.

"I need to go to the library," Jade said, keeping his eyes away from me. "I'll be home later."

"That's fine," I said and bolted, leaving him standing in the hall holding his portfolio. I wandered around campus for a while before I made my way to the train and went home.

"Maggie!" I shouted and slammed the door. "Maggie!" I yelled louder.

"What?"

"You've got to cover for me tonight," I panted.

"Rylan, calm down," she said. The tips of her hair were now pink. It was a strange thing to notice, but I was beyond crazy at the moment.

"No, I need to go out, like now."

"Why?" she asked. Her nails matched her hair.

I grabbed her shoulders. "You don't understand. I can't take this anymore. He's everywhere and I want him, but I can't have him because he's my fucking friend and our roommate. I don't even know if he's interested in me. I can't even think straight because I'm not getting enough blood to my brain. It's all moved down to my dick."

"Rylan, what are you talking about? You're not making any sense."

"I went to a life drawing class with Jade, and the model was a guy. All I could think about the entire class was a naked Jade."

The front door opened, and Maggie shoved me into my room and closed the door behind her. I heard her talking to Jade. A few minutes later, she opened the door and waved at me to come out.

"What is going on?" she asked. The shower turned on. Fuck. My stupid mind automatically informed me Jade was naked and the water was sliding down his chest and back and ass and…. I needed a hard slap upside the head so I'd stop thinking about Jade.

"Maggie, I need to go out and have sex before I fucking lose my shit," I rambled. "He's always here and… fuck, I told you, we just came from a life drawing class and the naked model was this beautiful guy, but all I could focus on was Jade. Before I knew it, I'd sketched several pictures of Jade's eyes. The professor was impressed with my drawing but told me I didn't quite capture the model's eyes. Jade tried to peek over my shoulder, and suddenly the professor knew whose eyes I drew. I had to shake my head and silently beg him not to out me. Oh God, Maggie, why is this happening? Jade is going to hate me. I fucking hate me. I don't want to like him like *that*!"

Maggie put her hand over my mouth. My heart was beating so hard it sounded like it had moved up to my ears.

"Rylan," she said slowly. "You need to calm down before you collapse and die right in front of me."

I nodded.

"I'm going to take away my hand, and you are calmly going to tell me what the fuck is wrong with you." She slowly lowered her hand. "Okay?" she said. "Take a deep breath."

I followed her instructions and felt my heart rate slow down. "I need to get laid, Maggie," I said in a low whisper. "Can you cover for me?"

"Oh," she said as the meaning of my words sank in. "I don't think it's a good idea to go out and get your rocks off with some nameless guy," Maggie scolded.

"I'm losing my mind," I whined. "I can't take this anymore. You don't understand. My hand isn't enough."

"Too much information," Maggie said, scowling at me.

"Maggie, please," I whimpered. "It's either cover for me or I'm going to jump him. He'll probably murder me, and you'll have to live with the guilt of my death. Jade will be arrested and sentenced to life in prison. No one wins, Maggie."

"Oh my God." She sighed. "You are such a drama queen. Fine, fine, go out and take care of business. I'll think of something to tell Jade."

I kissed her and took off to primp and prime for my evening out on the town. The boys wouldn't know what hit them. Secretly, I hoped being surrounded by beautiful guys would show me I was just horny and not feeling something for Jade. Shit. I put on my tightest jeans and hottest shirt and hit the town.

In the end, it didn't work. I kept comparing all the guys who came near me to Jade, and none of them could hold a candle to him. What the fuck was I going to do? How do you learn to stay someone's friend when all you want to have is more?

The cab pulled up to my house, and I scowled as I paid the guy.

"Rough night?" the cabbie asked.

"You have no fucking idea," I grumbled and slammed the door. It had been a total waste of money and time. I gave the guy a halfhearted wave and stumbled into the house half-drunk and really pissed off, knowing it was going to be another night with my hand. When I opened the door to my room, Jade was sitting on my bed. I checked to make sure I was in the right room.

"Maggie said you went out," he said.

"Um, yeah," I answered. I felt like I was on trial.

"Are you seeing someone?" I noticed he kept it gender neutral. It probably wasn't on purpose.

"No," I said. "Jade, I'm really tired and a little drunk."

"Did you hook up with someone tonight?"

"No," I grumbled. This was his fucking fault, and now he was interrogating me like I was a fucking criminal. "Why are you asking me all these questions?"

He remained quiet, watching my every move and making me incredibly self-conscious. I turned off the light. There was still enough moonlight streaming in the room so his outline was visible. He didn't move, and I could feel his gaze on me.

The logical part of my brain told me I should ask him what the hell he was doing in my room. The drunk, stupid part of my brain told me Maggie and I had spent several nights in the same bed and we were just friends. I was tired and he was in my bed. There was nothing left for me to do but get undressed.

I started with the shirt buttons. I'd never noticed how many buttons were on this fucking shirt. When I got the last one unbuttoned, I almost ripped the shirt off my body.

The belt proved to be more difficult, and I cursed it several times before I felt someone behind me.

"Jade," I murmured in a warning tone. He was too close to me, and I couldn't be held responsible for my actions if he touched me.

"Why didn't you sleep with someone tonight?"

The warmth from his palms on my shoulders seeped into my skin and made my blood boil. This didn't seem like normal straight-guy behavior.

"Jade, what are you doing?" I whimpered.

"I don't know," he answered. His warm breath caressed my neck. It took all my power to stay on my feet and not lean back into his body. Instead, I stepped away from him.

"Why are you doing this to me?" I asked.

Jade sat down on my bed. "I can't stop thinking about you."

I had no clue what to say to him. The silence in my room was deafening.

He lowered his head and cleared his throat. "If I made you uncomfortable, I'm sorry. I thought we... that you... shit, I'm sorry," he said again. He stood up, brushed past me, and kept his head down.

The alcohol fogged my brain, and I had no idea what the fuck was going on with Jade.

"Wait," I said and grabbed the door before he could shut it.

"Rylan," Jade said. "I made a mistake. Can we forget about this? It's fucking embarrassing."

I frowned. "Forget what? Did I miss something?" Jade kept his gaze locked on the floor. "Jade, talk to me. Please, I need to be sure I understand what's going on. I mean, I don't even know if there is something going on. Is there something going on?"

His eyes locked with mine. The intensity of his stare made me stumble back into the wall, or maybe it was the booze. He took a few tentative steps toward me until he was totally crowding my personal space. It certainly seemed like there was something going on.

Time stopped for me. I needed to think my next move through because I had forced myself to draw boundaries. He was supposed to be straight, my friend, and my roommate. And yet, right now, it felt like he wanted more. Those stupid boundary lines were blurring and the words *just friends* were slowly evaporating in front of my eyes.

But this was Jade, who had quickly found a special place in my life. Images floated through my head. He was the guy who ate chocolate cereal with me after we'd been on a ten-mile bike ride. He was the guy who sat on the deck with me and listened to me shout at the imaginary characters when they wouldn't cooperate in my stories. He was the guy who lay on my bed and wrote songs with me with his ankle hooked around mine. And every time I tried to shift away from him, he mirrored my movements, never letting me get too far away. All the random touches, the wrestling, the shoulder bumping, and the shy smiles started to add up in my head. Did he want something more from me?

He was standing so close to me, his warm breath tickled my cheek when he breathed out my name. "Rylan," Jade said in a low whisper.

"Yeah?" I squeaked.

"Help me out here," he said. "This is new territory for me."

"You sure?"

"Mmhmm," Jade said.

I took a deep breath. "I didn't sleep with anyone tonight because you weren't there."

He licked his lips. "I'm here now."

I groaned and erased that fucking stupid, imaginary boundary line when my lips dragged across his. He sighed and opened his eyes, staring straight into my soul. We kissed again, and I kept my eyes open, watching as his eyelashes fluttered against his flushed cheeks.

He danced his calloused fingers up my arms, across my shoulders and slid them into my hair. He tugged gently, and tilted my head back. His tongue glided over my lips, and I opened my mouth to him. The kiss was slow and gentle and made my fucking toes curl. I couldn't remember the last time I'd been kissed like this, maybe never. He nipped at my lower lip and then buried his face in my neck, sucking down hard until I felt beautiful pain blossoming where he was marking me.

"I didn't know. I didn't know," he panted into my neck, clutching me tightly.

"Didn't know what?"

"That it was supposed to feel like this," he said. "I feel you everywhere."

"Fuck," I whimpered, because I felt him everywhere too, and it scared the shit out of me.

He kissed me again, pressing me into the wall until I gasped for air.

"Jade," I whispered. He stopped kissing me and let his hands fall from my neck. His fingers tangled with mine and he slowly turned and led me back into my bedroom.

I stared at our hands locked together, and I never wanted to let go of him. That thought alone should have sent me running in the opposite direction. He let my hand drop, and we stood staring at each other, neither really knowing what the other wanted. He chewed on his lip and swallowed audibly. His hand moved toward the zipper on his pants. The unmistakable bulge of his cock was straining to be released. I stopped his hand.

"May I?" I asked politely. It sounded stupid, like we were sitting down to have coffee with Mrs. Morgan and asking permission to take a cookie off the fancy china platter she always used.

The second I brushed my hand over the denim, he groaned, and my uneasy politeness flew out the window. I wanted this. He'd tortured me for weeks by his mere existence. Now he stood fully hard in front of me, and I was acting like a fucking unsure virgin.

I popped the button and unzipped his pants, then reached in to grab hold of his cock. Jade's head fell back, and he whimpered. He dug his fingers into my shoulders, and his thighs shook. I pulled his jeans down and stared. This was all of my fantasies coming true, but all the times I spent jerking off to thoughts of him couldn't compare to the real thing.

"Rylan," Jade moaned.

I pushed him so he sat down on my bed. He kicked his jeans off, and I tugged at the waistband of his underwear. I was a little nervous that Jade would have a major freak-out if I pushed him too far, but he didn't even blink when I yanked his underwear off.

I dropped to my knees and spread his legs. He leaned back on his elbows, watching me. I slid my hands up his thighs, enjoying the feel of his muscles flexing beneath my touch. The closer I got to his cock the harder he panted.

His dick was thick and heavy in my hand, and I couldn't resist taking a minute to admire him. He whined and wiggled until I decided I'd teased him enough. I flicked my tongue out and took a small taste, licking around the crown.

He grabbed the sheets and raised his hips. I pushed down on his thighs to keep him still and wrapped my lips around his dripping cock, taking him as deep as I could. I followed my mouth with my hand, leaving no part of him untouched.

"Oh my fucking God," Jade croaked out.

I sucked harder, and I started to think he was going to rip my sheets to pieces or chew a hole in my pillow.

"Stop. Rylan, stop," Jade said hoarsely.

Panic curled in my stomach, and I froze. Was this when he was going to decide everything was a huge mistake and run away from me?

"I don't want to cum yet," Jade whimpered as he tugged on my hair until I looked up at him. His lust-filled eyes met mine, and something curled around my heart and squeezed.

"Can I fuck you?" he asked.

The words exploded in my head, and I let his dick fall against his stomach.

"I… I mean," he stammered, and his face flushed. "Only if you… shit. That was probably a stupid thing to say. I'm sorry."

I scrambled to my feet, almost tripping over my jeans as they dropped to my ankles. It was a fucking ordeal, but I finally managed to get them off along with my underwear. I yanked open the drawer of my bedside table, pulling so hard the thing fell to the floor with a loud bang. The bottle of lube landed next to my foot and the box of condoms spilled everywhere.

"Shit," I said and tossed the bottle and condom at Jade, hitting him in the head.

"Really?" he breathed.

I nodded frantically and climbed up his body. He flipped us over and hovered above me before settling between my legs. Memories of the first night I jerked off to him flooded my head. This was what it felt like to have the weight of his body on mine. It set my nerves on fire, and I couldn't help rocking my hips into him.

"Please slow down, Rylan," Jade warned. "Or this is going to be over before I can get the cap off the lube."

He opened the lube and covered his fingers in liquid. I licked my lips and opened my legs wider. He shoved a pillow under my hips, exposing more of me.

"Uh, Jade? How do you know all this?"

His cheeks flushed. "You've been driving me crazy. When I realized what I was feeling, I sort of did some research. Just in case."

"Oh," I groaned as he ran his slicked fingers down my cock, pausing at my balls and then rubbing over my hole. *He did research.* My heart skipped a beat or two, and I couldn't breathe. He wanted to be with me. Jade grabbed my attention when he rubbed my hole again.

After several more passes, he pushed in a finger, slowly twisting and watching all my facial tics.

"Another?" he asked quietly.

I panted out a pained yes and thrust my hips down. He wiggled another finger in and started slowly pumping them in and out of me. He soon had me begging for more.

The third finger hurt, but I bit the inside of my cheek to keep from screaming. I didn't want to freak him out. I concentrated on staying relaxed, but when he curled his fingers and hit my spot, the pain disappeared and sparks shot through my body.

"Jade," I groaned. He stopped moving. "No, don't stop," I whined. "I need more."

Jade rose to his knees, pulled his fingers free, and grabbed a condom. His dick was hard and leaking on my leg. He rolled the condom on and poured more lube in his hand, stroking his dick a couple of times.

He paused and stared at me. "If I hurt you...."

"Jade," I said and opened my legs wider, pulling my knees to my chest.

He lined up, pushed hard, and slipped inside me. The pain was intense at first, but I concentrated on his face. His red lips fell open, and his eyes rolled back. It was a lovely sight.

"Rylan," Jade gasped. His fingers drifted across my stomach and wrapped around my cock. He pumped me a few times, and I was on the verge of losing everything. I thrust my hips and Jade let go of my cock, digging his fingers into my skin. He pulled his dick out and pushed back in. He changed the angle of his thrusts, and suddenly he was hitting my spot, sending sparks flying up my spine. I moaned and my hips came off the bed, meeting Jade's every movement.

"Oh my God, baby, I can't hold off anymore," Jade panted. "I need to cum."

"Do it," I said, reaching between us to stroke my cock.

His breathing sped up, and I felt his thighs clench as his rhythm faltered. All my muscles tightened, and I felt the magic burn wrap around my spine. With a couple more strokes, we came within seconds of each other, my cum spurting all over my stomach and my name falling from his lips. Jade gasped and collapsed on top of me, smearing the wetness everywhere.

"Holy shit," he whispered. "Holy shit, baby."

My body tensed when he slipped out of me, and I worried he might race out of the room when he realized what we'd done.

He sat up, balanced on his knees, and removed the condom. He dropped it in the trash and ran a finger down my chest right through my cooling cum.

"You're a mess," Jade said. He leaned down and kissed me. "Shower?"

A small smile tugged at the corners of my lips as he helped me to my feet. We snuck down the hall trying to keep our giggles quiet. I couldn't help it. I was running naked down the hall with Jade Marin, my formally straight roommate, who I had firmly told Maggie I wasn't going to fuck.

The water was warm and soothing, and Jade couldn't keep his hands to himself. He pinned me to the shower wall and gave me one of the finest hand jobs I'd ever received while kissing me senseless.

We toweled off and crept back to my room. Jade gathered his clothes into a neat little pile and stepped into his underwear. He seemed unsure what to do, so I solved his problem by tackling him on my bed.

"Can I ask you something?" I said, hiding my face in his neck.

"Sure."

"Have you ever... er."

"No," Jade answered quickly. "I told you, I did research. Was it bad?"

He looked like he was starting to panic. I chuckled and dragged my lips over his neck. I rolled on top of him and grinned. "God no, it was you. How could it be bad? But, why me? I mean you had a girlfriend."

Jade wrinkled his nose. "I was never happy with her. I tried, but there wasn't a spark between us. At first I thought it was just Daria, so I spent a lot of time watching other women and there was nothing special. I mean, I appreciate beauty, but they didn't get me all riled up. I started to think there was something wrong with me, that I didn't know how to love someone. But then the first day I met you and Maggie, I knew. When you got out of your car something deep inside me woke up."

"The first time you saw me?" The thought made my entire body heat up. He had wanted me from the beginning.

"It freaked the shit out of me, but the trip to the grocery store was fun. Then you fell asleep in my bed. I, um, watched you sleep, and I knew." A shy smile spread across his face, and I wanted to know what the hell he knew, but I was too chicken to ask.

I sighed, and he wrapped his arms around me and held me tightly. I was in deep shit.

CHAPTER FIVE

SNEAKING QUIETLY around the house had never been one of my strong suits. I usually ran into a door or dropped something that made a ton of noise. Tonight was no exception when I had to go to the kitchen and find something to drink to relieve my cottonmouth. The plastic glass I fumbled made a terrible clatter when I dropped it on the wood floor. Maggie raced out of her room and almost ran into me.

"What are you doing?" she asked. I felt her gaze sweeping over my naked chest and landing on the hickeys. They must have glowed in the dark or something.

"Oh my God," Maggie said. "Did you bring someone home?"

"Er…. No."

She glared at me and made me feel like I was totally naked. The weird stare down lasted for a few seconds, and then her eyes widened.

"Oh, holy shit, Rylan. Is it Jade? Oh my God! You fucked. You fucking fucked already. Fuck, Rylan, are you fucking crazy? You told me you weren't going to get involved with our roommate." She ranted for a little longer about how fucking stupid this whole thing was and how she wasn't going to be there to pick up the pieces when one of us freaked out.

"I think I'm falling in love with him," I said quietly.

The statement stopped her in her tracks.

"What?"

"I love him," I said.

"Whoa," she said. She handed me the orange juice and left me standing in the kitchen. Maybe she had been sleepwalking and wouldn't remember this conversation in the morning.

I shook it off, went back to my room, and quietly pushed the door open. I held my breath, not knowing if Jade would still be in my bed, or if he had hightailed it back to his room. My heart soared when I saw the tips of his damp, sun-kissed hair spread out on my pillow.

"You scare the shit out of me," I whispered and kissed his cheek. I gently climbed over him and settled down again. He scooted closer, breathing into my shoulder. I sighed and closed my eyes, hoping he would be next to me when I woke up. I'd been known to have fantastic, realistic dreams when I was drunk.

So I couldn't be blamed that I was a little surprised when Maggie opened the door in the morning and I felt Jade wiggle next to me. I wanted to shout it to anyone who would listen that he'd stayed with me and it was all very real.

Maggie eyed us curiously. The only thing out of her mouth was we needed to get up for school. Even if she had been sleepwalking last night, there would be no pleading the Fifth to get out of this one.

"Rylan and I don't have class today," Jade said. It was news to me, but I wasn't going to argue with him.

Maggie shot a frigid glare at me, making me sink back into my pillow.

I think she scared Jade too, because his voice quivered when he spoke, quickly spilling the truth. "Okay, fine, we're skipping to work on some songs." Jade sat up straighter and spoke directly to Maggie. "Remember when we were watching YouTube the other night and you said we should post some of our songs?"

"Yeah," Maggie said.

"I think we should do it. I mean, if Rylan agrees, because I'm not doing it without him."

Maggie shrieked, and I looked at Jade like he'd stepped off the deep end. Maybe his blood supply was still located in his dick from all the sex last night and his brain wasn't working correctly.

The bed dipped when Maggie climbed in with us, shoving Jade against my hard cock. Jade sucked in a breath of air, but didn't move away. The curve of his ass rested against my cock, and every time Maggie bounced on the bed, there was friction. I managed to shift slightly, but my shoulders hit the wall. I was fucking trapped.

There was a lot of giggling and whispering, but finally, Maggie got out of bed and walked out of the room.

"Jade," I choked out.

I thought he would leave, but he turned around and straddled my hips, pinning me to the bed. He leaned forward to kiss me, but I turned my head away from him. "Morning breath," I groaned.

"Don't care," Jade said and caught my lips, shoving his tongue into my mouth at the same moment he drove his hips into mine. The friction was delicious.

"We don't have much time," I gasped.

"Not going to take much," he panted.

I slipped my hands between us and shoved our underwear out of the way so I could wrap my hand around our cocks. Jade rolled over so we were on our sides facing each other. His lips were near my ear, and he was breathing heavily. "When we have more time, I want you to fuck me."

My orgasm came without warning, filling my hand and covering Jade's cock with my cum. He moaned loudly, and I gripped him tighter, rubbing my cum everywhere. He grabbed the back of my neck and pulled me in for a sloppy kiss. His body shuddered and his dick pulsed in my hand. I milked him through his orgasm.

"Fuck," he said and rolled to his back. "I need a fucking nap."

"Maggie is not going to let you sleep after you told her we'd record something, so I propose you get up and shower before she comes back in here and sees you with your dick hanging out of your underwear covered in cum."

Jade laughed and tucked himself back into his underwear. "Don't worry. We have days. We need recording equipment before we can do anything. It's not like you have any of that shit lying around the house."

"Well, we don't have any in our house, but…."

"Your eyes are sparkling," Jade said and dragged his thumb across my cheek. "What are you up to?"

I shoved his hand away. "Shower, Jade," I said pointedly.

He frowned, gave me a quick kiss on the cheek, and climbed out of bed. He picked up his clothes and tossed them into my laundry basket. Maggie met him at the door. He kissed her on the cheek and whispered something to her. Within seconds, her face was bright red and Jade was laughing his head off. I wasn't even going to ask. It was difficult to make Maggie blush, but he seemed to do it on a regular basis.

She sat down on the edge of the bed. "Are you okay?"

"Yeah, I think so," I said. "I think I'm on overload. This is insane." I didn't need to elaborate. I'm sure she could see it in my face.

"I'm here if you need me," she said, grabbing my hand. "I'll always be here for you."

"Thanks, Maggie."

"Don't look so smug. We're still talking about this. You do not get to plead the Fifth on this one."

"Didn't even cross my mind," I said.

"Now go get cleaned up. I talked to Mrs. Morgan and she's waiting for us."

She pinched my thigh before she left the room. I collapsed on my pillow and felt that familiar spark shoot through my head. I rolled over and grabbed a notebook and pen from under my bed.

The words fell seamlessly onto the page. There was no struggle to yank them out of my mind, and I lost myself in the writing.

Before I knew it, Jade and Maggie were standing in the doorway, cleaned and dressed.

"I'll be over as soon as I'm done," I said without looking up at them.

"Why are we going over to Mrs. Morgan's house?" Jade asked Maggie.

"Mrs. Morgan has a small recording studio in her basement," Maggie said.

"Are you serious?" Jade said.

"Yep, her husband was a studio musician. She has a nice setup, and it got better when her lousy son decided to try his hand at being a rock star. He updated the equipment. Thank God, his career was short-lived. He couldn't play an instrument or carry a tune. He even tried rap. It was fucking horrible, but the studio is super cool and Mrs. Morgan has let us use it before."

"Hello?" I said. "I'm writing here. Go away."

Jade grabbed Maggie by the arm and hauled her out of my room. His excitement was catching. As I moved further into the song, it dawned on me I was writing a sappy love song filled with sentiments of happiness and hope. Maggie was going to know I'd gone crazy, but maybe it wasn't so bad to let go of my cynical side and be happy.

"Oh my God, I'm a lovesick puppy."

I gathered up my journals and started to leave the house when I figured I should shower. The stench of stale alcohol, sex, and sweat were not a nice combination, especially in mixed company.

By the time I got over to Mrs. Morgan's house, everyone was huddled in the basement discussing how the video would be shot.

"Why are you talking about a video?" I asked.

"The song is going on YouTube," Maggie answered.

"Oh right, well, maybe we should record the song first. Jade and I haven't had much practice. It might sound like shit once we lay it down," I said.

"We're not going to sound like shit," Jade announced.

He sent a smile at me that made my blood race. I sat down next to him, and Maggie started with all the technical stuff.

Mrs. Morgan was a huge help. She was the first person who had ever suggested I record my music, showing Maggie and me how the soundboard worked. Maggie devoured the information and quickly learned how to get the best sound out of me. Both women were hunched over the soundboard, speaking quietly and fiddling with the knobs. We did a few sound checks and adjusted our mics several times before we launched into the song. It didn't take long until Jade quieted his guitar, and I realized we'd made it through the whole song.

Jade scooted closer to me and gave Mrs. Morgan and Maggie the thumbs up.

"Come upstairs," Mrs. Morgan said. "I've got some champagne to celebrate."

I watched as she and Maggie disappeared out of the small room. I slid off the stool, but Jade stopped me by grabbing me around the waist and pulling me into a kiss. When he released me so we could both breathe, he touched my cheek, dragging his finger down my jaw.

"Thank you," he sighed.

"For what?"

"Making me believe again," he said. "And making my life better."

No one had ever said anything like that to me. I always felt I made life more difficult for everyone who knew me. My family would be the first to agree with my assessment.

"Can I show you what I wrote?" I asked timidly.

"Always," Jade said.

"You inspire me," I whispered. A sudden wave of embarrassment flooded my body. Christ, I didn't really mean to say that out loud.

I watched his eyes dart back and forth as he read the words I'd just written. Jade set the notebook on the table and grabbed his guitar. He messed around for a few minutes until he was satisfied with the melody.

Out of the corner of my eye, I saw Maggie slide back into the booth. Jade bumped my leg, signaling me to start singing. When the song was over, I couldn't breathe. Maggie was wiping tears from her face.

"I know it's early and crazy as all fuck," Jade said, "but I can't hold it in anymore. No one has ever made me feel so much. I love you, Rylan."

The three most dreaded words known to mankind hung in the air, and for the first time in my entire life, I relished them and happily returned the sentiment.

"I love you too," I whispered.

IT TOOK Maggie a week to work out the kinks with the recording and the video. I thought it looked fine the first time we watched it, but she was a crazy perfectionist, so we let her fuss and fume over everything. It's not like we did anything in the video except sit and sing.

"Okay," Maggie said. She paraded around our living room waving a disc in the air. "We are all gathered here on this couch for the debut of Rylan and Jade singing their first song, which is sure to be a number one hit."

I snorted. "I just hope we get one hit on YouTube so this wasn't a total waste of everyone's time."

"It wasn't a waste of my time," Jade stated. His ankle was already hooked around mine. I'd noticed it when we recorded the song. It was fast becoming a thing he always did when he sat next to me. It was comforting and made my stomach twirl.

"Are we ready?" Maggie shouted.

"Let's get this party started," Mrs. Morgan said.

"Right," Maggie said and pushed play.

The song sounded awesome, and Maggie had done a great job editing. The video didn't look any different from the first time I saw it, but I wasn't going to say anything to Maggie. I'm sure she'd gone frame by frame and tweaked the lighting or something. I had no desire to sit through a lengthy description of everything she did to the video.

Maggie and Mrs. Morgan swooned and played up the whole fangirl thing. I wondered if there was such a thing as fanboys? I chuckled, because I considered myself a fanboy of the guy sitting next to me.

"You two are absolutely adorable," Mrs. Morgan said. "And the music is just wonderful."

"I've got everything all set up and ready to go on the computer. Are you guys ready to upload?" Maggie asked. Her finger hovered over the keyboard, and I felt my stomach flip. This was insane.

"Rylan?" Jade looked at me and grabbed my hand. "Are you ready to be famous?"

I laughed and rolled my eyes. "Right. Famous. Push that button, Maggie Mae."

She made a grand gesture of wiggling her fingers as she hit the button. And suddenly, there was our song and our faces for the entire world to see. Christ. I felt ill. What if everyone hated the fucking thing and posted all sorts of hateful shit? My fragile ego would fall apart.

"Calm down, Rylan," Maggie said. "No one is going to send you hate mail."

Jade glanced at me. "How does she do that?"

"I have no idea. It's scary, though."

Maggie started chattering. "When are we doing the next recording? You should do 'From the Beginning.'"

"What song is that?" I asked.

She shrugged. "The one you wrote the day we recorded this one."

"You named the song?" I asked.

A blush stained her cheeks. "Yeah, you can change it. It seemed like a good title. I pushed record when Jade started to play. It's a great song. I listen to it all the time."

"She played it for me," Mrs. Morgan said. "She's right. It should be heard."

"Can we just see if anyone likes the first one we put up?"

"Okay, fine, but I was thinking about some other stuff too," Maggie said. She had her glasses on tonight, and her hair was tied back so you couldn't see the pink tips. This was grown-up Maggie at her finest. "You guys should consider singing live. I think it would be awesome."

Jade laughed. "We have, like, three songs in our repertoire. Pretty sure a set list needs to be a little longer."

"I've heard you guys singing way more stuff, and it's not bad to cover songs when you're first starting out," Maggie said.

"What do you think, Rylan? Do you think the world is ready for us to sing live?" Jade asked.

He was crazy.

"Just let me try," Maggie begged.

"Sure, Maggie. Have at it. If you can get us a live gig, we'll be there," Jade said. I kicked him in the shin. "Hey!" Jade shouted and rubbed his leg.

"I can't play in front of people. It freaks me out," I grumbled.

"Do you really think anyone would hire us without hearing us play? It's not like we have a demo tape or anything," Jade said.

"Good point," I said and high-fived him.

"If they saw you, they'd hire you without even listening to your music," Mrs. Morgan said. "The girls would go crazy over you two, and they'd be screaming so loud, they wouldn't even be able to hear the music."

"Mrs. Morgan, I'm surprised at you." Jade gasped and clutched at his chest. "Are you telling us the only reason we would make it in the music business is because we're hot? I thought you liked our music?"

"I love your music, but sex appeal sells, and if you've both got it, you should use it. There are a lot of talentless fools out there who are popular only because people find them visually pleasing," Mrs. Morgan said. "I've been around the music business, and trust me when I say you've got it all. I know what I'm talking about. I'm sure your PR manager lady will agree with me."

Maggie pursed her lips and nodded. Mrs. Morgan knuckle bumped her. This was another odd moment in my life. An eighty-year-old woman was talking about my sex appeal. We sure would have a broad fan base.

"Okay," Jade said.

"What?" I shouted and stood up. "Are you insane?"

"Possibly," Jade said. "Let Maggie have her fun. We can mess around with some songs and work out a short playlist. She's right. They don't all have to be original songs. We can do some covers."

"You're all nuts," I said. I was the only sane person in the room. I leaned back and let them scheme and plan.

As the night wore on, Jade got more and more excited about performing live. I'd always tried to exist in the shadows, and now they were talking about bringing me into the spotlight.

"Oh," Maggie squealed. "I forgot to tell you. I've set up a Facebook page for you guys, and I opened Twitter and Instagram accounts."

"What for?" I asked.

Maggie snorted. "Your fans are going to want some way to communicate with you."

"Our fans?" I rolled my eyes. "Who are these mysterious fans you speak of? Do we have a band name, in case we get famous?" I joked about it, tossing out strange mixtures of our names. "How about Rjayd? We could pronounce it Raid."

"Rylan and Jade will be fine," Maggie said. "Besides, it's what I've put on all the accounts and stuff."

"Maybe I want it Jade and Rylan," Jade said, grinning at me.

"Just Jade would be fine with me," I muttered.

He frowned. "I'm not a solo act."

His intense stare made my body temperature increase.

"Okay," I squeaked. "As long as we're in this together."

I had no idea what *this* was going to be, but I'd go along for the ride if Jade wanted to drive.

Listening to Jade and Maggie talk about the perks of being famous was entertaining. They were both crazy, but it was fun to watch them dream out loud. I sucked in a quick breath and asked Mrs. Morgan for a piece of paper and a pen. I needed to start carrying around a notebook or write things on my phone.

I scribbled the words down and smiled, because Jade did make me dream out loud.

"It's so good to see you smiling," Mrs. Morgan said. She handed me a cookie and sat down next to me.

"It's nice to be happy," I said.

She patted my hand and gestured toward Jade's ankle, tucked safely behind mine. "He's good for you, and I like him. You should think about keeping this one."

I glanced at him. He was waving his arms excitedly, talking about staging a live show. He had us playing Madison Square Garden next month, and Maggie was agreeing with him. His cheeks were flushed and his smile lit up the room. He took my breath away and made my heart bang against my ribs. I was crazy in love with a guy I barely knew. I guess that meant I was as insane as everyone else in the room.

"You are quite taken with him," Mrs. Morgan said.

"I am," I whispered.

"What's the name of the song you started writing?"

"'Dreamin' Out Loud.'"

Mrs. Morgan smiled and gave me a quick hug.

"I hate to break up this party," I said, "but I have a short story that needs to be finished by tomorrow."

Maggie frowned and looked at the clock on her phone. "I suppose I should do the assigned reading, even if it is boring as all hell. I don't understand why I need to take this history course when my major is public relations. I have no aspirations of becoming a dictator."

"I think you'd make a great dictator," I said.

She stuck her tongue out at me and proceeded to tell me it was my turn to make dinner tomorrow night.

"Dictator," I said under my breath.

"I heard that," she shouted. "And quit rolling your eyes."

Jade smiled at me and let Mrs. Morgan take his arm. "I'll be right back," he said.

When Jade left, my phone rang and Kelli's smiling face showed up on my screen.

"Hey, Kelli. What's up?"

She immediately asked if it was okay if she came out for a visit. She sounded worn-out and sad. I asked her what was wrong, but all I got out of her was she needed a change of scenery.

She had to tie up some things at home, so it would be about a week before she made it here. I told her she could show up any time and stay for as long as she wanted.

I hung up and stared at the darkened screen, wondering what was going on back home that had her so upset.

"Hi," Jade said. "Who was on the phone?"

"Hey. That was my sister, Kelli. She's coming to stay with us."

He sat down on my bed and ran his fingers through my hair. "Mrs. Morgan is very protective of you," Jade said. "She wanted to know my intentions. She told me, very sternly, not to hurt you."

It was nice to have someone so concerned about my well-being. I closed my laptop and stared at him, patting the bed beside me.

"I hope you're okay with everything I told Maggie tonight," Jade said as he sat down and snuggled into my side. "I have a tendency to get carried away sometimes."

"I like it when you get carried away," I said.

"Wouldn't it be something if we did hit it big?" Jade said. "Would you come on this crazy ride with me?"

"I would," I said. Jade started chattering about traveling the world and all the things we would do while we were on the road. He was so excited it was hard not to get swept up in the moment and dream along with him. I usually didn't allow myself to get so wrapped up in a dream. They always had a way of crashing down around me. I was a cautious dreamer.

Jade rolled over and stared into my eyes. "The best thing would be that I would get to do it with you," he said and kissed my nose.

"Sap," I said.

"Dream with me, Rylan," he said and rolled on his back. "Tell me something, anything. Tell me what's on your bucket list."

"Okay," I said. "I'd like to stand on a balcony in Paris at night with the Eiffel Tower lit up in the distance and shove my tongue down your throat."

"What else?"

"I want to sit outside at a café in Amsterdam and smoke a joint in front of everyone," I said, laughing. "Then I want to go back to the hotel and shove my tongue down your throat."

"You have very achievable dreams." He gave me a crooked smile. "Tell me a few more."

"Go to London and ride that Ferris wheel thing while kissing you for the entire circle," I said.

"I think it's called the Eye."

"And I want to go to Disney World." Jade burst out laughing. "Hey, I've never been there," I said, pretending to pout.

"I haven't either," he admitted. "Are you done with your homework?"

"Why?" I asked.

He leered at me, so I tossed my notebooks on the floor and let him strip me.

This was better than dreaming. It was real.

THE NEXT week passed in a flurry of studying and tons of homework. No one mentioned the YouTube video, and I resisted the urge to check it. There was probably nothing to check anyway. We were getting close to the end of the semester and Maggie was having a fit about her upcoming final. She was also very excited to have Kelli coming to the house.

I think the combined events sent her over the edge, which was why we were on a massive cleaning spree. I tried to tell her that Kelli wasn't a neat freak, but Maggie refused to listen. I spent several hours walking around the house carrying a bucket and wearing yellow gloves. Jade was busy with our laundry and cleaning the laundry room. Who the hell cleaned a laundry room?

When Maggie started rearranging the kitchen cupboards, Jade and I plotted our escape. I tried to reason with her, telling her I was just figuring out where she kept everything. She snapped at me and dusted a can of soup. We backed out of the kitchen and hightailed it outside.

"She's crazy," Jade said.

"She's nervous about my sister coming and her history final," I said. "This is how she copes. Wait until it's the end of fall semester and she has more than one final. It's scary. Last year, I stayed at a hotel for a few nights."

"How do we snap her out of it?" Jade asked.

"I have an idea," I said.

"You smell like cleaning solution," Mrs. Morgan said when she answered the door.

"Brownies," I said. "We'll be right back." She nodded and disappeared.

"What are we doing?" Jade asked, following me to the garage.

"Mrs. Morgan is going to make brownies, and you and I are going for ice cream."

"On our bikes?"

"I'm not going back into the house until I have dessert," I said. "She'll probably make us refold all the towels or organize the silverware drawer."

Jade jumped on his bike and took off for the nearest store with me in hot pursuit. It was warm outside, so we were going to have to be quick or we would be eating ice cream soup. But it would be worth it to snap Maggie out of this weird mood. I'd used brownie sundaes before, so I knew this would work.

The house was quiet when we walked into the place with ice cream and brownies in hand. I expected Maggie to swoop down on us and scold us for not cleaning the dust bunnies living under our beds. We found her standing in the middle of the living room staring at her phone. The cleaning supplies were scattered all over the living room floor.

"I have news," she said quietly.

"Um, okay," I said, setting the food on the dining room table.

"Promise you won't freak out, Rylan," Maggie said in a low voice.

I frowned at her, but held my tongue. She was probably going to make me clean under the fridge or something equally horrible.

"Maybe Jade should hold your hand or something."

"Maggie," I whined, feeling the irritation rise. I hated when she prolonged the agony.

"I got you guys a gig," Maggie said.

"What do you mean by gig?" I asked. My voice sounded squeaky and very shaky.

"I mean you play and they pay," Maggie said.

"Holy shit!" Jade shouted. "When?"

I think I heard three weeks, before the walls started closing in on me. I headed for the backyard, leaving Maggie and Jade shrieking and doing some odd dance while they raced around the room high-fiving each other.

I'm not sure how long I stood outside counting my breaths.

"What number are you on?" Jade asked.

"Two hundred and forty-four," I answered. He wound his arms around my waist, and I leaned back against his chest.

"This is a good thing, Rylan," Jade said.

"Is it? We don't even have a band. All we have is a guitar, a keyboard, a couple of songs, and absolutely no fucking clue."

"Think of it as an adventure," Jade said. He turned me around, pushed my hair away from my eyes, and raised my chin with his finger. "One that I would love to take with you."

He opened his mouth, pressed our lips together, and tangled his tongue with mine. I groaned and melted in his arms. He definitely didn't fight fair.

The peace of the moment didn't last long. We both froze when Maggie's shrieks filled the air again. "Rylan! Jade! Holy shit. Get in here. You have to see this."

What could she possibly want now? I was almost scared to go inside.

Mrs. Morgan stepped out on her deck, clutching her golf club. Maggie shouted again and Mrs. Morgan looked at us. We both shrugged and waved her over. I was pretty sure Maggie wasn't in mortal danger, and Mrs. Morgan deserved to hear the news about the gig.

This time Maggie was sitting at the dining room table staring at her computer screen.

"What's going on?" Jade asked.

"Yes, dear," Mrs. Morgan said. "You're going to give me a heart attack with all your screaming."

Maggie ignored us and pushed a key on her computer. Her mouth dropped open.

"Maggie," I said cautiously.

"I sat down to check my e-mail, because I haven't checked it lately with all the cleaning and studying and stuff. I thought someone had hacked my account or I got spammed or something," she said and pressed the button again.

"Maggie, you're not making any sense," I said.

"I know. I thought I was crazy too, but then I checked the site and there were all these comments."

"What are you talking about?" I asked.

"I hooked up your page to my e-mail account. But I was so confused. I checked the site a few times this week only the counter wasn't doing much of anything. I asked around and people told me the counters have a mind of their own. They told me to watch the comments, and holy hell, the comments are piling in from all over the place."

She pressed the button again, keeping her eyes focused on her screen.

"Maggie," I said. "You're freaking me out."

Jade walked up behind her as she pushed the button again.

"People just keep commenting," she squeaked.

"Is that... Is...?" Jade stammered.

"Yeah," Maggie said.

Mrs. Morgan bumped Jade out of the way and looked at the screen. "Holy cow!" she shouted.

"What is going on?" I asked.

"The comments keep piling up," Maggie said in a dazed voice. Jade reached across her and pushed the same button Maggie had been pressing.

I finally pushed my way close enough so I could see the screen. They had our YouTube page open and were staring at a long line of comments.

"Holy shit, Rylan!" Jade shouted. "Look at them all! And it looks like they're from loads of different users."

Jade hit refresh and scrolled through the comments.

"Someone must be spamming our site," I said. "There is no way we're getting that much traffic."

"Rylan, I've clicked on some of them, and they belong to different subscribers. It's not like they're new accounts. They're as legit as you can get on YouTube."

She scrolled down to the list of comments. I cringed and closed my eyes. *What if they were telling us we sucked?*

"You don't suck," Maggie said.

"Quit doing that," I snapped. Maggie frowned at me and bumped me with her shoulder. I turned around, and Jade was sitting on the couch, holding his head in his hands. I walked over to him and sat down next to him. I slid my finger under his chin, lifting his face so I could see his eyes. They were swimming with unshed tears.

"What's wrong?" I asked.

He closed his eyes and rested his head on my shoulder, reaching for my hand. "People actually like our music," he said quietly. "Ever since I was a little kid, my mom made fun of me for being a dreamer. Wouldn't it be something if this actually worked out?"

This was the first time Jade had really talked about his family. As far as I knew, his mother was no longer among the living, but when alive, she'd made his life a living hell.

"She always said I lived with my head in the clouds. She told me that dreaming wasn't for people like me, that it was a fucking waste of my time."

I wasn't exactly sure what Jade meant by people like him, but I didn't interrupt. He seemed like he needed to get this off his chest.

"She always told me I'd end up like my dad," he whispered. "I think she hated me because every time she looked at me, she saw him. Just because I physically resemble the guy didn't mean I'd end up like him."

I was dying to ask him questions, but when he turned his nose into my neck, I could feel the wetness of tears on my skin. All I wanted to do was take away his pain, so I wrapped my arms around him and rubbed his back. There would be time for questions later.

"I love you, Jade," I whispered. "I think you're perfect the way you are."

"Holy shit. Holy shit!" Maggie shouted. "You guys are not going to believe who commented. Holy shit."

The doorbell rang, interrupting Maggie's excitement. Mrs. Morgan pulled the door open, and my sister walked into our living room. My first thought was to untangle my arms from Jade. I was so used to hiding everything from my family it was second nature to shrink into the background when they were around. This time I stayed put.

"Kelli," Maggie said, rushing over to her.

"Hi, Maggie. Thanks for letting me stay here," she said, glancing at me. She smiled and bit her lip. "Hi, Rylan."

Jade let go of me, wiped his face with the back of his sleeve, then stood up and held out his hand. Kelli hugged him instead, whispering something in his ear. He blushed and looked over his shoulder at me, quickly settling back down next to me.

"So what was all the yelling about? The cab driver was concerned," Kelli said. "Thought maybe we should call the cops or something."

"Oh, holy shit," Maggie said again and leaped over to her computer.

Mrs. Morgan smiled at my sister and introduced herself. It was hard to hear over Maggie's screams.

I finally couldn't take it anymore and left Jade sitting on the couch to see what had Maggie so excited. I stared at the screen and she pointed at a comment.

"Who the fuck is tuv?" I asked.

"Not tuv, you idiot," Maggie said. "T.U.V. He's a rapper and songwriter."

"Oh," I said. "Should I care?"

"He's also a big-time music producer," Maggie said. "His real name is Trevor Ulysses Vance."

Jade flew off the couch and shoved me out of the way. Even Mrs. Morgan was gaping at the screen. I went and sat next to my sister.

The dark circles under her eyes were deeper. "Hey," I said. "You okay?"

She sighed and leaned against me. "Thanks for letting me come here. I needed to get away."

"Is everything okay at home?" I asked.

She chewed on her lip, but didn't say anything. I was going to try to pry more out of her, but she gave me a silly grin and poked me in the side.

"What?" I asked.

"So." She paused. "You and Jade?"

"Yes, me and Jade," I answered, cringing a little bit. I half expected some mean comment, instead she giggled.

"God, he's a hottie," she said. "What the hell are they so excited about?"

"Maggie posted a video on YouTube of Jade and me singing a song we wrote and apparently people like it," I said.

"How many hits?"

"Seven thousand or something," I said. I'd glanced at the screen, and all I saw was a seven and a zero. It was probably seven hundred.

"Try seventy thousand," Maggie said.

"Holy shit," Kelli said. "How long has the video been up?"

"I don't know? A couple of weeks or so," I answered.

"We need to put up another one and see what happens," Jade said. "Like right now."

"I agree," Mrs. Morgan said. "You should strike while the iron is hot."

"No time like the present. The iron is fucking scalding," Jade said and left the room. He came back carrying his guitar and several notebooks.

"But... but," I stuttered. "I have an assignment due tomorrow."

Jade handed his guitar to Maggie and told her to go get the studio set up and put the melting ice cream away.

He knelt down between my legs and stared up at me. "School will always be here, but this opportunity may disappear if we wait too long. I don't want to live with regrets anymore. Please. I can't do this without you," he said.

"Fuck, Jade, this is insane," I said.

"I know," he answered. He kissed my wrist and smiled at me. "T.U.V. likes our sound."

"I can't keep up with all this shit," I said. "We have a gig I don't know anything about. We don't have a set list or a band or much of anything. And now, some guy I've never heard of likes our music."

Jade put his hand over my mouth. "I know this is new, but, Rylan, we have each other. Take the chance with me, please."

How could anyone say no to him? He had me in the palm of his hand, and he knew it. But the thing I found most scary was I didn't want to say no to him. I think I was searching for some reassurance from him. I still didn't trust people with my heart, but since I'd met Jade, I'd taken countless leaps of faith, and so far things were working out okay. I just needed to keep one eye open in case the fucking roof caved in on me.

"Okay," I whispered.

Jade climbed into my lap and smashed his mouth against mine, driving my head into the back of the couch. He stood up on his knees, cradling my face and kissing me hard.

Kelli cleared her throat and Jade released me, turning so he could smile at her.

"Sorry," he said.

"Don't apologize," Kelli said. "Maggie keeps texting me. She told me to pry you two apart and haul your butts over to Mrs. Morgan's house, like now."

"You don't have to come with us if you don't want to," I said to Kelli. "I know you must be tired."

"Are you kidding, Rylan?" she said, leaping off the couch. "I wouldn't miss this for the world. I need something fun."

Between her and Jade, their excitement could light up the city of Chicago. Jade didn't let go of my hand until we were seated in the studio. The moment he dropped my hand, he hooked his ankle around mine, drawing a smile from me.

CHAPTER SIX

THE NEXT three weeks were insane. I barely knew when the sun rose or set. It was great having Kelli here. She cooked most of the meals for us and made sure we slept. She and Maggie plodded through all the e-mails and comments on YouTube. There were so many exciting comments even I was catching the Rylan and Jade fever.

It was thrilling and ego feeding to see comments begging for more music, asking where they could buy our song and when they could see us play live. We decided to set one full day aside to finish our assignments for summer session. There was no reason to toss away an entire class when we were so close to completing it.

Jade and I had it relatively easy compared to Maggie. We didn't have a final test to freak about, only a final project. Jade handed his portfolio in to his professor, and then told him he wasn't registering for the fall semester. I did the same thing. We agreed to try the music thing for one semester. If it didn't work out, we were heading back to school. My parents were going to fucking freak out. It would be one more thing to add to their list of disappointments when it came to their baby son.

Kelli told me not to worry about anything. She could handle Mom and Dad for me. It was nice to know I wouldn't have to face them with this news. They would probably try to have me committed. And truthfully, I wasn't ready to face them, and they weren't ready to talk to me. Forgiveness was a hard thing on either side of the fence.

We had several arguments about what songs to put up on YouTube. Maggie begged us to put up "From the Beginning," but I didn't know if I was ready to share that song with everyone. It was too personal.

"Jade, I wrote that one for you," I snapped. "I don't want to give it to anyone else."

It was selfish and maybe a bit childish, but if people didn't like that song, I didn't know if I could handle it. To me, if people attacked the song, they were attacking me personally.

"Rylan, every song you write is a part of you," Jade said. "I love that you wrote this song for me. I want to share it with the world."

"It's a beautiful song, Rylan," Maggie said.

They always ganged up on me.

"I don't want to put it up on YouTube yet. I want to sing it live first."

"I'm good with that." Jade looked at Maggie, and she nodded. "Okay, so we sing the song live and then put it up on YouTube. Rylan, you can't change your mind."

"You should make the video for the song when they sing it live," Kelli said to Maggie.

"Oh, yeah, that's a great idea," Maggie said. Jade agreed and I had to admit, it was a really cool idea.

We laid down three tracks that night, and Kelli joined Mrs. Morgan and Maggie as fangirls of Rylan and Jade.

It only took Maggie one day to get the next video ready for upload to YouTube. It was a song Jade had written a couple of months ago. I tweaked the lyrics, and it changed from a depressing song to an upbeat dance tune.

We filmed the video outside, chasing one another around the yard, laughing and smiling with Maggie and Kelli. Even Mrs. Morgan made a guest appearance. Life was good at the moment. I pretended not to notice. I was going to enjoy the ride. When the bad stuff came, I would be prepared and be happy I'd taken the chance. We celebrated with beer and pizza.

"Kelli and I are going to check out the bar this afternoon. We're meeting with the owner to finalize all the plans. He's very excited to have you guys playing."

"How can he be excited? He's never even met us?" I asked.

"Our reputation precedes us," Jade said.

Maggie cuffed Jade in the head. "He's seen your YouTube video, and I might have exaggerated a tiny bit."

I groaned, because Maggie's definition of exaggerating a tiny bit was definitely different from mine. It was safer for us not to know what she told the guy. Neither of us needed the extra pressure.

Jade and I spent the afternoon practicing and figuring out our set list. It wasn't like we had a vast amount of songs to choose from. To create a long enough set list, we would need to play all our songs.

We agreed he would do most of the talking to the audience. I needed time to get used to performing in front of people.

"I'm scared I'm going to freeze and end up staring at the audience."

"And they would love it," Jade said.

"Shut up," I said.

"You always put yourself down," Jade said. "Don't."

"He's right, you know," Kelli said.

"Old habits," I shot back at her.

"Rylan," Jade whispered and kissed me on the throat. "Well?"

Maggie came around the corner grinning like a loon. "It's going to be fine, boys. The venue is small, but nice. It's an all-ages show. We don't need a full band yet, but I think we should start looking for a drummer, and a bass and guitar player."

"Can we get through this first show?" I said as all the blood in my body drained to my feet. "If we absolutely bomb, we won't need any bandmates."

"Rylan," Maggie said. "You'll be fine."

"Easy for you to say," I grumbled.

"Go get dressed," Maggie said.

"Dressed?" Now it was time to panic. With all the practicing, we hadn't talked about what we were going to wear to the show.

"Your clothes are on your bed, Rylan," Kelli said.

Before I knew it, Jade and I were dressed in black pants and white shirts. I had on a tie. Jade's collar was open. He looked fucking hot. I was actually impressed the girls didn't try to make us wear something weird. This was nice, simple, and comfortable.

"Makeup time," Kelli shouted, before she came strolling into the room with a small cart. It was filled with bottles of goop, hair spray, brushes, and combs. There was even a flat iron. There was no way anyone was getting close to my hair with that thing.

Kelli fussed with our hair while Maggie dabbed on makeup. They both tried to get me to put on eyeliner, but I refused. We finally shooed the girls out of the room.

"Jade," I whispered.

"Yeah," he answered. He was still fiddling with his hair, mumbling about so much fucking hairspray he could poke someone's eye out.

When I didn't say anything, he glanced over at me.

"Rylan? You okay?"

"I'm fucking nervous," I said. "What if they hate us or no one shows up or I forget all the words? I'll look like a total moron."

"Maggie and Kelli will be there, so even if it's just them, we'll sing for them. Really, all I want to do is sing for you."

Well, that was a sigh-worthy comment and settled me down.

"Let's get moving," Maggie shouted.

There was a van parked in the driveway with a girl I'd never seen before sitting behind the wheel.

"This is Shannon. She's a film major and is going to help us do the video when you guys sing 'Dreamin' Out Loud.'"

I wasn't going to ask questions. Getting our stuff into the van would be a lot easier than trying to cram everything into Maggie's car. Jade and I probably would have had to jog alongside the vehicle.

We tried to talk Mrs. Morgan into coming along, but she told us she would be there to see us when we played at the United Center. Jade made her promise. She countered with a demand for backstage passes. Jade promised her dinner with us, a limo ride to the arena, and backstage passes.

"Blow their panties off tonight," Mrs. Morgan said to us.

"Shit, Mrs. Morgan," I said, grinning at her.

"Ha, I made you smile. Now think about what I said when you're freaking out. You're good, Rylan. You deserve to be up on that stage. Quit selling yourself short," Mrs. Morgan said. She patted me on the butt. "And if all else fails, shake your cute little booty. The girls and boys will die."

She waved at everyone and left me speechless.

Jade didn't stop laughing until we were on the freeway. "Should I be jealous?"

"Of what?" I asked.

"I think Mrs. Morgan was hitting on you," Jade said.

"You're it for me, babe," I mumbled.

"I have something for you," Jade said, digging in his pocket.

"What is it?"

He shifted closer to me and grabbed my wrist. "None of this would have happened without you." He slid a bracelet on my wrist. It was a black cord with a silver infinity sign. "I bought myself one too," he said shyly. He lifted his shirt cuff to reveal an identical bracelet.

He leaned toward me and pressed his lips against mine.

"I love you," we both murmured at the same time.

Several kisses later, we realized the vehicle was no longer moving.

"What the hell is going on?" I asked as the van inched forward. There were people all over the place, standing in a line that stretched for blocks.

"There's the bar," Maggie said, pointing at a small building.

"Did you see that sign?" Jade asked. He pressed his face against the window trying to see down the road.

I didn't see anything except a hell of a lot of people crunched together anxiously waiting for something.

"Keep down," Kelli said, shoving her hand in my face. "There's the parking garage the bar owner told us to park in."

"Go back," Jade said. "I think that sign had our names on it."

"Are you crazy? I'm not going back," Shannon said, glaring at him in the rearview mirror. "It would probably take us an hour to get around the block."

The parking lot attendant held up his hands, stopping us. Shannon rolled down her window.

"The lot is full," the guy barked, pointing at the lot full sign.

Maggie leaned over Shannon and hung out the window to talk to the parking attendant.

"We were told to park in here." She handed him a ticket, and he peered inside the car, eyeing Jade and me.

"So you're the ones causing all the ruckus tonight."

I swallowed and shrank back into the seat. The guy told Shannon where to go and waved us forward.

"You two stay in the van," Maggie said after we parked. "Kelli, Shannon, and I are going inside to find out what the hell is going on. This is crazy. They can't all be here to see you guys. Maybe we got the dates crossed or something else is going on tonight."

I leaned into Jade. He put his arm around me, pulled me close against his side, and kissed the top of my head.

"This is weird," Jade said. "Maybe Maggie did fuck up the dates, but I swear that sign I saw had our names on it."

"Why would someone have a sign with our names printed on it? We've never played live before. You're probably right. Maggie screwed something up. I'm never going to let her live it down," I said. Deep down, I knew Maggie hadn't done anything wrong. She was organized to a fault. If she didn't have roommates, her kitchen would probably be alphabetized.

Jade's fingers tangled with mine, and he grinned as he leaned in for a quick kiss. It quickly turned hotter when he dipped into my mouth with his tongue. I groaned when he shifted his weight.

"Ride me, Rylan," he murmured.

"Oh God, quit saying stuff like that," I whined.

Someone banged on the window. "Rylan, get off him!" Maggie shouted.

We separated and Jade glared at her when she flung open the van door.

"So, what's going on?" I asked. I snapped my mouth shut when a big guy opened my side of the van. He held out his hand to me so I shook it.

"Hi, I'm Dave," he said.

"Um, okay. Nice to meet you, Dave," I answered.

Jade had gotten out of the van and was deep in conference with Maggie. As soon as I got out, Kelli tugged on my tie to straighten it. She fluffed my hair and doused me with hairspray again.

"The club management sent Dave and a few other guys out here to help us," Kelli said.

"Help us do what? What's going on?" I asked. "Did Maggie fuck up the date or time?"

"No," Kelli said.

"So, what's going on, then?" I asked at the same time I heard Jade shouting.

"Holy shit," Jade shouted. "Really!" His voice reached an all-time high, and it made me incredibly nervous.

"Kelli?" I said anxiously.

She looked at me and chewed on her lip. "All those people are here to see you and Jade sing."

"You're lying," I said. "Jade?"

"Holy shit, Rylan. Can you believe this crap? Hi Dave," Jade said. "I'm Jade and this is Rylan. You might have to carry my boy inside. He's probably going to have a small freak-out."

Jade was now jumping around, asking if we could go outside and talk to the fans. Dave kept shaking his head. I couldn't breathe. The walls of the parking structure were sitting on my head, threatening to crush me into the ground. Kelli grabbed me around the waist and yelled for Jade. He was by my side in seconds, with his arm around my shoulder.

"Can you get us inside?" Jade asked Dave.

"That's what I'm here for," Dave said. It was then I realized there were two other large guys leaning against the wall. Dave called them over, giving them instructions to get our equipment and take it into the club.

"It's our first show, and we already have roadies," Jade whispered.

I giggled. He could always make me feel better.

"You good now?" Jade asked.

"Better," I said. "But fucking nervous. What if they hate us?"

Jade tweaked my cheek. "Obviously they're here because they saw our videos. They know what we sound like, so they must like us. I mean they had to pay to see us play. And besides, I don't think the club will be able to accommodate everybody."

That didn't make me feel any better.

"Babe," Jade whispered. "You can do this."

"Okay," I said. "As long as you stay close."

"Always," he whispered and touched my bracelet.

The word made my heart clench, and I suddenly desperately wanted to believe he meant it. Always. It was a word I'd never believed in before I met this guy. Now I felt hopeful.

The girls huddled next to us as Dave gave us instructions. It was crazy to think all those people outside were here to see us. Maybe they thought they were here for a different band. Now that would be funny if we got onstage and the audience went dead silent.

"Stop it, Rylan," Maggie warned. "All these people are here to see you and Jade."

"Yes, oh great dictator," I said under my breath. She smiled and squeezed my hand.

"You sure make my life interesting," Maggie said.

A lot of things happened very quickly. We were surrounded by a couple of large guys along with Dave, who hustled us forward like one big mass. A deafening noise greeted us when the people lined up outside figured out it was us coming out of the parking garage and heading into the club. I heard people chanting our names and shrieking louder when Jade waved in their direction.

"I told you I saw a sign. There it is," Jade shouted, jumping up and down so he could see over Dave. "It says *I heart Rylan and Jade*."

More screams greeted us when we entered the club. There were hundreds of people crammed into the dark, small place. Dave shoved his way down a small hallway, clearing out some kids who were now screaming at us. A door opened and some guy pulled us into a tiny dressing room with one lightbulb hanging on a string and two mirrors. There were metal folding chairs stacked against the wall.

Maggie grabbed a folding chair and sat down. "Wow," she said. "That was unexpected."

"You guys should get ready. I think they want you onstage as soon as possible. At least before the cops show up," Dave said. "I'll help you get out of here after your set is complete."

"Thanks, man," Jade said.

Dave took Maggie, Shannon, and Kelli outside, leaving Jade and me alone in the room. The screams and shrieks could be heard through the thin walls.

"Last chance to get off this ride," Jade said.

He pushed me up against the wall and leaned into me, dragging his lips across my mouth.

"I think I'll hang around," I gasped.

He nibbled at my bottom lip. "Then let's go out there and blow the panties off this crowd. And remember, the last song we sing is 'From the Beginning.'"

He kissed me again, licking into my mouth.

"Stop," I said, gently pushing him away from me. I had no desire to walk on stage with a boner. This was going to be stressful enough.

Dave poked his head in the door. "You guys ready?"

Jade nodded and bounced around the room. Dave handed him his guitar and gave us both a knuckle bump. I liked this guy and silently thanked the stars for sending him to us.

The lights blinded me, and the crowd was so loud my ears were ringing. We stood in the wings while some girl in a really short skirt introduced us. She leered at Jade and rubbed her boobs against him as she passed. I wanted to shout at her to get her grubby body parts away from my boyfriend.

The word stopped my heart for a brief second. We'd never discussed the boyfriend thing, never said the word out loud. He called me babe, but we'd never defined our relationship. I touched the infinity bracelet, and my stomach unknotted slightly. You didn't give someone jewelry if you weren't serious.

Before I knew it, Jade was escorting me out on the stage and shouting into the microphone. We'd worked up a few lines to say to the audience, but Jade was so far off script I was totally lost. He was talking to the audience like they were all his best friends. Another wave of jealousy flared through me. He was mine and I didn't want to share him with all these drooling girls.

"Hi, I'm Jade and this is Rylan," he screamed. "Thanks for coming to hear us tonight."

I don't think the crowd heard one word he said. Jade strummed his guitar and my mind focused back on him. It was time to sing. The audience settled down so I could at least hear myself think. When I stepped to the microphone and looked out at the blob of people clapping and shouting, a huge shot of confidence filled me. The screams got louder when I opened my mouth and started to sing.

Screaming our names and trying to touch us, girls draped themselves over the railing set up in front of the stage. Some tossed bits of paper on the stage. I opened one and saw a name and phone number scrawled on the paper. I smiled and handed it to Dave. He rolled his eyes and stuffed it in his pocket.

The most amazing thing I saw was some people in the crowd were actually singing along with the two songs we'd put up on YouTube. It was mind-blowing to think they had taken the time to learn the lyrics.

The short set we'd put together was over before I knew what happened. Jade pulled his stool next to mine and sat down, strumming his guitar. Maggie shoved her way closer to us and took out her camera. I spotted Shannon on the other side of the stage with her camera. She winked at me and gave me a thumbs-up sign. I had no idea where they stationed Kelli.

Jade nodded at me, telling me to speak.

"This is the debut of our brand-new song called 'From the Beginning.' We really hope you like it."

The crowd went crazy, screaming so loud I couldn't even hear the guitar. Jade smiled at the audience, picking the notes of the song until the crowd stilled. Our voices filled the room, melding together perfectly. He scooted closer to me and hooked his ankle with mine. I couldn't believe he was doing it front of everyone. But maybe no one was paying attention to our feet because the music was good. It was better than good, and the room exploded when Jade sang the last few lines.

From the beginning I knew you'd be my always

As long as you're here, we can reach the stars

From the beginning I knew you'd be my always

I swooned along with the crowd because he was staring at me when he strummed the final note.

We bowed, and the crowd surged forward just as Dave and his friends hauled us off the stage. Maggie, Kelli, and Shannon met us behind the curtain and hugged the stuffing out of both of us. The overexcited bar owner dragged us to the backroom, begging us to come back and do more shows. Maggie donned her business hat and took over the negotiations.

Jade was whispering to Dave, who rolled his eyes and finally nodded, scowling at Jade.

"Come on," Jade said. "We're going back out there. Dave said he and the guys could handle the crowds. We're going to see what happens."

I didn't have a chance to say no before they swept me back to the stage. Most of the crowd was still in the bar, dancing to our music.

"They're playing our songs," I said.

"Yeah, Maggie gave the bar owner a CD," Jade said.

"Cool," I said.

Some girls spotted us and screamed, almost knocking Dave off his feet to get close to us. They were all red-faced and very excited. We posed for pictures and signed some autographs, which was totally weird because I didn't know how to sign. Jade whispered to me, telling me to just sign my first name. That's how they knew us. I still couldn't get past the fact that someone actually wanted me to sign my name on a scrap of paper.

My hand started to cramp, and I was exhausted and starving. Dave finally held up his hands and told the girls we had to leave. The bar owner came back out and told a very excited crowd we would be back next weekend for three shows. Tickets would be available on Monday at 10:00 a.m.

Dave and his buddies got us back to our van before the screaming girls knew we were gone. Maggie talked to Dave for a few minutes while Jade and I got settled in the back seat. He shifted closer to me so I felt the heat from his body. He was sweaty, with messed-up hair and flushed cheeks, and I wanted to attack him.

I forgot I was tired and hungry and that there were three other people in the van. We slouched down in our seats and he ran his hand up my thigh. He slid lower and pulled me half on top of him.

"Are they always like this?" Shannon giggled.

"Um, guys," Maggie said. "Can you wait until we get home?"

"Drive fast," Jade panted.

When Maggie pulled into the driveway, Jade had me out of the van before it came to a full stop. We raced down the hall and into my bedroom. The door had barely closed before my shirt was on the ground and he was licking around my nipples.

"I need you," he panted and tugged at my pants.

"I'm yours," I groaned.

Jade had me facedown on the bed, and he spread out on top of me. His hard cock slid between my ass cheeks, and I wanted nothing more than to feel him push into me.

"Please, Jade, hurry," I growled.

He suddenly stopped and I whined, raising my ass. His full body weight came down on top of me and he licked my ear.

"I want you to fuck me," he breathed.

I always wondered if I could cum from someone just whispering in my ear. Jade came damn close to making that a reality.

"Jade," I gasped.

He climbed off me and sat up. My gaze drifted to his leaking cock and I shoved him backward and spread his legs, settling down between his thighs. I bent forward and licked his slit, slurping up the precum. He shouted and wrapped his fingers around my hair and pulled hard. The pain helped lessen the ache in my groin.

"Are you sure?" I asked.

"Quit talking," Jade said. He yanked on my hair again, trying to shove my face back into his crotch.

I licked him and he grunted, twisting his fingers tighter in my hair. I sucked him down and let my fingers drift to his balls. He let out a cute little squeak when I touched his hole.

"I need lube and a condom," I gasped. Jade twisted and yanked open the drawer, and sent it spilling to the floor. We were going to have to find a different place to keep the lube and condoms. I was getting tired of picking up all the shit from that stupid drawer every time we had sex.

Jade hung off the bed and finally found the lube and condoms, then tossed them on the bed. I managed to get the lube open and spill it all over my hand and his hip.

"Sorry," I said sheepishly.

"Rylan," he begged. "Come on."

I stroked my dick a couple of times, which almost proved fatal. I didn't want to cum before I was inside him. I'd never been this nervous or this turned-on in my entire life.

"Rylan," Jade said. "Make love to me."

"Okay." It sounded more like a squeak.

I ran my hands up his body and kissed him gently. My cock pulsed, reminding me of what was about to happen. I let my hand drift back to his balls again, rolling them until he was thrashing below me.

My fingers were still slippery with lube, so I went for it and pushed against his hole.

"Shit," Jade breathed out when I breached him. It took a while to get him loosened up, but when I finally hit his prostate, his hips rose off the bed and he shouted my name.

"I'm ready," he said.

I slipped the condom on and took a few seconds to gather my wits. It was now or never. I pushed hard, feeling the muscle give way and his body accept the intrusion.

"Holy mother fuck," Jade grunted.

"I'm sorry, Jade," I said.

He grabbed my thigh and squeezed. "Just give me a second."

This wasn't good. He had a pained expression on his face, and it was starting to freak me out.

"I'm okay," he said. "I'm okay."

"Are you sure? We can stop. I don't want to hurt you. I love you."

"Rylan," he moaned.

"Okay, just please tell me to stop if it hurts too much."

He pulled me down for a bruising kiss, and my hips automatically moved. I must have bumped against his prostate because he suddenly shouted yes really loud. Everyone in the house was going to know what we were doing.

Jade clawed at my back and begged me for more. I withdrew and pushed back in, agonizingly slow. This was probably going to kill me, but it would be worth it.

I found a nice rhythm, and much too soon, the burning wrapped around my spine. Jade already had his hand gripping his cock, pumping furiously. The sight brought my orgasm on full force. He came a few seconds after I did, shouting my name.

I was pretty sure I was dead. I shifted and slipped out of him. I took the condom off and tossed it in the trash.

"Well?" I whispered.

"It was interesting," Jade said.

"Oh God, I sucked. I came too fast. I'm sorry. I couldn't help it. I was already so close and you felt so good. Fuck," I said and buried my face in my pillow.

"Rylan, it was good."

"Are you sure?" I mumbled into the pillow.

"Yes. I mean, I definitely want to do it again, but…." He paused and bit his lip, looking at me with those ridiculous brown eyes. "I really like fucking you."

"Yeah, I like when you do that too." I felt my entire body go up in flames. "I just hope it was okay for you."

"Babe, how can you be so unsure about it? There's cum everywhere," he said, dragging a finger through the cum painting his belly.

"I don't top very often," I admitted.

He wiped his stomach off with my T-shirt and tossed it in my face. "Well, you can top me whenever you like."

I threw the shirt on the floor and let Jade cuddle me. I wasn't ready to admit it out loud, but the snuggling after sex was definitely a bonus. Usually it was awkward and no one knew what to say or do. Sometimes the guy would try to hang around, but I'd push him away and tell him I had a class or work or anything to get him to leave. But with Jade, I didn't want him to go away. Ever.

CHAPTER SEVEN

DURING THE week, we worked on new songs and some more stuff for the live shows. We invested in a couple of better amps and a new guitar. We practiced more dialogue, but I told Jade it was pointless. He hadn't stayed on script during the first show. I was sure he was going to change what he said every time we stepped onto the stage.

Maggie also made us venture into the world of social media. We tweeted and posted on our Facebook page about the upcoming shows. It was strange, but Maggie thought it was great. Jade rolled his eyes and posted a picture of me tweeting. People started following both of us.

The hits and comments kept coming on YouTube. None of us really knew what to think about all that shit. We did the three shows on the weekend. There were so many people wanting tickets, the bar owner pleaded with us to come back the next weekend.

After the show, Maggie had us meet a woman who wanted us to come on some weekend Chicago morning show. She said we were fast becoming the talk of the town.

It was exciting, and we stayed at the bar celebrating until the wee hours of the morning. It was totally irresponsible and stupid to think we could function on no sleep with a hangover.

Maggie opened the door and grunted something at us. I wasn't sure I could move. When Jade rolled out of bed, my brain felt like it was going to ooze out of my ear, and the room turned upside down. I cracked an eye open and stared at the clock. The sun was barely starting to rise. The only time I got up this early was when I was coming home from a night on the town. Maybe it would have been smarter to stay awake all night.

"Maggie said we'll feel better after we shower," Jade grumbled. "I don't believe her."

"This is your fault. You agreed to do this interview." I scowled and stomped down the hall to the bathroom. "And my scratchy throat is also your fault."

Jade started laughing. "Yeah, sorry about that, babe."

I didn't think he was sorry about anything. I tried to stay crabby, but thinking about the look on his face when he came down my throat last night was enough to put a tiny smile on my face.

The smile stayed on my face through the shower.

"Quit smirking," Maggie said as she tried to smear stuff on my face that would lessen the dark circles under my eyes.

"Can't help it," I rasped.

She rolled her eyes and shouted for Kelli to bring some more makeup and a cup of tea. They managed to make us halfway presentable, and I gulped down some tea. It made my throat feel a little better. The train ride almost did us all in. Maggie actually had a green tint to her skin when we got off the train.

The people at the television station were incredibly nice, and the makeup lady fixed us up even better than Maggie had. There wasn't a trace of last night left on our faces. A very jittery guy brought me some more tea to help my throat and then messed with my hair. They fussed over us like we were big stars.

The interviewer asked us tons of questions. Some were weird and personal. I could tell Jade was nervous, so I scooted closer to him and hooked my ankle around his. The cameras were focused on our faces not our feet. Jade immediately relaxed and charmed the shit out of the interviewer.

"Have you been signed yet?"

"Signed?" I asked.

"Yes, by a record label," the woman asked.

"Um, no," I said. "We just started all this."

She smiled and pointed at Maggie as she brought Jade's guitar on stage. We did a shortened version of "From the Beginning." By the end of the song, the entire crew was on their feet applauding. The next moment someone rolled out a giant cake blazing with lit candles.

"We were told it was your birthday today," the interviewer said, looking at Maggie and Kelli, who were standing off to the side of the stage.

I stared at everyone, not sure how to react. I'd actually forgotten it was my birthday. Jade patted my knee and smiled at me. God, I wanted to kiss him, but it would have to wait until we were away from the cameras.

The crew sang a quick happy birthday before some guy pointed at us, telling us we were live again and to wrap things up. The last shot was of Jade, Maggie, and Kelli shoving cake into my face. Jade's fingers ended up near my mouth. I used my tongue to lick the frosting off and hoped no one noticed since everyone's hands were on my face.

Jade's eyes fell shut and his breathing hitched. Maggie nudged Jade away from me and kissed my cheek. Kelli grinned and hugged Jade. It was a nice save. Although, I wasn't sure I wanted saving. I didn't care who knew about us.

They wrapped the show, and we thanked them for everything they had done for us. I was still in shock they had brought a cake on set.

"Were you surprised?" Maggie asked as we rode the train home.

"I forgot it was my birthday," I said.

"You up for going out tonight?" Jade asked. "You can't say no, because this is your twenty-first birthday. Everyone goes out. It's mandatory."

"Where are we going?" I asked.

"We thought we'd let you pick," Jade said.

I glanced over at Maggie and eyed her. There was a bar I loved. I'd been there a couple of times with a fake ID, and it was always fun.

"I know what you're thinking, Rylan, and I say let's do it," Maggie said. I grinned and my body buzzed with excitement.

We thought about going out for breakfast, but everyone was too tired. Kelli whipped up some birthday pancakes. They were the same kind my mom used to make me when I was a little boy. It made me feel weird.

Before I crawled into bed, Kelli pulled me aside. "Mom, Dad, and Lucas wanted me to tell you happy birthday," she said.

My throat tightened, and I looked away from her. "Thanks," I mumbled. I didn't know what else to say.

"Go get some sleep, Rylan, so we can rock the night away."

THIS WAS the first time I'd ever gone with a guy to the bar with the intention of going home with the same guy. I'd been out with people before, but we always went our separate ways to hunt for prospective bed partners.

"Wow," Jade whispered. I figured this was going to be an eye-opening experience for him. He'd never been surrounded by a mass of gay guys before. As we wound our way through the crowd toward the bar, several people took a long moment to stare at Jade and me. It made me feel extremely protective. I made sure to keep my hand on him at all times to show that he was with me.

"Drinks first, then we hit the dance floor," Maggie shouted. "Excuse us, birthday boy coming through."

For her comment, I got several slaps on the ass, two crotch gropes, and someone tried to kiss me. Jade wasn't having any of that shit. Jealous Jade was fucking hot.

We finally made it to the bar, where Maggie once again announced it was my birthday. The shots started to show up. I lost count after the third one. Thank God, Jade dragged me out on the dance floor before I lost the ability to walk. The music was thumping in my chest, and Jade was grinding against my ass. I wanted to strip down and fuck right on the floor. Jade had other ideas.

"I have to piss," Jade said.

"But I like this song," I whined.

"Come on, Rylan," he said. "I'm not leaving you by yourself. Someone will swoop down and take you away from me. These guys are like fucking vultures, and you'd be the main course."

"Never," I mumbled against his collarbone. "You own me. I have a bracelet to prove it."

Jade chuckled and dragged me off the dance floor into the bathroom. He didn't stop to piss; instead, he pulled me into a stall and kissed me.

"I thought you had to pee?"

He shook his head and reached for the button on my pants. "It's your birthday," Jade whispered.

"We're in a bathroom," I said, like Jade didn't know where we were. "And there's people in here."

"So," Jade said. "It's your birthday. They'll understand." He licked his lips, leaving them glistening in the dim light of the bathroom. When he slid his hands over the growing bulge in my pants, my last bit of self-control slipped away.

He popped the button on my jeans and slid the zipper down, then reached into my underwear to lift my half-hard cock out. My thighs trembled as Jade squatted and swallowed me down. I squealed and let my head bang against the metal wall of the stall.

"Happy birthday," Jade said, moaning around my cock. He bobbed and sucked and moaned some more.

This was going to be over before we really got going. "Jade," I grunted, tugging on his hair. "Jade, fuck, I'm going to cum."

He hummed, and that did it. I grabbed for something but came up with nothing. The force of my orgasm made my knees buckle and my dick fall out of Jade's mouth. He choked and some of my cum got on his face.

Jade spluttered and burst out laughing, collapsing against me. His spent cock was hanging out of his pants. I hadn't even noticed him jacking off.

"Fuck, that was hot," Jade said. "Happy birthday, babe."

We stumbled out of the stall, laughing and kissing. My shirt was half-buttoned and Jade had cum in his hair. Everyone in the bathroom was watching us. Some guy was pissing on his shoe.

"It's my birthday," I announced. Jade slapped my ass, and we staggered back to the dance floor.

The rest of the night passed in a haze of shots, some dancing that turned into heavy grinding, and openmouthed kisses. I think I remember Jade shoving his hands down my pants on the dance floor.

The next noise I heard woke me out of my drunken stupor. The bed dipped and someone touched my shoulder and gently shook me. I had to fight back the urge to puke.

"Rylan," Maggie shouted. Actually, she whispered, but it sounded like she shouted, because there was an angry drum corps marching around my head, banging the shit out of their drums.

"Hmmm," I grunted.

"Rylan, wake up. A morning radio show is on the phone." Maggie said. "They want to interview you guys."

"Huh," I groaned, trying not to move too much. My head felt like it was going to fall off. Maybe if it did, I would feel better.

"It's one of those radio shows," Maggie repeated.

Jade sat up so quickly Maggie fell off the bed.

"Give me the phone," Jade said. "I'll talk to them."

Maggie squealed and it felt like she punctured my brain with an ice pick.

"Oh my God, both of you shut the fuck up," I said. "I don't care if it's the fucking Queen of England. Get out of here and let me die in peace."

Jade scrambled out of bed and quickly grabbed a shirt to cover his junk. Maggie giggled as she handed him the phone.

I pulled the pillow over my head and went back to sleep. A few hours later, I only felt marginally better. I wandered around the house looking for everybody. I finally heard voices coming from the deck.

"I heard you on the radio," Mrs. Morgan said. "Was that Rylan shouting in the background? The guy who beeps out naughty words was having a field day."

"You listen to that station?" Jade asked.

"Sometimes," she said. "It's funny."

"Uh," I grunted. I grabbed a kitchen towel and put it on top of my head to shield the sunlight. Maggie breezed by me and handed me a pair of sunglasses. They were pink with rhinestones.

"Babe," Jade said when I stepped into the blinding light of the sun.

"Uh," I grunted again. Maggie handed me a glass of ice water. I sucked down the entire contents of the glass and collapsed onto a deck chair.

"Never again," I said. "If any of you ever let me drink that much again, I will personally kill each and every one of you very slowly."

"Noted," Jade said. "We're getting a ton of hits today on all the social media sites."

"I've noticed the hits go up every time you guys do a show," Maggie said. "Tomorrow night we put on a show in the largest place yet. I wonder how many hits we're going to get?"

They argued and giggled while I drifted in and out of consciousness. Kelli took pity on me and brought me a greasy cheeseburger. It made me feel half-alive. It was enough to make Jade insist on rehearsing some of the new stuff. He was focused on playing something fresh for the fans tomorrow night.

Nothing I tried worked. Even after the greasy food and several glasses of water, my hangover wouldn't let go. Frustration set in, but Jade pushed me to keep trying to find the right words to finish off the song. I wanted to throw my keyboard at his head.

He was lucky Maggie interrupted us.

"What's up?" Jade asked.

"Sit down," Maggie ordered. I sat, welcoming the opportunity, but Jade paced around the room. "Jade," Maggie snapped. He stopped and glared at her but sat down on the floor with his guitar resting across his lap.

"I just got off the phone with Trevor Vance. He and Andy Tremaine will be at the show tomorrow night."

Jade's red lips fell open. "Are you serious? You better not be joking."

"Does it look like I'm joking?"

I could hear it in the tone of her voice. She also had her hands on her hips and her brow furrowed. Maggie was not joking. She'd talked about Trevor before, telling me they had been conversing via e-mail. I never knew if you could trust this whole social media scene. For all

Maggie knew she had been e-mailing some person posing as Trevor. I knew she'd never mentioned Andy Tremaine.

"Rylan," Jade said. He poked me in the side when I didn't respond. "Did you hear?"

"Yep. Is this a good thing?"

"This could be a fucking phenomenal thing."

He leaped to his feet and tackled me to the floor, kissing my face, my lips, and my throat until I was moaning into his mouth.

"Hello," Maggie said. "I'm right here."

"Then go away," Jade said.

"You're in Mrs. Morgan's basement," she reminded us.

"Oh yeah," Jade said, sitting up. "We probably shouldn't fuck on her floor. Let's go home."

"Shouldn't you be practicing?" Maggie asked.

"I'm tired," I whined. "If you expect me to be any good at the show tomorrow night, I need a fucking break."

She rolled her eyes, and Jade pulled me up the stairs, across the yard, and into my room.

"God, I love you," he said before he latched onto my neck. I tried to squirm away because I didn't think performing in front of a big-time producer with hickeys all over my neck was a good idea.

"I need to see that you're mine," Jade said. "Please."

How could I fight something like that? I willingly tilted my neck, giving him more access.

He kept all parts of my body up for several hours. It was fucking worth it.

THE NEXT time I crawled out of bed, I was once again a fully functional person. It only took me twenty minutes to clean up the lyrics to the new song. Jade was pleased with me, but Maggie and Kelli were horrified with all the hickeys on my neck. They shouted at us for a full fifteen minutes.

"I'll keep my shirt buttoned," I said.

"Next time," Maggie poked Jade in the chest, "be a little more creative and hide them."

Jade looked at me like I was a chocolate dessert. My stomach twirled and my skin turned bright red. The ride to the show was pure torture with Jade whispering in my ear all the places he was going to mark me.

I was sporting a semi by the time we got to the venue. I wanted to kill him. Everyone was going to notice, so he offered to jack me off in the car. Maggie almost blew a gasket.

"Two of the biggest record producers are going to be at this show. You two are *not* going to have sex right now. Get it under control, or I'll cut it off," Maggie snapped.

My erection died immediately.

The show was fierce. The songs were tight, and we were both feeling the energy. The fans were out in full force, waving signs and singing the lyrics. I swear I saw a sign that said RheartJ. It freaked me out a little bit, but I decided it must have been something else, like the normal I heart Rylan and Jade. There were always tons of those signs.

When the set ended, Dave hustled us off the stage, offering his congratulations. He was sure Andy and Trevor enjoyed the show. With all the excitement, I'd actually been able to put them out of my mind.

Dave shut the door, leaving us alone. Jade pressed me against the wall, unbuttoned my shirt, and sucked on my collarbone like he did after every show. He moved to my lips and kissed me so hard it made my lips tingle.

"That was fucking awesome," he mumbled.

"Yeah, it was. Do it again," I panted and licked his ear, shoving my hips forward.

He sighed and kissed me again. We sprang apart when someone banged on the door. A guy in a very expensive gray suit burst in without waiting for an invitation. Another guy dressed in baggy jeans and a white T-shirt followed him into the room.

"Hello, gentlemen," the gray-suit guy said. His gaze paused on my open shirt. "I'm Andy Tremaine, and this is Trevor Vance."

Jade ran his fingers through his hair and straightened his shirt collar. I tried to discreetly wipe the spit off my lips and button my shirt. I don't think it worked.

We all shook hands and chatted about our music and the show. I liked Trevor. Andy projected an icy demeanor that lodged him in a social class above where everyone else in this building stood. Maggie and Kelli bursting into the room didn't help our social status. Mr. Tremaine frowned and picked imaginary lint off his jacket. Maggie started to introduce herself, but Andy waved her off.

"We'll be in contact," Andy Tremaine said.

Maggie stared at the guy's back as he walked away from her. I couldn't tell if he liked the show or if he absolutely hated us. Maggie looked like she wanted to pounce on him and scratch his eyes out. Jade frowned and stalked out the back door. The screams started the second the girls caught a glimpse of him.

"Well, that was strange," I said to Kelli.

"Rylan, you guys were great," she said. "Andy Tremaine is an asshole if he couldn't see that."

"I'm glad you're here."

She sighed and sat down next to me and rested her head on my shoulder. Maggie sat across the room and stared at her phone.

"Twitter is going crazy again," Maggie said. "The fans loved the show, and there's pictures of Andy Tremaine watching you perform. I don't think he cracked one smile during the entire show."

"Trevor seemed to enjoy it," Kelli said.

"I'm fucking beat," I said. "Tell me we have a few days off before the next show."

"We do," Maggie said. "I only have one more show booked, but I'm sure it wouldn't take much to get you more shows. People have started calling me."

Her phone interrupted our conversation. She didn't recognize the phone number, but answered it anyway. Her face paled, and she repeated the word yes several times before ending the conversation.

"Maggie," I said carefully.

She took a deep breath. "We're going to Los Angeles."

"What?"

"That was Andy Tremaine. He's invited us out to LA to talk business. Apparently, he loved you guys."

I flew across the room and kissed her on the cheek.

"I have to find Jade," I said, then burst out of the dressing room door and raced down the hall. All I needed to do was follow the screams to find him. Girls surrounded him and took pictures as he signed autographs for them, but when he spotted me, his eyes lit up.

I sidled up next to him and took some pictures with more of our fans. Finally, I waved, and Dave hustled the girls away.

"How do you feel about Los Angeles?"

"What are you talking about, Rylan?" Jade asked.

"We have a meeting with Andy Tremaine in a couple of days. He's flying us out to Los Angeles."

He slid his fingers up my face and held my cheeks in his hands. Dave cleared his throat and gave us a shove into an office, then quickly closed the door.

"Are you serious?" Jade asked.

I nodded. "He just called Maggie."

"Holy fuck, I thought he fucking hated the show," Jade shouted and pulled me into a tight hug.

"Apparently not," I said.

The next two days passed in a haze of packing and practicing new songs. We talked to Maggie and told her it was time for her to decide if she was registering for school or working with us.

She left us in midsentence and walked out the back door. An hour later, she came back with Mrs. Morgan in tow. Apparently Mrs. Morgan had convinced her you only live once and school would always be there for her. This opportunity might never come around again. I loved that woman.

Mrs. Morgan made us a celebratory meal. Kelli told me she had to go home for a few days to deal with her own decisions. I told her she was more than welcome to hang with us. She'd done her fair share of shit for Jade and me, and we wanted her along for the ride.

We said our good-byes, made sure Mrs. Morgan was going to watch our mailbox, and made it to the airport with plenty of time to spare, only to be held up at security. We were the last people to board the plane.

The flight was uneventful, except Jade tried to get me to become a member of the mile high club. I promised him that when we struck it big and got to fly on private jets, I'd make his wish a reality.

"I won't forget," he murmured and fell asleep on my shoulder.

There was a dude holding up one of those signs by the luggage carousels. It said the Marin and Blake party. Jade spotted the guy immediately. I sort of forgot I had a last name. In the last few months, I'd just become Rylan.

The limo guy was talkative and welcomed us to sunny LA. Maggie climbed into the front seat so she could pummel the driver with questions about Los Angeles. Between the two of them, I wasn't sure who talked more.

Jade and I sat leaning against each other in the backseat. I had no idea what to expect, and it made me nervous. Feeling Jade next to me calmed my nerves.

We had to go through all sorts of security checkpoints to get up to Andy Tremaine's office. It was worse than airport security.

We were down to the last roadblock. A small woman with fire-engine red hair and cat-eye-shaped reading glasses sat at a desk beside a giant set of double doors. She stared at us, giving both of us the once-over. It felt like she was stripping us down to our underwear. She pursed her lips and tapped her nails on her desk before she picked up the phone.

She rose, opened the doors to the office, and pointed at some chairs in front of a giant desk. Andy Tremaine, big-time music producer and creator of stars, had his back turned to us.

When he spun his chair and faced us, he made me feel like I was a slab of meat up for inspection. Maggie squeezed my hand, and Jade hooked his ankle around mine. It comforted and calmed me.

The meeting started with Andy telling us everything his team thought we could achieve in the next year. The amount of money being tossed around was staggering. He had to be exaggerating.

"Because you boys write most of your own music, it will increase your monetary value. In short, I want to sign you gentlemen. I think it will be a lucrative partnership," Andy said. "If you agree to certain conditions."

"What sort of conditions?" Maggie asked. She moved to the edge of her seat and stared at him.

"Well, Ms. Stewart, I'm going to be quite blunt. I know Rylan and Jade are together, and I don't think it's financially wise for you gentlemen to be out as a couple. I think it will hurt your earnings potential."

I slid down in my chair just as Jade tucked his leg back under his chair. It was hard to pretend it didn't hurt when he moved away from me. Plus, this whole thing was stupid. Why was it so stinking important to be fucking dating a girl? Did everyone he signed get interrogated about their sexual orientation? The sad thing was this guy would probably be thrilled if I were fucking every girl in sight.

"Why does it matter that we're together?" Jade asked.

"I was at your concert, Mr. Marin. Your audience is primarily young female fans. They want to believe they have a chance with you."

"That's…," Jade snapped his mouth shut and crossed his arms over his chest. Tension in the room was thick.

I shifted in my chair and focused on the floor. There was a dark spot on the carpet by my foot. I dragged the sole of my shoe across it and wondered if it was the blood of some other performer who had signed with Andy Tremaine. He seemed to want control over more than my music.

Maggie finally spoke up. "We have a few conditions as well." I couldn't wait to hear what our conditions were.

"First, if Rylan and Jade agree, as far as the girl thing goes, I would take on the role as Rylan's girlfriend and Kelli would take on Jade. The fewer people who know the truth, the better, right?"

"Who's Kelli?" Andy Tremaine asked.

"My sister," I piped up. "She was the other girl with us at the show, and she's been hanging out with us since this all started. The fans in Chicago know who she is."

"Okay, this might work," Andy said. "But you girls will have to sign a confidentiality agreement, and we'd pay you, of course. Is Kelli available right now? She should fly out here so I can formally meet her."

Maggie nodded. "I'll call her. I'm sure she can be here by Sunday."

"That would be fine," Andy said.

"Second, we have a few guys back in Chicago who have been providing security for us. If they agree, we'd like them to stay with us. Rylan and Jade are comfortable with the guys, and it would just make things easier. Since you want to keep everything on the down low, again, the less people who know the better."

Andy nodded. "Anything else?"

"Third, we want some say in who will be playing in the band. I think there should be some sort of chemistry within the band."

"Is that all?" Andy asked. He actually seemed impressed with Maggie. I was impressed with Maggie.

"Obviously, since the guys write the songs, they would like a little creative control when it comes to picking the songs on the album. Also, if videos are made, we want input on them as well. And if this doesn't work out, Jade and Rylan want the rights to the songs to revert back to them immediately."

"Have you done this before?" Andy asked.

She smirked. "I'll let you know if I think of anything else."

"Take the contracts back to the hotel. Read them over and talk about it. We'll meet Monday morning, and you can tell me your decision. I'll have my people draw up something for you and Kelli as well."

We all nodded and shook hands. Andy handed Maggie a thick envelope as we exited his office. The limo was waiting to take us back to the hotel. I didn't dare sit next to Jade, so I let Maggie crawl in between us. This was all happening so fast, and I wasn't sure what to think about all the restrictions being put on us.

Maggie spent the evening poring over the contracts. She sent a copy to an entertainment lawyer she knew. Between the two of them, they changed the wording in several spots, and they decided Maggie should renegotiate the royalty percentage from the sale of the album.

We didn't even have an album.

"What do you think?" Jade asked as he plopped down next to me on the bed.

"I want to sign," I said. "But I hate the part about the girls."

"They call them beards," Jade said, studying his hands as he talked.

"I'm sorry," I whispered.

"What for?"

What was I supposed to say to him? Sorry for making your life harder because I was a guy and normal people weren't supposed to fall in love with members of the same sex? I buried my face in the pillow and fought the tears threatening to spill.

Our dreams were staring us right in the face, but they came with giant ropes attached.

"Rylan," Jade whispered. "It's okay. I want to be with you, and if we have to hide it for a little while, then we'll do it. It shouldn't be that big of a deal. I mean, I do want to jump you on stage, but so far, I've controlled myself."

He laughed and poked me in the side.

"You're not upset about this?" I asked.

"I think it's stupid he finds it necessary to pretend we're straight because he thinks it will affect our sales. He doesn't even know us," Jade said.

He rested his head on my shoulder and sighed.

We hung out at the hotel the whole day. I didn't feel like sightseeing. Kelli showed up on Sunday with Dave and Brent. We went out to dinner and explained the entire situation to them. Dave rolled his eyes and Brent shook his head.

"They really want you to have fake girlfriends?" Kelli whispered.

"Beards," Jade said. "And yes, that's exactly what they want."

"Sucks," Kelli said. "But if it helps you guys, then I'll do it."

Monday morning found us all gathered in Andy Tremaine's office. Dave and Brent leaned against the wall with their arms crossed over their barrel chests while Jade and I stood behind the chairs of our soon-to-be fake girlfriends. Jade's thigh was pressed against mine.

After we'd gone around the room doing the introductions, Andy brought out the contracts. Maggie pointed out the things she had changed, and they started the negotiations. Dictator Maggie held fast to her wants and got Andy Tremaine to agree with all her demands, but he wouldn't back off on the girlfriend thing.

"If…." Maggie stressed the word loudly. "If Jade and Rylan need us, we will be there for them."

Andy stared at us for a few long minutes. He pushed a button on his phone and the red-haired guard lady came inside and took the marked-up contracts. She returned in a few minutes with a fresh pile of papers.

The room was quiet except for the scratching of Andy Tremaine's pen. When he finished, he pushed the stack of papers toward the edge of his desk and set a pen down on top of the pile.

"Are you ready?" Jade whispered in my ear. It sent a shiver down my spine.

I laced my fingers with his and pulled him toward the desk. A tiny smirk spread across his face as he looked at our hands.

I quickly signed and initialed all the pages. Jade took the pen next and did the same thing.

There were also contracts for Maggie and Kelli and Dave and Brent. They all signed them. I glanced at Jade and tried to remind myself this was a great thing for us. I plastered a bright smile on my face and silenced that little voice in my head shrieking about Andy Tremaine owning me for one year. Maggie had refused to back off and let him have two years. If the girlfriend clause stayed, then we were only signing for a year. I guess Andy figured a year was better than none.

The red-haired lady came back in carrying a tray of glasses and a bottle of champagne. Drinks were poured and after several toasts, Andy Tremaine leaned back in his chair, dismissed everyone except Jade and me, and we got down to business.

"We want to get started as soon as possible. We're fast-tracking your first album release so we can get you out on tour. You're going to be an opening act for a few months, and hopefully, if all goes as planned, you'll move forward to headlining your own tour."

Jade glanced at me and bounced around in his chair.

"You should go back to Chicago, pack, and tie up any loose ends before you get back here at the end of the week. You'll be meeting with a stylist and a vocal coach. Most of your time will be spent in the studio. Trevor is getting his team ready to start work on the single and album."

We both nodded.

"The girls don't have to come out unless you want them here, but it would probably be a good idea for them to hang out with you. You'll be staying in a house close to the recording studio."

"Okay," we both said.

As we walked out of his office, I suddenly thought about my parents. I wondered what they would think of me now. I was pretty sure Kelli would pass on all the news about my new career. I wondered if she would tell them about her new career as a fake girlfriend.

"Hey," Jade said. "You okay?"

"I'm good," I said. "Just worried about what my parents will think when they find out what my sister is doing."

He never asked me much about my family. I think he could tell it was a sore subject for me.

Thankfully, I didn't have a lot of time to dwell on these problems.

We went back to Chicago and played one more show. Andy and Trevor came to the show and made the announcement that we had been signed and to watch for the single and album to come out soon. We hadn't even discussed what song we would be releasing as our first single.

The crowd went crazy, and we spent two hours after the show signing autographs. My cheeks hurt from smiling, and there were spots flashing in front of my eyes from all the pictures.

The next day we were back on the morning show that gave me the birthday cake to make the big announcement.

"That was incredibly fast," the interviewer said.

We grinned like idiots and let Andy Tremaine answer all the questions about the signing. We kept repeating how excited we were to be signed.

We also did a couple of radio shows over the phone. We put the phone on speaker and shouted out thank-yous to the fans in Chicago. Finally, we were packed and ready to go to Los Angeles. Mrs. Morgan had us all over for Sunday dinner.

"Now, don't you let them bully you into doing things you don't want to do," Mrs. Morgan said sternly. "I know you're not thrilled with the girlfriend clause, but you'll have to make the best of it."

"I know," I said.

"I am so proud of you," Mrs. Morgan said. "If you need me, you can always call."

She hugged me and wiped a few stray tears off her wrinkled cheeks.

"Bring Jade over here," she said to me. I waved at him, and he sauntered over with a lazy smile plastered on his face. He kissed me on the cheek.

Mrs. Morgan shooed me away so she could have a few words in private with Jade.

I was going to miss Mrs. Morgan.

CHAPTER EIGHT

THE MOMENT the plane touched down in Los Angeles we hit the ground running. A driver met us by the baggage claim and barked orders at some scrawny kid who helped us with our luggage. The driver led us to a giant SUV and hustled everyone into the vehicle. All he told us was we were heading to our new home.

The house was in a gated community surrounded by palm trees and pretty gardens. The driver pulled up to the house, unloaded our luggage, and sped away. Trevor Vance was sitting by the front door. The first thing he did was give us our own keys to the palace.

Maggie and Kelli couldn't stop squealing.

"This will be your home for the next few months," Trevor said. We exchanged guy hugs and Trevor gave us the grand tour. The house had everything a person could possibly need. Even the fridge was stocked.

"Everything in this house is for you to use," Trevor said. "I wouldn't advise any wild parties, but it's your place."

"Thanks, man," Jade said.

"Here's your schedule for tomorrow. Andy actually gave you the day off to get settled. You should feel honored," he said. The sarcasm dripped from his voice. I immediately liked this guy even more.

We asked Trevor to hang for lunch, but he said, unlike us, he did not have the day off.

Trevor pulled me aside. "If you need to talk, I'm here. I know this whole hiding thing is going to be tough on you guys."

"Thanks," I said. "I appreciate it, Trevor."

"Don't let it destroy you," he said.

When Trevor left, Maggie and Kelli claimed their rooms. Jade and I got the master suite. I'd secretly been worrying about the sleeping situation. I'd gotten used to waking up next to him. I didn't want that to change. In here, we were safe from prying eyes. This was our space where we were allowed to be ourselves. I was quickly learning those spaces were precious and needed to be protected.

We spent the afternoon investigating the house, staking out our territory, and hanging by the pool. It was a good day, but the night was even better. Jade fucked me into the mattress. Walking was going to be an interesting adventure tomorrow.

The next day dawned bright and early when Andy's assistant called Jade and shouted at him to get moving. Time was money or some shit. We found out the woman's name was Ms. Loe. Jade immediately started calling her Ms. Blow.

By the time we were dressed and ready to go, our driver was leaning on the horn. The first item on our to-do list was to meet our vocal coach. Ms. Diaz was very nice but a little on the eccentric side. She answered the door wearing a plastic tiara and a long dress with parrots and flowers splashed all over the place. The plastic jewels in the tiara matched the jewels embedded in her long, pointy nails.

We spent the next hour making weird noises. At one point, she made me lie flat on my back, tilt my head back, and grunt. I thought she was going to step on me, but she poked the toe of her sneaker into my diaphragm and frowned. In the middle of a loud grunt, she dismissed us and told us she would see us both next week.

"Do not be late," she said, shaking her finger at us. "We have a lot of work to do."

"We'll be here," I promised.

"Fuck," Jade said, when we got into the car.

"Agreed," I said. She made me feel like I couldn't sing a note. It made me more nervous to meet with our team at the studio.

The studio was much larger than Mrs. Morgan's recording space. I missed the intimacy of the little room in her basement.

"Hi." Trevor waved us inside. It was nice to see one familiar face. "How did you like Madame Diaz?"

"She was interesting," Jade said.

"Interesting is an understatement," Trevor said, laughing. "What was she wearing?"

"A plastic tiara and a wild dress with parrots and flowers."

"Yo, LD," Trevor yelled at a bald guy across the room. "You owe me twenty. She had on the tiara."

The guy flipped him off, but then dug a crumpled bill out of his front pocket and tossed it at Trevor's head.

"LD, Mike," Trevor said. "This is Jade and this is Rylan," he said, patting me on the head.

We exchanged hellos and sat down.

"We're just going to hang out and play some tunes this morning," Trevor said. "Andy is really pushing to get a single laid down and released, so we need to hear what you've got."

I frowned and poked at my throat and diaphragm.

"What's wrong?" Jade asked.

"Nothing," I said.

"Rylan, you can sing. Ignore Ms. Diaz."

I stared at him. "You're turning into Maggie."

He laughed and handed me a guitar. "Sing, Rylan."

"Will you sit next to me?"

"Always," he said and pulled his chair closer to me. Trevor rolled his eyes, but didn't say anything.

The session went great. Mike and LD got really excited when we sang "Dreamin' Out Loud" and "From the Beginning."

"Would you consider working on lyrics with me?" Trevor asked. "I have a few ideas for you guys I'd like you to look at."

"Of course," I said.

We left Jade, Mike, and LD hunched over a computer watching our YouTube videos and talking about the arrangement of the songs.

Trevor and I wrote two songs in the next few hours. He was pleased with our work and made me promise to show the stuff to Jade as soon as possible.

"Let's break and get something to eat," Trevor said.

"Do you guys know a good tattoo parlor?" I asked.

Jade looked at me like I'd lost my mind.

"What? I just signed a fucking record deal. I want a tattoo to commemorate the moment."

The boys all snickered and decided it would be a good bonding experience for us all to get tattoos. I was going to get a heart with music notes on my hip for Jade.

Jade decided to get the same heart on his arm, weaving it into his tribal band. There would be small hearts with music notes dripping from the band, with the larger heart in the center of his bicep.

It was a great afternoon. Mike flat-out refused to get a tattoo, stating he didn't want to mar his perfect skin. LD called him out.

"All right," Mike said. "I hate needles. They make me woozy."

"Woozy? What the hell does that mean?" LD asked.

We found out what woozy meant when I had to have the fan turned on me so I wouldn't pass out. They all teased me for being a wuss. Jade came to my defense, telling them this was my first time.

The tattoo artist snickered, and the conversation turned to stories of losing your virginity. I didn't want to get in on this conversation. I was pretty sure none of the guys wanted to hear about my first time. I sighed and turned my face away from them, concentrating on the hum of the needle.

The tattoo artist gave me instructions on how to care for my new tattoo. Trevor reminded me to listen closely. If anything got infected, Andy would freak out. Jade promised he would keep an eye on my tattoo and report any redness or swelling immediately.

We parted company and headed off to the next stop on our list. We were meeting with a stylist. I had no idea what to expect from that meeting. Our driver dropped us in front of a building and gave us the suite number of some woman named Ella.

"I can't believe all this shit is happening," Jade said.

"Me neither."

The elevator binged, and Jade bumped me inside and pulled me into a quick hug as soon as the doors closed. "I love you," he whispered. "And your new tattoo."

We broke apart before the elevator doors opened and walked down the hall, knocking shoulders until we were standing in front of Ella's suite. Before Jade could open the door, a woman bolted out, almost knocking us over and bawling her eyes out. Someone from inside the office called her a stupid bitch and told her to never come back again.

"Holy shit," Jade said.

I was absolutely positive I didn't want to meet this woman.

"Oh, hello," a woman said. "Are you my next appointment?"

"I'm Jade Marin, and this is Rylan Blake," Jade said as he pulled me by my sleeve into the woman's office.

"Come in, come in. Oh, you two are fabulous," she said. "I'm Ella K, as in the letter K."

Ella was a tall, slender woman with long brown hair and dark piercing eyes. Her entire outfit was coordinated, from her earrings to the tips of her shoes. She dropped the bundle of skirts she was carrying on a cart and stared at us. I was pretty sure the woman had X-ray vision.

"I'll start with you," she said to Jade. She pointed at a chair and told me to sit, while she whisked Jade through a curtain.

I sat down in the chair and took in my surroundings. There were racks and racks of clothing lined up against one wall. Piles of shoes, purses, and hats covered another wall. Most of the clothing looked like it was for women. I shot a text off to Maggie. She sent me Ella K's Wikipedia entry.

Most of her clients were women. If Jade or I came out looking like girls, I was going to kill Andy Tremaine. The curtain rustled, and I held my breath. Jade stepped out wearing black jeans, motorcycle boots, a white button-up shirt, and a black suit jacket. As far as I was concerned, Ella was fabulous.

She motioned for me to come back behind the magic curtain. She dressed me in skinny white jeans that were so tight I could barely breathe. She frowned at the new tattoo, but didn't say anything. Thank God the pants sat low on my hips, so the fabric didn't rub against the heart.

On top, I got a black shirt and a tie. It wasn't much different from how Maggie had dressed me. My shoes were white Converse tennis shoes. I would have preferred the motorcycle boots, but Ella said we couldn't be too matchy-matchy.

She sounded like Maggie and Kelli when they were talking about clothes. She took tons of pictures and wrote down different designers and other pieces of clothing she thought would suit us. Jade burst out laughing when Ella dressed me in these weird checked pants and some odd floaty top. This time I did look like a girl. Even Ella giggled into her hand.

"No," I said sternly and went back behind the curtain.

"Okay," Ella said. "All done for now."

I wanted to collapse in a chair. I'd never tried on so many clothes in my entire life.

"You better hurry," Ella said. "Your next appointment is in thirty minutes."

"What are we doing now?" I asked.

"You're getting your hair and nails done," she said. "Off you go."

"What the hell are they going to do to my hair," Jade said as we walked down to the car.

"I have no idea, but if they try to shave it off, I'll kill them."

"You too," he said as he touched the lock of my hair that liked to curl into my collar.

Jade climbed into the car, and our driver scowled at us. "Try to keep your hands to yourself when you're out in public," he said to Jade.

"What the fuck are you talking about?" Jade snapped.

"I was told to report any funny business by you two," the guy said.

"You know what," Jade said. "I think we'll find another ride. You've been nothing but a fucking jerk, and we don't have to put up with your shit."

"You think I'm bad?" the guy said, laughing. "Wait until it comes out that you two are fags."

Jade flew at the guy. I managed to get my hands around his waist and pull him out of the car, saving the driver who promptly flipped us off.

"You better call Andy," Jade said. "If I call, I'll probably tell him to fuck off."

I called Trevor, who immediately asked where we were. He told me he'd get us another driver. "Don't worry, Rylan. I never liked that guy. He's a jerk to everyone."

"I swear I don't even know what we did to set him off," I said.

"It's okay," Trevor assured me. "I'll call Ella and have her contact the salon. You'll only be a few minutes late."

Jade was leaning against the building with his head hanging down. "I'm sorry," he said.

"For what? The guy was a total douche. I don't even know what set him off," I said.

"I touched your hair."

"You can fucking touch my hair anytime," I said.

We didn't have to wait long before a car pulled up in front of us. A guy with short gray hair waved at us, so we climbed into the car.

"Before we go anywhere," I said. "My name is Rylan Blake, and this is Jade Marin. I don't know what Trevor told you, but if you have a problem with us, then get it out so we can call someone else."

"I'm problem-free. My name's Pete Savoy," the guy said. "Nice to meet both of you."

He winked at me, and I felt better. Jade still eyed him cautiously, but he visibly relaxed when Pete told us the windows were tinted so it was difficult to see into the car. Jade slid closer to me and grabbed my hand. Pete smirked.

"Thanks," Jade said. "It's been a long fucking day, and now we're going to get our nails done or some shit."

"You'll love it," Pete said. "I promise."

The salon wasn't bad. The lady massaged my hands and told me I had nice cuticles. Jade fell asleep in the chair with his head in the sink and foil in his hair. I took a picture and put it online. He was going to kill me, but the fans ate it up.

When we came out of the salon, my hair was a little lighter and Jade had more golden highlights. We also had less hair on our bodies. The eyebrow plucking was horrible. That shit fucking hurt. Jade threatened the stylist with bodily harm. She laughed at him. He resorted to begging, quickly switching to bribery when the begging didn't work. I think he was up to buying her a car when the woman proclaimed his eyebrows perfect.

I laughed until my sides hurt. When the woman finished with Jade, she attacked my eyebrows. It was worse than getting the tattoo had been.

Maggie and Kelli were excited about our makeover and made us relive the day several times. By the fourth time of describing all the outfits we tried on and Ella K's office space, Jade was asleep, drooling on my shoulder.

The days and nights began to merge together. We grabbed sleep whenever it was possible. If we weren't in the studio, we were at photo shoots or interviews or out shopping or trying to write new music.

Andy started having us go out in public with the girls more and more. He called it laying the groundwork. It was okay, because so far, he let us go out as a group.

Kelli flew home a couple of times, but she never told me why she went back. She always looked exhausted when she returned. The only thing I could get out of her was that Mom drove her crazy.

Jade and I barely spent any quality time together. I started to think Andy was doing it on purpose. Even if we were alone, we were both too tired to do anything.

After one particularly long day, where nothing worked, Jade snapped and stalked out of the recording studio without a word to any of us. Trevor pulled me aside.

He hesitated at first, trying to piece together a sentence. "I'm just going to say it," he said. "Have you two had any privacy lately?"

"Um, not really," I whispered.

"Take tomorrow off," Trevor said.

"But, what about Andy?"

"I'll take care of Andy," Trevor said. "We can afford to take one day off."

Trevor wasn't much of a guy for hugging, so I punched him in the shoulder and bolted out of the studio. Jade was waiting by the door.

"Well?"

"It worked. We have tomorrow off."

"We owe Maggie big time," Jade said.

I rolled my eyes. I owed Maggie so much I'd never be able to pay her back, even if we both lived for a thousand years.

When we got home, she told us she and Kelli were going out for the evening with Ella K and wouldn't be back until tomorrow. I couldn't stop the smile that spread across my face. "You really shouldn't be so happy that your girlfriends are leaving for the evening," Maggie said.

I fake sobbed on Jade's shoulder.

"You boys behave," Kelli said. The girls blew us kisses as they giggled and whispered on their way out the door. Pete waved from the car. Jade slammed the door before the girls were in the car.

"So," Jade said, dragging his finger down my chest. "What should we do?"

"I don't know? Watch TV? Take a nap? Fuck in the pool?"

"I like the third one," he said. We raced through the house, shedding our clothing as we ran. We were naked before we dove into the pool. Jade swam over to me and pushed me up against the side of the pool, then kissed me hard.

"I need you so much, Rylan," Jade murmured. His hard cock rubbed against my hip. I slipped out of his grasp and went underwater and took his dick into my mouth. A muffled shout came from above the water. He didn't let me stay under long. He wrapped his fingers around my hair, and yanked me out of the water and claimed my mouth the moment I surfaced.

The kiss ended, and Jade stared at me for a few seconds before he turned and climbed out of the pool, dripping water everywhere as he ran into the house. I wasn't sure what just happened.

My questions were answered when Jade came back outside, carrying towels and a bottle of lube and condoms. His muscles rippled and his cock bounced as he walked, making my mouth water. He unfolded a towel and covered one of the deck chairs.

"Rylan," Jade said in a low voice that made my dick jump to attention.

I climbed out of the pool and went to him. He took another towel and wrapped it around me, dabbing at the droplets of water running down my skin. He dropped the towel and chased the drips around my skin with his tongue. He sucked my nipples until I was squirming with each lick.

"Bend over," he whispered.

One day he was going to make me cum without touching me.

He ran his calloused fingertips down my back and up again, each time moving closer to my ass. When I finally felt lube drizzling down my crack, I was so hard if I touched myself, I would cum. Jade was taking huge gulps of air, so I figured he was just as excited.

He took his time, opening me up with his fingers. He had me reduced to begging for him to please fuck me.

"Can I ask you something?" Jade said.

"Now?" My voice rose several octaves.

"It's important," he muttered. "I, um, had the test and I'm clean, and I was wondering if you...."

He paused and buried his face in my neck.

"Oh," I said, finally getting what he was talking about. "I'm clean."

"Really?" Jade said. "I would like to... with you... I mean... only if you want."

"Are you saying you want to be exclusive?" I asked. My voice may have cracked.

"I don't want anyone else, Rylan," Jade said. "Ever."

"Oh," I gasped. It was extremely difficult to have this conversation with his dick pressed against my hole.

"Does that mean?"

"Yes," I panted.

"I love you so much," he said as he pushed his dick inside me. The deck chair groaned from our weight.

"Holy fuck," Jade said. It felt like he didn't move for five minutes.

He took his time, draping his body over my back and kissing my neck and shoulders with each thrust. His breathing got more labored, and he started to bite me.

"Rylan," he gasped.

I pushed back against him, encouraging him to speed his thrusts until all I could feel were his fingernails digging into my skin, his cock slamming into me, and his wet kisses against my overheated skin.

I came fast and hard. Jade wrapped his arms around my waist, keeping me plastered to his body. He moved his hips a few more times before I felt him release into me.

"Oh fuck," Jade groaned, but he didn't move. He finally slipped out of me and stood up. I stayed bent at the waist until his cum dripped out of me onto the towel below.

"You are beautiful," he said. He draped a clean towel over me when I shivered. "Are you cold?"

"A little," I said.

"Let's go inside," he said. His brown eyes held my gaze until he blinked and a few tears slid down his cheeks.

I caught one with my finger. "Um, is something wrong?"

"No, everything is perfect. That's what scares me," Jade said. He grabbed me and pulled me hard against his body. "I can't lose you," he mumbled.

"You won't," I said.

Later, I told him he might lose me because if Maggie found out I sucked him off in the kitchen and let him cum on my neck and chest, she would probably kill me. We made sure there was no sign of cum anywhere.

THE DAY off did wonders for everyone, and two weeks later, we were staring at a completed album. Andy and Trevor were still arguing about the first single, but that was up to them. Jade and I were pleased with all the songs.

We spent three days shooting the cover of the album. The first day of the shoot the photographer complained about the light and refused to take any pictures. The next day Andy decided he didn't like our outfits and argued with Ella K. He was a stupid man. We never did change our clothes.

On the third day, I wanted to take a picture with my phone and call it good. I worried we were going to be here for a fourth day, but as the sun was setting, everyone agreed on a shot.

At least I was getting used to having cameras in my face all the time. Trevor warned us it was going to get worse.

When they made the final decision for the single and the release date of the album, we did more interviews. We also made sure to tweet teasers from the photo shoot. The online fans ate it up. The next morning, Andy called us to come over to his office. It always made me paranoid when he summoned us.

"Sit down, gentlemen," Andy said as we walked into his office. "I just wanted to thank you for all your hard work. I'm giving you a week off before the single releases. You can do whatever you like."

"We all want to go back to Chicago," I said.

We'd talked about it earlier in the week, hoping Andy would give us a few days off. I wanted to go home and relax. Kelli was going to go home to the farm for a few days and come back to spend the rest of the week with us in Chicago. Andy thought it was great that the girls were going with us.

"After the single drops, we're going to start getting together a band. Trevor has a few guys in mind, so we'll bring them in and see what you think," Andy said.

"That sounds good," Jade said.

"I don't have to remind you to—"

Jade interrupted him. "We know. Behave and don't go anywhere unsavory."

The only place I wanted to go was to our house to hang out and relax. Of course, things didn't always work out as planned.

THE MOMENT we landed in Chicago, we were mobbed. I had no idea how anyone knew we were coming to town.

Fans stalked us all the way back to the house. I was beginning to think we should have brought Dave and Brent with us. We tried to accommodate the fans by signing autographs and letting them take pictures, but it never stopped. Our street was constantly filled with cars driving past our house. Girls lined up in our front yard. Once, when they started getting too close to our house, Mrs. Morgan threatened to spray them with her hose. She would have turned them into popsicles.

The cops were called more than once. They set up barricades and tried to control the crowds, but girls still managed to elude them. We found a few peering over the fence when we were sitting in the kitchen.

After two days, we'd all had enough. Andy told us to come back to LA. He had potential band members for us to meet. I was totally disappointed with the whole mess. What the hell was going to happen when the album dropped?

That question was answered three days later when we released the first single from our album. It shot to the top of the charts within two weeks. Andy and Trevor had finally agreed on "Dreamin' Out Loud" as the first single. We kept the homemade video up on YouTube, but Andy said since the song was such a success, we would be shooting a new professional video. Maggie and Kelli told Andy we should use clips from the original video. He was so impressed with that idea he listened to more suggestions from the girls.

The single exceeded the expectations of everyone. Andy didn't say much, but Trevor made a big deal about it, taking us all to an exclusive club with one of those back rooms reserved for important people. I had never really believed those were a real thing. Trevor tried his best to keep Jade and me separated, but there was way too much alcohol involved. We didn't blatantly make out or anything, but there was a lot of groping under the table. Jade tried to kiss me, but I managed to turn him away before there was any lip-to-lip contact.

Some fuzzy videos and pictures found their way to the Internet, but to me, it just looked like we were partying. I didn't think it was a big deal. Andy kept his mouth shut, but the way he eyed us was enough to keep Jade from hooking his ankle with mine when we were doing a radio interview.

After the interview, Pete picked us up to bring us back to the studio. We were meeting with some musicians who Trevor thought would be good in our band. I couldn't believe we were going to have a band. It was strange enough to hear my lyrics intertwined with professional musicians playing backup for us. On two of our songs, we actually used a string quartet. It was fucking awesome.

Pete had the radio tuned to LA's most popular music station. Jade was holding my hand and staring out the window. The stoplight turned red and Pete stopped the car. The DJ came on the radio and started talking about this hot new band making a huge splash in the music scene. He babbled some more about the talented duo and then announced the title: "Dreamin' Out Loud" by Rylan and Jade.

"What?" Jade shouted and sat up. "Pete, turn it up!"

The first notes of our song blared from the speaker, and suddenly the car was filled with Jade and me singing. Jade shrieked and rolled down the window, shouting at the carload of girls next to us.

"Turn your radio on!"

The girls glanced at us, and he shouted it again, telling them the station call letters. They turned up their radio so it was blaring along with ours.

"That's us," he screamed, yanking on my shirt so the girls could see me. I waved.

They started squealing and taking pictures of us hanging out the window. Pete hollered at us to get back in the car because the light was green. We waved at the screaming girls, who were still sitting at the light.

"Holy shit," Jade said. "It's us."

It was silly because we knew our single was out there, but to hear it played on the radio when neither of us was expecting it was spectacular. Jade called Maggie and shouted into the phone, holding it in the air so Maggie could hear the song.

She squealed as loud as those girls. I think I was in shock, but I managed to tweet about the experience. When the song ended, Jade eyed Pete in the rearview mirror. He glanced around and nodded. Jade pulled me down and kissed me until I was gasping for air. Our red swollen lips were going to be hard to hide from Andy, but we didn't give a shit. In my head, hearing my song on the radio made me a legitimate musician. Suddenly, I had no desire to go to the studio. I wanted to go home and spend the day with Jade celebrating our success, but Andy wanted to meet some potential band members. There was no way for us to get out of it.

The studio was packed with people. The moment we opened the door, all eyes focused on us. Andy spotted us and waved us to the back office. We had to meander through a long line of people before we were face to face with Andy. He pulled us into a small office and closed the door.

"I've got some great news. The preorder sales for the album are phenomenal," Andy said. "I just got off the phone with Daniel Jay. You boys are going to be opening for one of the biggest acts in the world. They are already touring, but we'll hook up with them in a month."

Somewhere deep inside my head, I knew this was wonderful fucking news, but at the same time, it made me want to puke. We were going on tour in one month. We didn't have a band or a stage show or much of anything.

"Holy shit," I murmured and sank to the floor. Jade was close behind, leaning against my shoulder. I waited for Andy to yell about the body contact, but I think he was blinded by dollar signs floating in front of his face.

"We don't have a lot of time, so we're going to be working nonstop. We need to get the band together in two days so they can start learning the songs and we can start staging a show," Andy said.

Jade said something, but all I heard was a loud roaring in my ears. He must have grabbed my shoulders before I tipped over.

"You need to quit doing that," Jade said. We were standing in the bathroom, and Jade was holding a damp towel on my forehead.

"Sorry," I mumbled. "It's been a crazy day."

"When was the last time you ate?"

"I don't think I remember," I mumbled, sticking my nose in his neck. He smelled good.

"Let's get you some food and then check out our potential band members."

"Okay, don't get too far away from me," I said.

"I won't," he promised. "Ever."

Jade ushered me out of the bathroom and told Andy we needed food. It was going to be a long fucking night.

CHAPTER NINE

THE NIGHT lasted three long weeks. Once again, we were working so hard I didn't know when one day ended and the next one started. Maggie and Kelli were also wrangled into working. Andy had them assisting Ella K with our wardrobe, and she was almost as bad as Andy. He also had Maggie running around the country setting up promotional opportunities for us when we were on tour. I still couldn't believe we were going on tour.

There was so much to get done and so much to remember. The songs were the easy stuff. They were actually trying to choreograph dance moves for us. Jade rolled his eyes a lot. I knew he'd change the shit during the concert, so why the hell did I have to learn it. Our staging person yelled a lot and pulled her hair. By the time the entire show was staged, she was a wreck. I think we gave her a permanent twitch, especially after our first dress rehearsal.

Like I tried to tell her, when Jade got in a groove, he changed everything. I'd learned to just follow along with him. The shows in Chicago had always been interesting. One time, he took a picture of the audience and tweeted it. Another time, he told a fan to tweet everything about the show. He posted her Twitter name and she got a shitload of followers. A few times, he jumped into the crowd, making Dave and Brent freak out. I stayed on the stage and watched as Dave tried to grab Jade and put him back on stage.

The only thing that stayed the same in the set was the order of songs, which would make our new band very thankful. Our band started with the auditions of almost fifty different people. We'd reduced the final number to three. Ethan played guitar and probably every other instrument known to man. He was amazingly talented and had the looks to match. His dark hair hung over his eyes, giving him that mysterious bad-boy persona. His biceps were impressive and made me drool. Jealous Jade made an appearance the first day we met Ethan. Jade stuck close to me, even going as far as sliding his fingers under my shirt, touching the small of my back when I tried to have a conversation with Ethan.

It would have been easy for me to pull Jade aside and assure him I was his forever, but it was a little fun to fuck with him.

Our new drummer was all sinuous muscle and long limbs, and he had a British accent that almost made me wet my pants when he spoke. Jens and Jade hit it off immediately, and now it was my turn to be jealous, until Jens started talking about all the babes lined up outside.

The news of the tour sent our fans into a frenzy. They hung around in huge clumps outside the studio. Andy regularly sent us out to talk with them. Word got out that we were nice, and more and more girls started showing up. Sometimes, all we did was shout a quick hello before Dave and Brent hauled us into the studio. More than once, we had to change locations because there were so many people lining the streets it wasn't safe for us.

The bass player was the strong, silent type. He made me shiver when he talked. Not only did he play the bass, he had a voice that matched. I think Brody could make anyone shiver.

The big question was how much information to tell them before they accepted their new positions. They might not want the job when they found out about us. Andy didn't want to tell them anything, but they were going to be part of our inner circle, and I needed to be able to trust them.

We decided to invite the guys to the house for dinner and drinks so we could discuss things in private. We didn't tell Andy about the meeting. As far as he was concerned, they were already in the band.

I was a nervous wreck and Jade was no better. He'd never had to out himself to anyone, and he had no idea how to do it.

"Let's just see how the evening plays out," I said, giving him a kiss on the neck.

"Okay," he agreed. "They all seem like nice guys. I think it will be just fine."

I didn't have the heart to tell him sometimes people changed when they heard the word gay. I still found it strange I had to tell people whom I was dating. Straight people didn't have meetings to announce who was in their beds.

Pete brought Ethan, Jens, and Brody over early in the evening. We asked him if he wanted to hang out, but he was going to be busy driving Trevor around tonight, so he declined.

"Rylan," Pete said. "It's going to be okay."

I sighed loudly. "I hope so."

"Trust your instincts," he said.

I nodded and waved, then watched as his taillights disappeared into the night. Everyone was in the dining room, gathered around the table. I made a quick decision to expose our secret quickly, like ripping off a bandage. There was going to be no stammering or trying to find the right words to bring this out into the open.

Jade was on the other side of the table, watching me move toward him. I gave him a sweet little smile, and it was like he read my mind. He stood up and opened his arms. Maggie gave me a wide-eyed look, but then she winked when I slid under Jade's arms and let him embrace me.

"We have a secret," I said, eyeing everyone at the table. "If you want to be a member of the band, we need to know that you will stand beside us."

They were silent for a few seconds.

"I thought we were having dinner," Brody said. "I'm starving."

"Is that all you think about?" Ethan asked.

"Pretty much. I like food. Oh, I guess I think about playing the bass at Madison Square Garden and everywhere else. And sex. I think about sex too."

Ethan started laughing, and Jens joined him.

"So," I said. "Does this mean you guys want to join Jade and me?"

"Just on stage," Jens said. "I mean, you're both really fit, but I like the birds, er, ladies. Speaking of which, how do you two fit into this story?" He gestured at Maggie and Kelli.

"Maggie is my real best friend and my current fake girlfriend. Kelli is my real sister and Jade's fake girlfriend," I answered.

We spent the rest of the evening eating, drinking, and getting to know each other.

"So, how do you do it?" Ethan asked. "It can't be easy."

"The girls are part of the contract," I said. "We get yelled at a lot. It's hard to hide how I feel about him."

"I knew the moment I met you guys. Jade is very protective of you. I think he thought I was hitting on you," Ethan said.

"Were you?"

"If you weren't head over heels for him, I'd probably give it a shot." Ethan smiled.

"Are you gay?"

"I like to think I fall in love with the person, not the gender."

We were going to get along just fine. In fact, we all got along so well, Andy thought there was something wrong with all of us.

It was nice to have more people in our corner. I don't think I could have hidden my feelings for Jade from the band. We were spending a lot of time in close quarters, and sometimes I needed to be aware of Jade when I was getting stressed. Having the band know about us made things a lot easier.

Rehearsals were a lot of work, but having the boys on stage with us made me feel like a big-time act. Maggie and Kelli did their jobs by showing up at different times to come see us at rehearsals. There was always a camera around when that happened.

Sometimes, we all left together. Sometimes, Andy had Jade and Kelli go out for dinner and Maggie and I would do something else. I hated being apart from Jade, but it was part of our job.

Two days before we left for our tour, we were hanging out in the safety of the house in LA. Maggie was talking to Mrs. Morgan, telling her about the tour. She put her on speaker so I could hear her.

"I know what's going on," Mrs. Morgan said. "I follow you all on Twitter."

She voiced her displeasure that we weren't coming to Chicago on this leg of the tour, and reminded us of the promise we made to her.

"Jade and Rylan have no control over what cities they visit," Maggie said.

"Well, hurry up and get here before I croak or something," she said.

"You're not going to croak," I said.

She snorted. "When your time is up, it's up."

"Are you sick or something?"

"Well, no, but I want to see my boys," she said.

"I'll see what I can do," I said.

We talked for a few more minutes before Mrs. Morgan had to say good-bye. She was going out to lunch with her no-good son.

"Was that Mrs. Morgan?" Jade asked when he came into the room.

"Yeah. She's concerned she may die before we play in Chicago," I said.

"Andy wants us to come to the office," Jade said.

I groaned. "Can't we have one day off?"

"He probably wants to go over all the rules and regulations we must abide by during this tour. Pete's waiting for us."

Ms. Loe, Andy's red-haired guardian, let us by without so much as a glance. She may have smirked at us. I never knew if she was happy or mad when we came to the office. I think she liked to keep me guessing, because sometimes she even seemed friendly, but most of the time she just freaked me out.

"Hello, gentlemen," Andy Tremaine said as he spun his chair around to face us.

"Hi, Andy," Jade said and sat down.

"This won't take long," Andy said. "I wanted to let you know you have both totally surprised me. We were going to save these until after the first leg of this tour, but there's going to be more, much more."

He grinned at us and slid two pieces of paper across his desk. We both picked them up and turned them over.

Jade stared at the check in his hand. I forgot how to breathe. I wasn't expecting this much money. I wasn't expecting anywhere close to what was on this check, but since I couldn't breathe, I was going to expire before I could spend any of it.

"Rylan," Jade said and punched my arm.

"Uh," I grunted. My heart seemed to be beating again, and my lungs were taking in air.

"I want a car," Jade said.

"Me too," I agreed.

"Let's go shopping. Can someone drive us?" Jade asked.

Andy laughed and made a quick call. "Downstairs. Behave, there'll be photographers."

I rolled my eyes. There were always photographers.

"Where to, gentlemen?" Pete asked.

"Porsche dealer!" we both shouted at the same time.

"You want a Porsche?" I asked.

"Always have," Jade said, grinning at me.

"Good choice," Pete said.

The salesman was a total dick to us, basically waving us off as two young kids who didn't have a pot to piss in. Pete disappeared for a few minutes and came back with a different guy in tow.

"Take a break, Monroe," the new guy said.

"Yeah, take a fucking break, Monroe," Jade said, sneering at the jerk. I couldn't help but laugh and hope Monroe's salary was based on commission.

Pete winked at us. I knew he'd probably called Andy to vouch for us, but I didn't give a damn. This new salesman, Derek, was awesome. We strolled around the showroom floor, looking at the different styles of Porsches. Jade may have been drooling when he crawled into a convertible 911 Carrera Cabriolet.

I found myself standing in front of a 911 Carrera. I wanted a top on my car that didn't come off.

"I want it," I said.

I'd never been frivolous with money, but I really wanted this car, and all I'd been doing for the last few months was working my ass off. This was a reward. A very expensive reward, but fuck it, you only live once, and I could afford the damn thing.

My car was midnight blue, and Jade's convertible was metallic black. We signed a bunch of papers. Pete pulled out two cashier's checks and told us the cars were a bonus from Andy. I almost passed out.

After spending over two hundred thousand dollars, I was starving. We made Pete come out to eat with us. His phone beeped in the middle of lunch, and he excused himself.

"I've been thinking," Jade said. He folded and refolded his napkin several times.

"About what?" I asked. The tablecloth covered our feet, so I inched my foot forward until I found his foot.

"Hey, guys," Pete said. "Ella wants me to bring you over to this store to pick up some new clothes."

We quickly finished lunch and took a ride over to some exclusive shop for men.

Ella must have called ahead and cleared out the store for us, because there was a closed sign hanging on the door. The salesman was buzzing around the store, pulling items as his phone beeped. Ella must have been texting him.

"We never finished our conversation in the restaurant. What have you been thinking about?" I asked as we headed into the dressing room again.

"Well, we should probably pick a few places to buy houses," Jade said. "If you want."

"What?" I asked.

"Um, we won't be staying in Andy Tremaine's rental house forever, so I was just thinking about it. I mean…." Jade's face turned bright red.

"You want to buy some houses together?" I asked.

A sweet, crooked smile spread across his face. "When I gave you that bracelet, I meant it."

"Let's go home," I said, dropping the clothes onto the nearest display table.

"But...." Jade paused and looked at me.

"If we don't go home this second, I'm going to jump your bones right in this fucking store. I don't think Andy would be impressed."

"Right," Jade said.

The sales guy who had been helping us came around the corner with an armload of shirts.

"Sorry, but we have to go," I said. "I promise we'll be back, and when we do, we'll ask for you." I looked at his nametag. "Dustin. Remember that name, Jade, or just pack up all the stuff Ella wants and send it to her. She'll know where to find us."

We raced out of the shop, startling the photographers waiting to ambush our shopping trip. Jade waved and jumped into the car. I climbed in after him, and we took off. I pulled him down and kissed him.

"Guys," Pete warned.

"Right," I panted. "Sorry." I sat up and stared at my cock straining to get out of my pants.

I sent a text to Maggie. The girls were out shopping and we would have the house to ourselves.

I think Pete broke the sound barrier getting us home. We barely made it into the house before our clothes were off and Jade had me pinned to the wall.

"You know," he whispered. "I've heard it's fucking sexy as hell to fuck someone up against the wall."

Whoever said that was a fucking idiot. It was a lot of work to get in the right position for wall sex. I wasn't some pixie, lightweight girl. Jade was a strong guy, but to hold me in the air while fucking me was too much work. Plus, I was going to have wall burns on my back. In the end, we settled with Jade sitting on the floor leaning against the wall and me facing him, riding him. It was a great position. We finished right before Maggie and Kelli walked through the front door.

"What is this spot on the rug?" Kelli asked.

Jade barked out a laugh and slammed our bedroom door.

"Do not tell them anything," I said, covering Jade's mouth with my hand. "Maggie will call the cleaning crew, and I don't want anyone else around tonight. I need to spend time with you."

Jade licked my hand. Within ten minutes, he had me flat on my back with my legs over his shoulders. After we finished, Jade passed out and couldn't be moved. I was starving and needed some food. As I walked by Maggie's room, I heard crying. I tapped on the door, but she didn't answer.

"Maggie? Can I come in?" I asked and knocked again. She sniffled, but didn't answer. I opened the door. She was sitting on her bed with her laptop in her lap and tears were streaming down her face.

"What's wrong?"

"Nothing," she mumbled and wiped her face with her sleeve.

"No pleading the Fifth," I said.

She groaned. "Fine, but it's stupid. I was tweeting like I'm supposed to do, and some assholes started attacking me. I'm just tired. It usually doesn't bother me. I mean I don't know these stupid people. Why should I give a shit what they think about me?"

I scanned the screen and people were calling her all sorts of shitty names. Some told her she should die.

"Maggie, how long has this been going on?" I asked.

Maggie snorted. "The moment I was introduced as your girlfriend. Not all the people are this bad. It just got too mean tonight."

She clicked off the screen, and YouTube came up. My name was plastered all over the screen. "What are all those videos?" I asked.

"You don't know about these?"

"No, I don't have time to mess around on the Internet. I barely have time to breathe anymore."

"These are the RheartJ shippers," she said. It was like she was talking in a secret code, but then she clicked on a video. Images of Jade and I together played across the screen. The way he looked at me during some interview made my stomach do a somersault. Playful touches and teases during an old concert I didn't even realize happened were highlighted and slo-mo'd.

"There are tons of these RheartJ videos all over the Internet. There's stuff written about you guys being in love and theories that Kelli and I are beards. Some people have way too much fucking time on their hands."

We watched a few more.

"Fuck," I said. "Andy hasn't said anything. Maybe he doesn't know about this shit."

Maggie gave me a look that told me I was an idiot. "If you're a fan of Rylan and Jade, you know about RheartJ. I'm sure Andy knows, but what the hell is he supposed to do? He can't shut down the Internet."

"I'm sorry," I said. I knew she would shout at me for apologizing, but I didn't know what else to say. This whole thing was turning into a gigantic headache, all because I loved Jade.

"Rylan," Maggie said.

"I know, but I am sorry you have to go through all this shit. I don't understand how people can hate someone they don't even know."

"They are jealous that I know you," she said.

"That's crazy," I said. "When are you and Kelli hooking up with us?"

"Not sure yet," Maggie said. "We meet with Andy tomorrow to discuss our schedule. I know we're not going right away. He said he didn't want any distractions for the first couple shows. Promise me you'll be mellow and maybe you won't need us."

I snorted. "I'll always need you."

"Just try to have some fun. Be friends with Jade onstage. You can be lovers behind closed doors," she said. "I know it sucks, but it's better than nothing."

She leaned against me and softly cried on my shoulder. It wasn't often Maggie let the world get to her. Usually, she was propping me up. It was my turn to be her rock.

A few hours later, Jade found me in Maggie's room holding her. She had finally cried herself out and fallen asleep on my arm. I didn't dare move.

"Hey," Jade said. "Is everything okay?"

"Did you know about all this RheartJ stuff and that people attack Maggie and Kelli online?"

Jade sighed and sat down on the bed. "Yeah, Kelli gets upset about it sometimes. I tweeted a few times pleading with people to knock that shit off, but it only fueled the fire. I don't look at the shit anymore."

"It's horrible," I said.

"I don't know how the girls can handle it," Jade said. "Reading some of the shit people write makes me want to punch them in the face. I doubt they would ever have the guts to say it to our faces."

Jade curled up next to me, and we stayed in Maggie's room for the night. Early in the morning, Jade shook me hard, shouting something about our cars being delivered. It was hard to get excited when Maggie and Kelli were being called whores. Maggie bonked me on the head and told me to get over it. She was just having a bad night, and if I really was worried about her I would let her drive my shiny new car. It was the least I could do. We raced around town until Maggie was due at Andy's office.

Jade and I were leaving late that night, and I didn't know if I'd see her again before we went, so I gave her a kiss on the cheek and a hug. Of course, someone captured the moment and posted it online, gleefully stating our relationship was a fake. I sighed and waited for the shit to hit the fan again.

When I got back home, Jade was waiting on the front step, sitting on a pile of luggage. Pete was picking us up in less than an hour.

"I think I got everything," Jade said.

I didn't care. If I forgot something important, someone could send it to me.

"Nervous?" Jade asked when we boarded the plane.

"Always," I said.

"I'm here for you," Jade said.

I bit my lip and looked down at my feet. I wanted to kiss him and snuggle into the warmth of his body, but we'd probably get tossed from the plane.

"Thanks," I whispered and pressed my knee against his thigh.

Our first show was in Seattle. When we walked into the arena and saw all the seats, Dave had to physically carry me to the stage. I didn't want to know how many people were going to be at the show that night.

Ethan, Brody, and Jens raced up to the stage and jumped around like maniacs, screaming about the enormity of the moment. It made me feel faint.

"Scope it out," Jade said to Dave as he placed me in a chair. I had no idea what Jade wanted scoped out. A few minutes later, Dave waved at Jade from the side of the stage.

"Come on," Jade said, pulling me out of the chair by my arm.

I followed close behind him. Dave pointed at a door and Jade pushed me inside the small dark space. He wrapped me in a tight hug, kissing my neck and whispering to me. "I love you, Rylan. We deserve this."

His soft voice assured me. We did deserve to be here. We'd worked damn hard to get this far.

"Let's blow their panties off tonight," Jade said.

"I'd rather get your panties off," I whispered.

Jade groaned and pressed his lips against mine. I sighed and kissed him back, enjoying the few seconds of privacy.

That evening, the roar that greeted us when we stepped onstage almost made me wonder if the headline act had followed us. I could barely hear the beat of the drums. This was our first live show with a band behind us. It was an experience I wasn't going to forget.

The set was going as planned. Jade sounded great. His banter with the audience was perfect, and he looked so hot I wanted to fly across the stage and hump his leg. We were in the middle of a costume change and the sight of sweat trickling down Jade's bare back made my dick twitch. Ella K giggled.

"Darling, should I flash my boobs to get you under control?" Ella asked.

"What?"

"You're practically drooling. Quit looking at Jade," she said, smacking me on the ass.

Ms. Ella K used to freak the shit out of me, but now that I'd gotten to know the woman behind the name, I liked her. She was funny and could make me laugh when I wanted to scream or cry. She was a lot like Maggie, and I was thankful Andy had set it up so she was helping with our clothes and makeup during this tour. I secretly thought she was also hired to keep me from jumping on Jade when he was half-naked.

"Sorry," I panted.

"It's hard enough to get you into these pants without your junk in the way."

"Oh my God, Ella," I said. "Shut up."

She laughed and shrugged, patting me on the butt again before I went back out to another huge roar from the audience.

After the set ended, I was so fired up I made the mistake of hugging Jade on stage. The hug must have lasted too long or something because Kelli and Maggie were at our next show and put on display for the media.

The rest of the month was a crazy blur of huge crowds and shows that rocked the house. With each new city, the fans were growing. It was hard to go anywhere without people following us around or asking for an autograph. It was getting to the point neither Jade nor I could go anywhere without security.

Most people were incredibly nice, but there were the rude ones we had to put up with on occasion. Maggie and Kelli took the brunt of the abuse. The moment the comments about Maggie and Kelli crossed the line, we left. There was a huge outcry, but when we posted online why we left early, most people understood. The comments in public slowed, but the online abuse never ended.

At the last concert we were contracted for, Andy and Trevor showed up, and hung out backstage. Both looked incredibly pleased. After the show, Andy took us all out for dinner and drinks at some fancy restaurant. Jade and I were exhausted, and I needed contact with him, but Kelli was sitting between us.

"Well, boys, I have news," Andy said. "It seems our leading act doesn't like playing with you anymore. Says you take too much away from them. So, we are going to do a few test shows in smaller venues where you will be the headliners."

I rubbed my ears because there was no way I had heard him correctly. Jade leaped out of his chair and hugged the shit out of a very startled Andy Tremaine.

"Holy fuck!" Jade shouted. "Thank you, thank you, thank you."

"Is this real? This isn't some joke, is it?" I asked.

"It's real, Rylan," Andy said. "We have a few venues in mind. We should know in a few days, and then the real work begins. We are going to need to work up a full show."

"Oh my God," I said.

"Hold it together, Rylan," Jade whispered. "I won't leave your side."

I frowned and looked at the distance between us. Kelli stood up, and we shuffled chairs around. For once, Andy was too happy to give a shit.

A LOT of things happened in the next month, and not all of them were good. The numbers for the album were fantastic. The concerts sold out so fast we had to add more shows. Andy started talking about doing a second album as soon as possible. We hadn't even been writing anything. I don't know how Andy expected us to put out a new album when we didn't have any downtime.

We were working hard to get a long enough set list for a full live show. The hours were brutal, and everyone was on edge. We all started to think it was absolutely insane that we believed we could stage an entire show in a month.

Two weeks before the first show, Ms. Diaz had to be brought in to help me with my voice. My throat hurt from all the singing. She silenced me for two days. It was weird not being able to talk out loud. I communicated by text messaging or pantomiming when I didn't have access to my phone. Jade did all the singing at rehearsal. It made me feel like a prop on stage, but at least I knew where I was supposed to stand and sit during the show.

When Ms. Diaz let me off silent mode, she had me do vocal exercises, insisting I warm up properly before I sang. I was discouraged and upset because I still believed she didn't think I could sing.

One particularly bad day, she signaled to me and had me sit down away from everyone else. She knelt in front of me. The feather from her purple hat tickled my nose.

"Rylan, my darling, you need to relax when you sing. You have a beautiful pure voice, and I want to hear you."

"What?" I asked. She looked at me and pinched my cheeks. "You like how I sing?"

"Of course, honey, you have a lovely voice," she said. "You just don't always use the tools you were given."

"I thought you hated my voice," I whispered.

"Darling," she said, standing up and pulling me with her. She squished me in a tight hug. I could hear Jens and Ethan snickering. "You are my star."

After she let me go, I threw my shoe at Ethan. It only made him laugh louder.

"That woman could suffocate a person with her boobs," Ethan said.

"Don't I know it," I said, but after her compliment, I felt more confident about my voice, and it showed in the rehearsals.

THE SHOWS were fabulous. More and more people were talking about us. Calls came in from magazines for photo shoots, TV talk shows wanted us as guests. We were the "it" boys and Andy took full advantage of our popularity by accepting as many invitations as we could handle. Cities started to blur together. But with all the good things, the downside reared its ugly head all too often. The rumors on the Internet were going crazy, and reporters started asking us uncomfortable questions about the closeness of our friendship.

Jade laughed and said things like who wouldn't want to kiss this boy. I'd be lucky if he let me, but I don't think my girlfriend would approve. He always pushed the limits with everything. I kept my mouth shut.

During concerts he teased me mercilessly, by sneaking up behind me and whispering dirty things into my ear. He didn't do it every show, but the bastard could recite a fucking grocery list and my dick automatically jumped to attention. The people in the first few rows got a nice little show. There were so many pictures of my crotch online that I might as well be a porn star. The band teased me continuously about having a second career to fall back on if pop star tanked.

On the night of our last solo sold-out concert, Ella and I argued about the pants she had me wearing.

"I'm tired of seeing pictures of my dick all over the Internet," I whined. "Can't I wear something a little looser?"

"I like the pants," Jade said. He snuck a quick kiss.

"Not helping." I scowled at him and shifted my dick into a better position. Ella snickered.

"One day, Jade," I threatened.

He laughed and finished getting dressed. I frowned when Ella tossed me a long sleeved shirt. "It's hotter than hell tonight." I could tell by her frown I wasn't going to win an argument with her. I discarded my T-shirt and slipped into the new shirt, leaving several buttons open. Ella raised an eyebrow but I ignored her and took my place on stage.

The drums pounded in my chest and the audience screamed when the spotlights hit us. Jade stared at me and almost missed his cue to sing. Ethan kicked him in the shin to get him to open his mouth.

I wasn't sure why Jade was so worked up tonight. Maybe it was because it was our last show in the smaller venues or maybe because the audience seemed to be especially overheated tonight.

"Jesus, Rylan," Ethan whispered in my ear.

"What?"

Ethan raised his eyebrows. "Your shirt is see-through."

I chanced a glance at Jade. His face was flushed and his pupils blown. He stalked toward me like he was going to claim me in front of four thousand screaming fans. The rip of the guitar pierced the air and Jade started to sing. I covered my mouth with my hand and smiled, because I could see the unmistakable outline of his dick pushing against the zipper of his pants. It was his turn to have his cock plastered all over every social media site.

"Holy shit," Ethan whispered in my ear. "You're a dead man."

"Yeah," I said with a shaky voice. I kept my eyes on the audience during the last two songs.

We took our bows, blowing kisses and waving, before we raced off the stage. I started to head to the dressing room, but Jade grabbed my arm, stopping me. He dragged me over to Dave and whispered something to him. Dave started to shake his head, but when he looked at Jade, he swore and took his phone out.

I tried to wiggle away from Jade, but he had a viselike grip on my wrist. Dave was doing his best to shield us from all the people backstage. He finally got Brent's attention and waved him over to us. Dave whispered something to him, and Brent paled slightly.

"Are you fucking serious?" Brent asked.

"Dead serious," Dave said. He reached into his pocket and slipped something into Jade's hand.

Brent headed down the hall and checked a few doors before he nodded. Dave poked his head in the room and then looked over his shoulder several times.

"I can buy you fifteen minutes," Dave said to Jade.

Jade had me pressed up against the wall before the door shut.

"Um," I stammered.

"No talking," Jade said and bit my throat. If I thought he was hard when we were on stage, I was wrong. His dick felt like a steel rod pulsing against my thigh.

"Jade," I moaned. "We are going to get in so much fucking trouble."

"I don't fucking care. I can't believe you wore that in front of everyone. I could barely remember the fucking lyrics, you little shit."

"I didn't know the shirt was see-through." I gulped.

"You're fucking lucky I didn't jump you and fuck you right on that stage," he said, and then his eyes narrowed. "Or maybe that's what you wanted me to do."

I gasped as the thought of him kissing me in front of all those people flew through my brain. The RheartJ shippers would die a thousand deaths.

He was rutting against me, searching for friction, but I needed more. I needed him naked and inside me. I needed to feel his burning hot skin against mine. I did want him to claim me in front of everyone. I was getting tired of playing all these games. It was getting to the point where I didn't talk in interviews anymore because I was scared I would say the wrong thing.

"Off," he whined, tugging at my pants.

We were all hands, trying to rip at each other's clothing. When he finally pressed his naked chest against mine, I moaned. Jade put his hand over my mouth. "We don't have much time."

He turned me around, and I put my hands on the wall, bracing for impact. I was ready to take my punishment. Instead, he ran his hands up my back and turned my head so he could kiss me.

"The clock is ticking, Jade," I whined. "I need you."

He gave me a wicked smile and traced my spine with his fingers, then paused for a few seconds to drizzle some lube down my crack. I didn't ask where he got it. His fingers were in me, pumping and twisting before I could properly moan.

"Jade, please," I begged, moving in time with his fingers. "Now, c'mon."

He fumbled with the condom, but finally, with one hard push, he was in me.

"I love you, Rylan," he whispered into my neck.

"Fuck me," I murmured.

Soft grunts and the quiet slapping of skin was the only sound in the room. I felt my orgasm shoot through me as he finished me off with a quick hand job.

"You do realize everyone saw your heart tattoo."

My mouth dropped open, and my hand automatically fell to my hipbone. We were dead. Andy didn't know about the matching heart tattoos.

Dave knocked on the door just as we finished getting dressed.

It wasn't until we were walking down the hall that I noticed Jade was wearing my shirt. It made my dick twitch and I had to count the light fixtures to keep from getting another full-blown erection. Maggie gave me a strange look before her mouth fell open.

"Shhhh," I hissed. "Maybe no one will notice."

"That's like saying no one would notice if you shaved these pretty blond locks of yours," Maggie said.

"Oh God," I muttered. She was right. The fans knew if I wore one of Jade's T-shirts on a date with Maggie or if Jade was wearing my coat when he was out buying a coffee. I could have worn the fucking thing one time, but they sure as hell could spot it.

Jade glanced back at me, and I rolled my eyes, fingering the cuff of my shirt. The shithead burst out laughing, clinging to my sister as we headed outside to be photographed by the stupid paps. I was hoping the fucking paps would get bored and go home, since we were fifteen minutes late.

"Smile pretty for the cameras," Maggie whispered and kissed me on the cheek. The paps blinded us with flashes.

When we got back to the hotel, Andy had left six different messages. Dave told us to bite the bullet and call him back. We ended up on Skype with Andy. He shouted at us for forty-five minutes and made sure to tell us we were to report to his office the moment we landed in Los Angeles.

CHAPTER TEN

I KNEW we were in deep shit when Andy's red-haired guard frowned and gave me the evil eye before opening Andy's giant doors. I tried to diffuse the situation by smiling at Ms. Loe, but it didn't work.

Andy sat at his giant desk, watching us like a hawk when we walked into his office. It made me feel like I'd stepped into the principal's office. I reminded myself I was an adult who was making this man a ton of money. I took a deep breath and straightened my shoulders.

"Gentlemen, please, sit down," Andy said.

We sat.

"There's been a lot of chatter online lately," Andy said.

Jade and I glanced at each other and shrugged.

"This RheartJ stuff needs to calm down. Everyone thinks you boys are together. Showing off that tattoo of yours didn't help matters, Rylan."

The blood drained from my face and Jade shifted uncomfortably, immediately unhooking his ankle from mine. I stared at him.

"We are…," I started. Jade kicked me. "Ow!" I shouted and glared at him.

"I think you should be more affectionate in public with the girls," Andy said.

"Would a sex tape leak help you out?" I said under my breath.

"This isn't a laughing matter, Rylan," Andy shouted.

"I never said it was. We're doing the best we can. We can't control what people are writing on the Internet." I glanced at Jade, but he wouldn't even look at me.

"You fuel the rumors," Andy said.

"I don't understand what the hell the problem is? We're selling out concerts, the album is doing great. Who cares about our private lives," I said.

"Right now, it's only speculation, but if you out yourselves, everything could be over. Are you willing to take that chance? Are you willing to give this all up just so people know you're together? Trust me, I've seen it happen before."

Jade said nothing and it irritated me. What was more important to him? The fame or me?

Andy handed a piece of paper to each of us.

"You have a few days off. Here is what you and the girls will be doing."

I scanned my paper. Jade's name was absent from my itinerary. Maggie and I would be hanging out in New York City while Jade and my sister hung out at Disney World. I fucking hated this.

"This is crazy. Jade is my best friend. I don't want to go to New York with Maggie. We planned to hang out in LA and lie low."

"Not happening," Andy said.

I kicked Jade's chair. "It's just for a few days, Rylan," Jade mumbled.

I closed my eyes and stood up, almost knocking over the chair. "Is that all?" I asked.

Andy nodded. "I expect you at the airport bright and early with a smile plastered on your face and Maggie draped over you."

I crumpled the paper, stuffed it into my pocket, and made sure to slam the office door a little harder than usual. Ms. Loe actually gave me a sympathetic nod.

"Rylan," Jade called, chasing after me. "Wait."

"Leave me alone," I grumbled.

"Rylan." He grabbed my shoulder and spun me around. "It's just for a few days."

"Fuck off, Jade," I said. "Go talk to your girlfriend."

Pete waited for us with the car. I frowned and climbed into the front seat, leaving Jade in the back by himself. I spent the car ride texting Maggie. She met me at the front door and tried to drag me into her bedroom. I headed for the pool.

Jade and Kelli were scheduled to leave that afternoon. Maggie and I wouldn't leave until tomorrow. I stayed outside while Jade packed for Orlando. We didn't even say good-bye.

When I heard the door slam, I went to our room, lay face down on the bed, and cried. The morning came early. Ella showed up to make sure I looked presentable. I put on one of Jade's T-shirts. Ella spent ten minutes trying to talk me out of wearing it. The fans would know it was his.

"That's the fucking point," I argued.

"Oh, Rylan," Ella said. "At least put a shirt on over it."

"Fine," I said and slipped into a button-up shirt. I left it wide open. I didn't give a fuck. I needed it.

Pictures showed up online the minute we stepped off the airplane. Maggie let me have a couple of drinks on the flight, so I was pleasantly drunk. It was easier for me to deal with the stupid paparazzi. Dave tried to stay out of sight, but if anyone got too close to us, he'd swoop in and herd them away. We made several scheduled stops on the way to our hotel. I forced a smile to my face and let Maggie drag me through several shops. We stopped for coffee. I didn't know how excited fans could be to find out what the hell I ordered at the coffee shop. I really wanted a shot of tequila or at least a cold beer.

Two hours later, Dave finally gave us the thumbs up. It was time to go to the hotel where we had a few hours to ourselves before we had to go for our scheduled dinner date.

Andy had some secluded secret date set up at some dark and romantic expensive restaurant. Of course, the cameras were on us the minute we arrived at the restaurant.

Secluded and secret, my ass.

Maggie ducked her head, hiding behind her newly dyed purple tips as the flashes from all the cameras went off. I sort of wished the ground would open up and swallow me whole.

The RheartJ fans analyzed the shit out of the new photos. They said I looked miserable. They were right.

Back at the hotel, Maggie surfed the web to find out what Jade and Kelli were doing. The pictures were everywhere. They were having a great time, and it made me feel sick to my stomach. They were at Disney World, posing with Mickey Mouse and a bunch of other characters.

"That was supposed to be Jade and me," I said. "It was on my bucket list."

Maggie closed her laptop and handed me a mini bottle of whiskey.

"I don't even know what to say," Maggie said. "It wasn't supposed to be like this. I swear I didn't know it would be this bad."

"It's been no picnic for you either," I muttered. "I don't know how you deal with all the hate on the Internet. I can't even look at that shit anymore."

My phone chirped. It was a text message from Mrs. Morgan. On one of her trips home, Maggie had hooked Mrs. Morgan up and taught her how to send text messages. She was worried about us. The pictures popping up on the Internet weren't helping.

"You created a monster," I said, flashing her my screen.

"She's worried about you. I'm worried about you," she said.

"This is what Jade wants. I don't have a choice," I said.

Maggie pursed her lips but held her tongue. I wasn't up for an argument. I emptied the minibar and passed out, feeling no pain until someone was banging on the door, yelling my name.

"Rylan," Dave's voice came from the other side of the door. "Open up."

I wondered what Andy had planned for us this morning. It was too fucking early to leave the room, and I felt and looked like shit. There was no way I could pull off the happy boyfriend shit with Maggie when my boyfriend was miles away with my sister, running around with Mickey Mouse. I pulled open the door, ready to shout at Dave.

"Jade," I gasped. "What are you doing here?"

He pushed me into the room, grabbing me around the waist and pulling me forcefully against his chest.

"I missed you," he said. His mouth found mine, and he kissed me hungrily.

"How?" I whimpered. He held my face in his hands and stared into my eyes.

"I couldn't do it. We were supposed to go to Disney World. It was on your list."

"You remembered," I gasped.

"Um," Maggie said. "I'll go find another room."

"Where's Kelli?" I asked.

"She stayed in Orlando. The bungalow is really secluded so no one will know I left. We took about five hundred pictures yesterday, so she'll keep posting them over the next few days. Everything will be fine if it stays nice and sunny."

"I don't give a fuck anymore. I need you," I whimpered.

"I saw the pictures of you online. You were wearing my shirt," Jade whispered.

"I hate this," I mumbled.

"I know, but I'm here now," Jade said.

"Why do you want to keep doing this?" I asked.

Jade sighed. "Do we have to talk about this now?"

"We've never talked about it at all," I said.

"Fuck," Jade said. He sat down on the couch and pulled me next to him. "Are you sure you want to hear all this fucking shit?"

"I need to hear something."

"I'm scared to come out. What if Andy's right and everyone turns against us? What the hell would I do then?"

"You can do anything," I whispered.

"And make this obscene amount of money?"

I wanted to shout at him that money wasn't everything. I mean, it was good, but fuck, we had plenty of money already, and the royalties would keep coming for at least a little while.

"Look, I had a less than stellar childhood and the fucking money is great. I can finally take care of my sisters and myself. I don't ever want to be without money again, and I'm scared if I quit, I won't have anything again."

It was hard to hear him say that when I was sitting in front of him. I wasn't with him because he was a famous pop star or had loads of money. I would do whatever it took to make sure he had everything he wanted and needed, but I could see it deep in his eyes, there was no arguing with him.

"No matter what we do, there will always be people who hate," I said.

"Someday, I'll tell you all the disgusting details of my life."

"Do you wish I was a girl?" I asked.

He snorted and twirled a lock of my hair around his finger. "Well, it would make my life less complicated, but no," he said. "I love you."

"You're just too ashamed of me to say it in front of people," I muttered.

"Please give me some more time, Rylan," he begged.

He stared at me with those big brown eyes, and I caved, sliding my lips across his cheek and down to his mouth. Jade moaned and rolled me onto my back, then climbed on top of me. His hard dick dug into my thigh.

I decided he was the most important thing in my life. The other stuff could wait. I still didn't like what we were becoming, but at the moment, none of that shit mattered. He left Disney World to come to me, and I needed to hang on to that thought.

"Make love to me, babe," Jade whispered.

My muscles tensed and I flew off the couch to find the lube. It wasn't often he asked me to top, and I was going to take advantage of it.

The sex was slow and loving. There were soft kisses and gentle caresses. I made him stay on his back so I could see his face the entire time I was in him. He came whispering my name over and over. I told him I loved him.

It broke my heart to think that because we were both guys, our love was somehow devalued.

As I was cleaning up, he ran a finger over all the hickeys on my neck.

"I think you're part vampire or something," I said. "Andy is going to know we did something crazy when the close-up pictures of my neck flood the Internet."

"What's he going to do? So he yells at me. He always yells. It was worth it," Jade said. "I had to see you."

I fell asleep wrapped around him. Word on the Internet was that we were both holing up with our girlfriends getting some much-needed alone time. The RheartJ shippers had their own theories, which included Jade and I sneaking off to an undisclosed location. Our crazy fans should consider a career as detectives. Although they had no concrete proof, their theories were freakily close to our reality.

Jade left two days later. How he managed to sneak back into Disney World without anyone noticing him I would never know. If I didn't know the details, no one could drag them out of me. I was in awe of him, though.

After the separate vacations and hundreds of photos posted, things calmed down for a few days. We all relaxed, which was a huge mistake. The paps nailed us together outside the studio. I guess I looked at Jade wrong, or right, depending on which camp you were in. The RheartJ stuff went crazy. There was nothing we could do to stop it, and Andy was getting seriously pissed off. I didn't know what else to do. We couldn't even talk to each other without pictures ending up online.

Andy pushed us to spend more time with Maggie and Kelli. It was starting to get to me. I loved Kelli to death, but I wanted to kill her every time she put her hands on Jade.

I felt like I was constantly on the edge of a major freak-out. We never seemed to get a break anymore, which meant we didn't get enough alone time. The pressure to crank out some new songs for the new album and get ready for the tour of larger venues was killing everyone. Andy still hadn't told us where we were booked. Supposedly, he was telling us tonight and announcing it to the world the next day.

Most bands got a break between albums and touring, but we were working nonstop because Andy wanted to keep pushing forward. Money was flowing like mad, and I had to admit, I liked that part, but I didn't get to enjoy it.

It had been another stressful, long day, and I was at the end of my rope. Andy brought Kelli over to the studio so she and Jade could leave together. Andy had Kelli sit on Jade's lap, and they tweeted a bunch of lame pictures. I stood out in the hall and tried to get my emotions under control.

Kelli poked her head out the door to tell me I was wanted inside again.

"Stop acting like you enjoy kissing Jade so much," I snapped at Kelli.

"Oh for fuck's sake, Rylan," Kelli said. "Andy is on my case every five minutes. Do this. Do that. Make it look real. Shove your tongue down his throat. Next thing they'll be asking for is a fucking sex tape. I don't know how much more I can take."

She had a point. Jade and I had an interview yesterday with some fucking magazine, and Ella made a point of putting the interviewer between us. I fucking hated all this shit. At first it was a game, but now it irritated me. I couldn't remember all the rules.

"We go back on tour in a few days," Jade said. "So you guys get a break."

"Wrong," Kelli said. "Andy told us he wants both Maggie and I to be there for the first month of shows."

"Oh, that's just fucking great," I said. I tossed a pile of lyrics on the floor, left the room, and slammed the door for the effect. I knew I was playing the drama queen, but this was slowly driving me crazy. I was losing myself, and I didn't know what the fuck I was doing anymore. It wasn't fun, and if Andy was trying to break us up, he was doing a great job.

"Rylan!" Kelli shouted.

"I'm going home. Tell them I had a headache or something," I said. I got in my car, turned the music up, and drove around for two hours.

The house was quiet when I got home. Jade was asleep on the couch, curled up in a ball. I was actually surprised to see him at home. I figured Andy would have had Jade and Kelli stay at some hotel. There was a slip of crumpled paper in Jade's hand. I took it and scanned it. It was a list of our upcoming shows. They were all major venues.

Mrs. Morgan would be pleased. The United Center was listed. The last show on the list was Madison Square Garden. We were going to be playing Madison Square Garden. Big acts played that venue. Jade and I had only been a band for a little over a year. It was crazy. I stumbled to my room, staring at the crumpled piece of paper.

I lay in bed with the paper sitting on my chest and stared at the ceiling.

There was a quiet knock on the door. "Go away," I shouted. Jade never listened to me, and he walked in and sat on the bed. He laid his hand on my shoulder and squeezed.

"Rylan," Jade said. "It's only a few months."

"It's always only a few months."

"We have three months of touring, and then we get a vacation. We'll go somewhere secluded. Just you and me."

"Right," I snapped. "There is no way they'll let us go anywhere without the girls and our own private paparazzi. They've probably got us booked for separate vacations on the opposite sides of the world this time, so there's no chance either one of us can sneak away."

"Rylan," Jade said.

"I don't want to do this anymore. It sucks. I don't give a shit about the money."

I flipped on my stomach and buried my face in my pillow. He climbed on top of me and started massaging my shoulders. I could feel his cock pressing against my ass. It felt good, but I wasn't done being angry.

"I need this," Jade whispered against the back of my neck.

I jerked and shoved him off me. He hit the floor with a loud thud.

"Why?"

"Are you kidding, Rylan?"

"By this," I gestured wildly, "you mean the money and the fame."

"Rylan," Jade said.

"Fuck off, Jade. I hope you're fucking happy with your money."

I slammed the door and ran into Kelli.

"Shit, I'm sorry," I said.

"Rylan, I need to talk to you," Kelli said.

"Can we go downstairs?" I asked. "What's going on?"

"I wanted you to hear this from me. I asked Andy if I could go home for a few days. He said no. I told him to fuck off. He's now decided that Jade and I are going to break up. He thinks it would be good for him to sleep around or some shit."

"Kelli, I'm sorry about this afternoon."

"Don't worry about it," she said. "I don't know how you've held together this long."

"Is everything okay at home?"

"Yeah, Rylan, it's fine. Um, Lucas is going to be a dad," Kelli said.

"Really?"

"Yeah, he and Kate finally worked things out, and they're going to get married."

"Was anyone going to tell me?"

"Ry, they know the kind of pressure you're under. I'm telling you," Kelli said. "I just need to go home."

Her eyes filled with tears and she started sobbing. I knew there was something she wasn't telling me, but she was too upset for me to press her anymore.

"When are you leaving?" I asked.

"Tomorrow," she said.

"So soon."

"It's for the best, Rylan," Kelli said. "I need to go pack."

Everything was falling apart, including me. I grabbed something to drink from the fridge and went out by the pool. The night was calm, but the sounds of the city were always close by. The lights and pollution hid most of the stars from view. I looked at my phone and called Andy, putting him on speaker as I searched for Maggie.

"We have a few days off before we go on this tour," I stated to Andy. "Maggie and I would like to go back to Chicago. I need to be away from all this."

"I think we can arrange that," Andy said.

"Good," I said and clicked off my phone. I didn't really give a shit if he couldn't arrange it. I could fucking arrange it.

Maggie was sitting in the laundry room on top of the dryer. She smiled sadly but gave me a hug when I told her we were going back to Chicago for a few days. I didn't go back to my room. I stayed with Maggie, sleeping spooned against her. I felt terrible.

In the morning, Jade showed up and said good-bye to Kelli. He wouldn't talk to me, but scowled at me when Maggie and I hauled our bags to the front door.

"You're welcome to come with us," I said. "I need some quiet before we hit the road again."

Jade left the room.

"Let's go," I said sadly. Pete was waiting for us. I sat between the girls. Kelli laid her head on my shoulder and Maggie held my hand, staring out the window. Maggie cried when Kelli left us standing at our gate. All I could do was apologize for putting her through all this shit.

WE'D BEEN back in Chicago for two days, not doing much but sleeping. Jade called a few times, but I refused to talk to him. I knew it was childish, but I was pouting. He could have fucking come home with me.

"Are you okay?" Maggie asked.

"Not really. I've never been so happy and fucking miserable at the same time," I said. "What about you?"

"The same."

"Sucks," I said.

Maggie sprawled on my bed and stared at me. "I'm worried about you."

"Yeah, I'm worried about me too. I think we've had this conversation before," I said. I took my shirt off and tossed it in the corner. "I'm worried about Jade and you too. And something's up with Kelli, but she refuses to talk about it."

"This isn't what I thought it would be like," Maggie admitted.

I snorted, because it wasn't even close to what I thought being a pop star would be. I'd been on Twitter earlier, and there were pictures of Jade out with some stupid movie star. It made me jealous and angry. Kelli had barely left, and already they had Jade dating someone else.

You'd think I'd be used to it by now, but it was different when it was Kelli. She knew about us. This actress didn't know Jade belonged to me.

"I talked to him," she said. "It wasn't his idea."

"And yet, there he is, kissing some woman he barely knows." I frowned and clicked off the picture, switching over to Twitter. I scrolled through hundreds of tweets.

"It's getting worse," I said.

"What is?" Maggie rolled on her side to make room for me on the bed.

"The hate," I said.

"I stopped looking online. Now I only check my private e-mail."

"I'm sorry, Maggie," I said, wrapping my arms around her.

"Quit apologizing. You have no control over what people say about me or you."

"I don't know what else to do."

"I'm tired," Maggie said. She closed her eyes, and I stroked her hair. Not many people would do what she was doing for me. She shouldn't have to do this. I shouldn't be forced to have a fake girlfriend, to hide my feelings for someone who I loved deeply, because society wasn't ready for us. Or so everyone said. I was starting to believe no matter what we did, or who I dated, fake or not, we could never satisfy everyone. Some people liked to bitch.

My phone buzzed, and I pulled it out from under my pillow. Jade's face was looking back at me. I almost shoved it back under my pillow, but I hadn't talked to him since we'd been back in Chicago.

"Hello," I said quietly. I shifted Maggie out of my arms and pulled the blanket over her.

"Rylan," Jade whispered.

"Yeah, you called me. Who else would it be?"

"You haven't been answering your phone."

"I needed a break," I said.

"I miss you," Jade said, his voice cracking. "Babe, I miss you so much."

I could tell he'd been drinking.

"I'll be back in a couple of days. You should get some sleep."

I shut off my phone before he could reply.

Mrs. Morgan found me sitting on the deck, staring at the sky. There weren't a lot of stars here either. Maybe they didn't exist anymore. I used to wish on shooting stars all the time back on the farm. Out in the country, in the dark of the night, you could lie on your back and map out the constellations. In the city, I was lucky I could see the North Star.

"Rylan," Mrs. Morgan said. She was carrying a bottle. I eyed it suspiciously.

"It's only water," she said.

"Too bad," I said.

"You look like someone stole your lunch money."

"I'm losing him," I said. "And I don't think there's anything I can do to stop it."

"I don't have the answers," she said. "You'd think after eighty years on this earth, I'd know something about love."

"We're going to be playing here," I said.

She sat down and smiled. "I know. I follow a lot of people on Twitter. I think they know things before you do."

I laughed. "Do they know I'm here?"

"I don't think so. Things have been focused on Jade these last few days."

"Right," I said.

She touched my hand and leaned back in her chair, staring at the night sky. I pointed out the North Star and described what the sky looked like at the farm.

"I would like to see that before I become one of those stars in the sky," she said.

"I bet Kelli would love to have you come to the farm," I said.

"I bet your family would love to have you come home," she said quietly. I didn't respond.

We stayed on the deck until the sun rose and Maggie found us.

"Have you been out here all night?" Maggie asked.

"Yes," I answered.

"I'm going to sleep," Mrs. Morgan said. "I'll see you when you come to Chicago." She kissed me on the cheek and walked back to her house.

"I called Andy," Maggie said. "Instead of going back to LA, we're flying directly to Phoenix for the show. Jade is...."

I sighed and held up my hand. I had no desire to know what Jade was doing or who was going to be draped over him the next time I saw him.

"Could you please call Ella and have her set up something for Mrs. Morgan at the Chicago show?" I asked.

"Sure, Rylan, no problem."

She left me sitting on the deck. I didn't move until dinnertime. Maggie forced pizza down my throat, yelling about how I looked too tired.

"I stayed up all night," I said. "I am tired."

"Go to bed, Rylan," Maggie ordered. "I'll pack your shit. We have to leave before the crack of dawn."

I dragged my ass to bed, only to be hit with nightmares of losing Jade. Maggie woke me up at 2:00 a.m. when she crawled into bed with me. She stroked my hair, and I tried not to think that it should be Jade who comforted me. But if Jade was here, I probably wouldn't be having these shitty dreams.

Maggie poked me before the sun was even up, telling me to get in the shower. I went through the motions of making myself presentable. I didn't do a very good job. Maggie handed me sunglasses and a hat before we left the house.

There were a few fans at the airport. I did my best to smile for the pictures and sign some autographs. When we got on the plane, I put my headphones on and fell asleep before we were in the air.

It was way too bright and sunny and fucking hot in Phoenix. Pete was at the airport to make sure I made it to sound check. I was nervous to see Jade. Of course, the first glimpse I got of him was with some woman. She had her arm around his waist and my stomach plummeted into my shoes. I didn't think I was going to survive the day.

Ella was the first to spot me and wrap me in her long, spindly girl arms. It should have been Jade. I could sense the minute he looked at me. I decided to ignore him and let Ella usher me into the dressing room.

She chattered about the clothing and the changes. I knew it all by heart. We'd rehearsed so many times, I was pretty sure I could do the damn show drunk.

Dave poked his head in the door and told me it was time to get on the stage. The sound check was uncomfortable and stiff. As soon as Ethan strummed the final chord, I jumped off the stage and raced down the hall until I found a bathroom. The cool water I splashed on my face calmed me down, but me fucking whole body ached. He was so close but so far away.

The door opened and Jade stepped inside. His face was flushed, and there was a faint bite mark on his neck.

"Rylan," Jade said, reaching for me.

"I can't," I murmured. I started toward the door, but he blocked my path.

His fingers slid up my bare arm. All I could think of was that he touched that girl with that same hand. I backed away, but he mirrored my movements until he had me against the wall.

"Jade, please," I said.

"I can't do this without you," he whispered. The heat from his body surrounded me, and I gave in. I didn't have the strength to walk away from him. I leaned into his touch when he pressed his chest against mine.

He smashed his mouth against mine so hard my teeth rattled, and I drew blood when I bit his lip. I wanted to hurt him, to make him feel as bad as I was feeling. My fingers dug into his arms, leaving red dots. He pulled my hair, keeping my lips anchored against his mouth. He sucked on my tongue. There was a knock on the door, and I shoved him away from me.

Dave carefully opened the door. Jade grabbed the back of my jacket before I could get away from him.

"Can you get us to the hotel?" Jade asked.

Dave nodded, whisking us away before anyone noticed.

We took different cars to the hotel and entered through different doors. We didn't make love. We fucked. Hard.

That night, with me sprawled on his chest, Jade called Andy and told him to get rid of the girl. She was too much of a distraction. For once, Andy agreed, and the woman disappeared.

I relaxed and tried to enjoy the shows, but in the back of my mind I knew what was coming. With each day that passed, our contract was getting closer to ending, and there was talk of a new one being drawn up for us to sign. The money was going to be astronomical, but once again there would be giant ropes attached to us, weighing us down. I sighed into Jade's hair and went to sleep. Tomorrow was Chicago, and I wanted to be on top of my game.

Ella had outdone herself. We arrived in a limo to pick up Mrs. Morgan. Ella also picked out a gorgeous gown and sent a couple of her assistants to make sure the dress fit perfectly. When I went to the door, Mrs. Morgan opened it before I could ring the bell.

She beamed at me. "You look tasty," she said, patting my butt as we walked to the car. I swear everyone in the neighborhood was outside watching us.

"You look lovely," I said.

"I know."

Jade held the door for her, and she got into the limo. I thought we would let Mrs. Morgan sit in the middle, but Jade pushed me in the car and followed behind. He immediately hooked his ankle with mine.

We ate at a swanky restaurant. No one interrupted our meal for an autograph. When it was time to head to the arena, Mrs. Morgan asked about Maggie.

"She's waiting at the arena for us," Jade said. "She'll show you around backstage and introduce you to everyone while we're getting ready. You can do anything you want."

"I just want to see you boys sing," Mrs. Morgan said.

The show was awesome. Chicago was excited to see us back home. This was the first place we had played, so they claimed us as hometown boys. I thought the show was a dream, but when I came off the stage, everyone gave me a strange look. I had no idea what the hell was going on with them, but it made me nervous.

The phone call from Andy came in the limo on the way back home. Andy was so pissed off about the show I thought he was going to have an aneurysm. I didn't know what the fuck he was so mad about until he shouted something about a blatant lyric change. He screamed about money and target markets and other things that in the whole picture of life didn't matter one bit to me.

He told Dave to bring us to his hotel after we dropped off our guest at her home.

"I'm sorry you had to hear that," I said to Mrs. Morgan.

"He's quite the prick," Mrs. Morgan said.

"Yeah, he is," I agreed.

I walked Mrs. Morgan to her door, glancing over at Maggie's darkened house. I missed the simplicity of the place.

"I wish I could tell you everything will be okay," Mrs. Morgan said.

"Me too," I said and hugged her tightly. She told me she had a great time and that it was the best concert she'd ever been to. She was very glad she hadn't croaked.

"Are you sick?"

"No, but you never know," she said. "One day you're here, and then, you're not."

"I better go," I said.

"Rylan, you need to follow your heart," she said.

I climbed back in the car and slumped in the seat. Jade reached for my hand, but I slid my hand into my pocket, pretending to look for my phone.

"I didn't do it on purpose," I said. "I got caught up in the excitement of the show and the way you were looking at me. I'm sorry."

Jade shook his head and kissed me.

There were fucking fans at Andy's hotel, so we had to sneak in through the delivery entrance. Going through all this work to get shouted at seemed really foolish. Dave and Brent got us up to Andy's suite without anyone noticing us.

Andy scowled at us when we walked into the room. Maggie was standing in the corner next to the bar, sipping on a drink. I joined her and grabbed a beer. I waited for the shouting, but it never came. Instead, Andy made me listen to a thousand different sound clips of the lyric change. Most normal people wouldn't have noticed, but the RheartJ shippers were having a field day. Twitter may have blown up.

He finally shut his laptop. I thought we were finished, but Andy turned his attention to the lyrics of a new song I'd written. Jade sat there like a stupid lump, not chiming in to support me.

"You know, Rylan," Maggie said, swirling her drink. "All you need to do with the song is add in a few oh girl lines and stop sneaking in those gender-specific words during the concert. You've done it before."

"I did it once!" I yelled. "And I didn't mean to do it. I got caught up in the moment and it just slipped out."

"It just slipped out," Maggie repeated the words in a tone of voice that made me want to kick her in the shin. "The fans analyze the shit out of every fucking word you utter. For fuck's sake, you can play the part of straight boy for a few hours."

"What?" I shouted, and threw my can of beer across the room. It smashed into the wall, splattering liquid everywhere. "I play the part all the fucking time. I can't get away from it. I may as well be dating you in real life. I don't know who the fuck I am anymore." It sounded like Maggie was jumping ship and siding with Andy.

"Quit fucking yelling at me. Can't you control your emotions?" Maggie snapped. "Stop looking at Jade like he's the center of the whole fucking universe."

I gasped at her words. He was the center of my crumbling universe, and she fucking knew it. I tripped over my feet and banged into the table.

"Oh," Maggie whimpered. "Oh, my God, Rylan, I'm sorry." She ran her hands through her hair, tugging at the ends. Tears filled her eyes and dripped down her cheeks. "I can't do this anymore. I'm turning into you," she shouted, pointing at Andy. "I'm done. I'm going home."

She raced out of the room, and I sank into a chair. Jade tried to hook his ankle around mine, but I jerked my leg away and listened as the door slammed loudly.

After two more hours of Andy shouting at me and Jade staring at the ceiling, Ella interrupted the meeting and said we'd had enough. Our flight left tomorrow at the crack of dawn, and we needed to get a few hours of rest. Andy frowned and dismissed us with a wave of his hand.

I tried to call Maggie, but it kept going straight to voice mail. When the car pulled up to the hotel, Dave stopped me from getting out of the car.

"Let Jade go up first. We'll go in through the back entrance," Dave said.

"Fine," I said, sinking down in the seat. I didn't have the strength to argue with him. I pushed redial and stared at my phone, willing Maggie to answer. It went to voice mail again.

Jade was waiting for me in my room.

"Rylan," he whispered. I shook my head and let him lead me to the bed. He gently laid me back and covered me with his entire body. I clung to him like a dying man taking his last breath.

"I'm losing it," I cried.

"We'll make it," Jade whispered. "We only have a few more shows left. I promise we'll take a long vacation away from all this shit."

His words vibrated against my throat, and I arched into him. He moaned and moved my shirt away, then bit down on my collarbone and sucked until a red mark blossomed. I concentrated on his touch instead of all the bad stuff surrounding us.

I didn't sleep much that night and it showed when I looked in the mirror in the morning.

Jade was sitting at the table staring at his phone when I got out of the bathroom. "Did you tweet about Maggie?"

"No," I snapped and tossed my suitcases by the door.

"Well, someone tweeted from your account that you're a free man." He flipped his phone around so I could see the screen. I stared at the tweet. I'd even put a smiley face. At least Maggie would know it wasn't me. I hated those fucking emoticons.

"Jade, I can't take much more of this shit," I said. "My whole life is based on lies."

He sighed and rubbed his eyes. He opened his mouth, but his phone buzzed. "They're waiting. You're supposed to go down the back stairs."

"Of course I am," I growled and grabbed my bag. The door opened and I slammed into Dave.

"Hey, man," he said. I held my hand up and headed down the hall to go out the back entrance like a dirty little secret. I shot a text to Maggie pleading with her to call me.

Pete got out of the car and popped the trunk so Dave could toss my luggage in the trunk.

Dave got in and I gave him a confused look.

"They want you to show up separately," he said.

I closed my eyes and leaned against the window. Maggie didn't call me, and Jade and I didn't sit together on the plane. There was a new girl sitting next to him. It was a long flight.

The airport was packed with fans, and security deemed it unsafe for us to interact with that many people. I think Dave could tell I wasn't up for posing for pics and signing autographs. Andy was livid, but Dave barked at him, telling him he was in charge of security and he wasn't risking us getting hurt.

"Thanks," I whispered to Dave when we were tucked in the car. All I got was a barely there nod, but I knew he heard me.

The fans hadn't figured out which hotel we were staying at yet, so it was smooth sailing checking in to our rooms. I tossed my shit on the extra bed and collapsed, pulling the pillow over my face. Maggie still hadn't answered my texts, and I was getting worried. I had no idea where she had gone.

Mrs. Morgan answered on the third ring.

"Beth," I said. It was still hard for me to use her first name.

"Rylan," she said. "Are you okay?"

"Not really, but is Maggie at home? She won't answer her phone or my texts, and I'm freaking out."

"She's sleeping on my couch," Mrs. Morgan said.

A wave of relief loosened some of the knots in my shoulders. At least I knew she was safe.

"She's disgusted with herself. She wouldn't tell me what happened, but I think I have an idea."

"I don't know how much more of this I can take," I murmured. Before I could take another breath, I started to cry. "I have to go. Tell Maggie I love her."

I hung up before Mrs. Morgan could say anything else. This was not going to be a good day. I glanced at our schedule. We had a sound check and two interviews, plus a meet and greet before the show. I wanted to hide under my bed.

I must have fallen asleep, because when I woke up, Jade was gently shaking me. "You need to clean up," he whispered in my ear. His tongue snuck out, tracing around the shell of my ear, making me squirm.

"Shower with me," he said.

For my own sanity, I knew I should stay away from him. Sometimes it felt like Andy installed cameras in our rooms to keep track of our every movement, but I desperately needed to feel Jade.

"How did you get over here?" I asked.

"Dave," he panted, and turned my head so he had access to my lips as he backed me toward the bathroom. "Andy wants to talk about the new contract as soon as possible."

I stopped and stared at Jade. "I don't want to discuss that right now," I said.

"Rylan, please," Jade whined. "He's only asking for two years, and the amount of money would set us up for life."

"I need a few days to think about this shit," I said.

"We can do this for two more years. Only two years and then we could do whatever the hell we wanted."

For the first time since I'd met Jade, I was happy when my phone rang. I stepped away from him, mumbling that I needed to take the call. I left him standing with his shirt askew and his pants undone.

"Hey," I whispered into the phone to Maggie.

"Are you okay?" she asked.

"No, I don't know what to do. Jade wants to sign the contract and continue with this fucking charade. I don't know if I can do this for another two years."

"I can't tell you what to do," she said.

"I know," I whimpered. "I miss you."

The line went silent and my chest hurt with every breath I took. I was surprised when my phone buzzed again. Maggie had sent me a video.

Remember when things were simple.

I pushed play. It was Jade and me in Mrs. Morgan's studio messing around with "From the Beginning." It was the night we wrote it. The song was rough and all raw emotions, but it was fucking perfect. When the song ended, I almost shut my phone off, but the video kept playing.

"I know it's early and crazy as all fuck," Jade said. "But I can't hold it in anymore. No one has ever made me feel so much. I love you, Rylan."

The three most dreaded words known to mankind hung in the air, and for the first time in my entire life, I relished them and happily returned the sentiment.

"I love you too," I whispered.

I closed my eyes and turned my phone off. The world could give me a few minutes peace. It fucking owed me for letting me believe that Jade was my always.

The next few concerts were tense, but we held it together and gave the audiences a great show.

We were in New York City on the eve of what was supposed to be the greatest night of our lives, and I was fucking miserable. The moment we got into the hotel, I fell asleep with my head resting on the table. Jade woke me up when he busted into the room, shouting about the new contract.

"Have you read it yet? They're offering us the fucking world, Rylan," Jade screamed in my face. "We'll be touring all over the world. Think about it. Remember all that stuff you told me you wanted to do with me. It could come true."

I laughed. "They would never let us stand on a balcony in Paris or ride the Eye without some unnamed woman. Kelli's gone, Maggie's gone, and now there's a new girl following you around," I snarled.

"I'm not cheating on you," Jade snapped.

I pounded my fist on the table and stood up. "What the fuck do you call it? You're shoving your tongue down these girls' throats. And I have to see it over and over on the Internet, on TV, in the magazines and newspapers. It's fucking everywhere, and it hurts."

He pushed me and I stumbled back into the wall. I tried to twist away from him, but he grabbed my wrist and pulled me back toward the table and those fucking contracts.

"Let go of me, you fucking asshole," I shouted. With one hard yank, I pulled my arm out of his grasp. My bracelet snapped and fell to the floor.

It was like watching something dying in slow motion. I dropped to my knees and stared at the infinity charm lying on the floor. Infinity was a hell of lot shorter than I realized.

"Rylan!" Jade screamed. "I'm sorry."

I looked from the broken bracelet lying on the floor to Jade. It seemed so symbolic, that the choice I was about to make was already made. It was written in stone. I wasn't going to sign the contracts.

"I'm sorry," Jade said again. He kept repeating the words as he scooped the bracelet off the floor. He tried to hand it back to me, but I shook my head. I think he stuffed it in his pocket.

"Fine, Jade. If you think it's for the best, then I'll sign after the show tomorrow night." It was another lie to add to the mountain.

"Okay, Rylan, that would be great," Jade said quietly. I thought he'd be more excited. After all, it's what he wanted.

I nodded and twisted the doorknob. Jade tried to hug me, but I sidestepped his grasp. "I'm exhausted. I'm going to sleep."

Dave glanced at me when I walked out of Jade's room.

"You okay?" he asked.

I shook my head. "Can I talk to you?"

Dave stood up and called Brent, telling him he needed a break. Brent was there in five minutes. "I'll be in Rylan's room if anyone needs me."

Dave followed me into my room. I went straight to the minibar and grabbed the first bottle I could wrap my fingers around.

"Rylan," Dave said. "What's going on?"

"You've been a great friend."

Dave studied my face, got up, walked over to the minibar, and grabbed his own bottle. "I have a feeling I'm going to need this."

I chugged my bottle and frowned. I sat down on the edge of the bed.

"I have no right to ask you this, and you can tell me no," I rambled. "Whatever you decide, I would appreciate it if you could keep it to yourself."

"You're not signing, are you?"

"No," I said. "Tomorrow is my last show, and I was wondering if you could help me get out of the arena when it's over."

"Have you talked to Jade?"

"I've tried, but he wants to sign. I can't do it anymore, Dave. There's been so many lies that I don't even know who I am anymore."

"Rylan, I'm sorry," Dave said.

"You don't have to apologize," I said.

"Yeah, I do. I think all of this is total bullshit, Rylan. I wish there was something I could have done for you."

"They would have fired you," I said. "Having you around made it a little more bearable. I do appreciate it."

He stood up and patted my shoulder. I tried to keep the tears inside, but they insisted on leaking out of my eyes. Dave pulled me into a big bear hug. When he walked out of the room, his eyes were wet too.

This was going to hurt so many people, but if I stayed, it would be worse. I curled up in a ball and lay in the middle of the large bed. I missed Jade already, and my wrist felt naked.

I managed to avoid Jade most of the day. We did separate interviews and separate meet and greets. Sound check was quick, and then Dave whisked me away, citing something that sounded plausible. We went back to the hotel and did a shot of tequila. Close to show time, I ventured over to Jade's room.

The contracts sat on the table ready for our signatures.

"Did you sign it?" Jade asked.

"Uh, I told you, I'd sign after the concert," I lied again. Last night had solidified my decision, and today I had accepted my future. This wasn't the life I wanted, and if I didn't get out now, I would end up hating him. I already hated myself for giving in to all their demands. I couldn't be a dirty little secret anymore. I was done with the lies.

"Okay," Jade said. He reached for my hand, but I pulled away, pretending to fuss with my tie.

"I can't believe we're playing the Garden," I said.

"Yeah, me neither," he said.

His phone buzzed, signaling that the car was downstairs ready to whisk us away. I headed to the door, but he grabbed my arm and spun me around.

"It's all going to work out," Jade said. I couldn't make myself turn away from his kiss. Just because I was leaving him didn't mean I didn't love him. I would always love him. He tried to deepen the kiss, but I shoved him away.

"Andy will know," I said and stepped away from him. "I don't need him shouting in my face before the show."

He frowned but agreed with me.

Jade was amped up and the ride to the arena was tense. Maggie sent a text wishing us luck. I couldn't even reply. What the fuck was I supposed to tell her? This was it for me, my swan song. When the last note played tonight, I was walking out of Jade's life and away from a multimillion dollar contract. People were going to think I'd lost my fucking mind, and maybe I had. I knew if I stayed, I *would* lose my fucking mind.

The closer we got to the arena, the more traffic slowed us down. There were people everywhere. When we'd done our sound check earlier, I swear some of the same people were still here, standing in the pouring rain.

Most normal acts would be driven into the underground entrance, but management loved to let the fans have access to us. The driver stopped the car and our bodyguards surrounded the car with bulk and umbrellas. I sighed, and Jade patted my knee. I flinched and quickly opened the door. The fake smiles came easy now. I'd been perfecting them for a year.

A loud roar from the crowd went up as we were quickly ushered inside the building. Jade bumped me and placed a warm hand on my shoulder. I twisted away from him, shrinking from his touch because Andy was always watching. My mind flashed back to the unsigned contracts, and suddenly I didn't give a shit. What the hell more could he do to me? After tonight, he no longer owned me. I leaned over and whispered in Jade's ear.

"I will always love you."

He cocked his head and gave me a confused look. I shrugged and let Dave practically carry me into the building, where we were hustled into the dressing rooms for hair and makeup.

My phone buzzed again showing another text from Maggie. She was worried. I sent her a smiley face. She was going to know something was up, because I hated those stupid emoticons.

We signed some autographs, posed for some fucking pictures, and goofed around with the lucky fans who were given backstage passes. Time passed in a whirl of makeup brushes and hairspray. We were given last-minute orders about costume changes and some other shit. I pretended to listen to all the instructions. Don't stand so close to each other. Flirt with the girls. It was the same shit they told us at every show.

"Hurry up and get changed," Ella shouted at us. She hustled us out of makeup and into the dressing room where everything was neatly laid out for us.

"Fifteen minutes," Ella said before she closed the door.

We were alone. We were never alone anymore. I turned my back on Jade and stripped off my jeans and shirt. The click of the lock sliding into place sounded like an explosion, and I was sure someone was going to be pounding on the door in a second, shouting at us to open the fucking thing.

His warm hands slid up my spine bringing me back to the first night we made love.

"Jade, please," I whimpered when he pressed his body against mine. "They're going to fucking kill us."

"*They* are not here right now, and I've missed you so much."

He ran his hands down my back, slipped his fingers in the waistband of my underwear, and slowly pulled them down. The logical side of my brain told me to fight him, to say no and get dressed for the show. My heart told my brain to shut the fuck up. This was probably going to be the last time, and I was going to take whatever he was offering.

He buried his face in my neck, ran his tongue across my shoulder, and bit down hard. I hissed but let him mark me. It would be visible when I wore my white T-shirt.

The unmistakable sound of the top popping off a lube bottle filled my ears. The tearing of a condom wrapper caught my attention, but I understood why he was using one. I didn't need to have fluids leaking out of me during our performance. His wet fingers spread me apart, and I leaned forward and grabbed the edge of the table. He pressed two fingers into me. We really didn't have time to mess around, and I didn't care. He could have shoved into me the minute he slicked his cock.

"Just do it," I growled. The physical pain would be a welcome distraction to me.

He twisted and wiggled his fingers for a few more minutes. His cock nudged against me, and he grabbed me around the waist and shoved hard into me. I bit my lip and stifled my shout. It burned, and the ache spread through my entire body. Jade stilled, waiting for me to adjust.

"Fuck me," I begged.

He groaned, and it was then I felt the desperation in him. His hands were everywhere, running up my back, digging into my hips and tugging on my hair. He bit me again, and I arched into him, meeting his frantic thrusts. When I tried to grab my cock, he slapped my hand away and wrapped his slick hand around my erection, and twisted and ran his thumb through my slit until I wanted to scream.

"Almost there," he gasped. He tightened his grip on me, and I grunted.

"Now, Jade," I moaned, and watched as my cum covered his hand.

He bit down on my shoulder again and collapsed on top of me when he came.

"Five minutes" came a voice from out in the hall.

"Christ," Jade groaned.

"Yeah, Christ," I said as he pulled out and I examined his marks in the mirror. "I look like I was attacked by a vampire or have leprosy or something."

Jade shrugged and tossed a towel at me so I could wipe up any remaining jizz. We quickly got dressed. I watched him out of the corner of my eye. Did he know what was coming?

This once magical ride had been reduced to a bunch of angry people shouting about insignificant things. The worst thing was Jade wanted to keep the lies going. Too many people had already been hurt by this roller coaster ride. It was my turn to get off.

"Hey," Jade said. "You okay?"

I nodded because I didn't trust my voice.

"You ready, then? It's Madison Square Garden, babe!"

Jade unlocked the door, and Ella burst into the room. She fussed and fiddled with our hair, straightened our collars, and gave me an exasperated look when she spotted the hickeys on my collarbone and throat. I pointed at Jade. She pulled a tube of cover up out of her pocket, but I waved her off. She didn't even argue. Instead, I got an eye roll and doused with hairspray.

Jade bounced out of the room and headed down the hall, high-fiving everyone who saw him. I hung back and tried to calm down.

Ella touched my back. "Rylan, it's going to be okay."

When I looked into her eyes, she gasped and covered her mouth. She knew.

"Please," I begged. "Don't tell anyone."

"Oh God," she whimpered and turned her back to me.

"I have to." I felt like I owed her an explanation, but I didn't have the time. I touched her hand and frowned because Jade was shouting at me. It was time to slide into my pop star persona.

Ella pulled me into a quick hug. Ella K never hugged anyone. Jade gave me a weird look, but I shrugged it off. We stood shoulder to shoulder for a few seconds, and then he turned to face me and rested his forehead against mine. I had to bite back the tears. He wanted to say something, but he swallowed the words and knuckle bumped me. What the fuck?

The music signaling our walk to the stage started. I was surprised to see Andy waiting in the wings. God, I wanted to lean in and tell him to fuck off, but it would have to wait until after the show. He hugged us both and I went stiff as a board when he touched me.

"It's been a great year, boys. I can only hope the next year will be just as lucrative for us all."

"Fat fucking chance," I said under my breath.

The thumping of the drums pounding in my chest sent adrenaline racing through my blood. We sprinted out on stage to a roar so loud I couldn't even hear my own voice over the microphone. I took a minute to scan the audience. The RheartJ signs were out in full force. I was always surprised Andy didn't set up checkpoints to search the fans and take any unsavory signs away from them. He liked to believe he could control everything.

Jade talked to the audience, thanking them for a great year. I smiled and flirted with some girls in the front row, posing for pictures and shaking hands, until Jade came over and grabbed me by the arm and hauled me back to center stage. The set started, and I went into autopilot, playing my part perfectly.

The costume changes were quick. Our harmonies were spot-on, and the banter with the audience was light and charming. Then the house lights dimmed, the audience settled down, and Jade and I sat alone in the middle of the stage. He picked up his guitar, and I watched as his calloused fingers slid down the neck. My body remembered how his hands felt the first time he touched me. I remembered everything from our first awkward kiss in the hallway to waking up snuggled against his warm body. I wondered if I went back, knowing what I knew now, would I still choose to kiss him? I stared at him and took a deep breath. Thoughts of our first time invaded my mind again. It had been good. And even though things were pretty shitty right now, I figured, with time, I'd come to appreciate the time we'd spent together.

Things had been simple before we put those songs up on YouTube and Andy Tremaine found us. I heard Jade tell the audience that this past year had been a dream come true, the best year ever.

He continued to talk about the past year. I had to close my eyes and count silently in my head to keep from falling apart. Most of the days had been good, but lately, the lies were taking over everything and I didn't know where the lies ended and I began. Kelli was back home and Maggie was in Chicago. I missed them.

He plucked a few notes, but stopped and stood up. I eyed him when he shuffled his stool closer to me. He also fucked around with his mic stand before he settled back down. A shy smile spread across his face, and I almost died when he hooked his ankle around mine and started to sing "From the Beginning." We usually didn't sing that song anymore. Andy thought it gave too much away. My throat felt like it was collapsing, and I could barely breathe. The heat from his ankle actually calmed me down, and I was able to join him on the chorus.

The audience went bat-shit crazy when the song ended. My entire body shook as we bowed. It got worse when I felt Jade's hand sneak under my shirt. I reminded myself he had chosen to sign a contract that would keep our secret hidden behind a wall of lies.

I took a deep breath and pulled away from him. Jade got a funny look on his face when I picked up my microphone and held it to my lips. This was when we were supposed to blow kisses to the audience, smile, and get off the fucking stage.

The audience quieted, and I stepped further away from Jade. Dave was in front of the stage, and he gave me the thumbs-up signal. He was probably going to get fired for helping me, but I was so grateful he hadn't ratted me out.

"Thank you for everything, for believing in our music," I told the audience. My voice filled the entire arena, and I had to take another deep breath. "It really has been one hell of a ride." I caught a glimpse of Andy freaking out behind the curtain, waving his arms and making a slash signal over his throat. When I didn't shut up, he started yelling at one of the sound guys to kill my microphone.

"I'll never forget this night as long as I live, but I'm handing over my spotlight to Jade." My voice cracked and the tears started to drip down my cheeks.

Several girls in the front row started sobbing. It was difficult to think when everyone was freaking out. Everywhere I looked, people were unhappy, but I stared straight ahead, because I knew if I saw Jade, I'd fall apart. I squeaked a few more words out, but suddenly my microphone went dead, so I shook my head, walked to the center of the stage, and set my microphone on my stool. The houselights went down, and the only light shining was on that microphone. The crowd erupted, and I raced to the edge of the stage and jumped toward Dave. I thought I heard Jade screaming, but I couldn't turn back. I'd made my choice. It was over.

A huge part of me hoped he would jump into the crowd and run after me to confess his undying love and whisk me away from all this shit. I wanted our story to end like every good romance novel. But it was Dave who grabbed my arm and shoved his way through the crowd, getting me away from the screaming fans.

"Run, Rylan," Dave said. I raced down the hall, through the maze of hallways, until I spotted another exit door. Dave was hot on my heels, shouting at people to stay the fuck away from me. He caught up with me when we made it to the door to the underground garage.

"There's a car waiting," Dave said.

"Thanks, man," I said, shaking his hand.

"Rylan," he said and pulled me into a bear hug. He knew the story. He knew everything, and he protected me until the end, and I would forever be indebted to the man. "I know. Now go."

I ran outside and climbed into the waiting car that whisked me away from this stupid lie of a life I'd been living.

The doorman at the hotel recognized me when I jumped out of the limo. I waited for him to say something, but he only tipped his hat. I asked him to get me a cab and have it wait at the coffee shop down the street. I'd be there in fifteen minutes.

My ears were still ringing from the crowd. The hotel was surprisingly quiet. I quickly gathered my stuff and shoved everything back into my suitcase. I had spent the last year living out of a fucking suitcase. We were always on the move. I sighed and shoved some more clothes into it and quickly zipped it closed before I changed my mind.

The last thing to pack was my journals, and I almost had them in my bag when I stopped. I didn't need these anymore. They were for him. All the lyrics I'd written were for him, and I couldn't take them with me. I threw them in a plastic bag and jotted a quick note. It was a garbled message at best, one I didn't think he would understand.

I never did any of this for the money. It had always been for him. It hurt more than anything I'd suffered through in my life to think that the money was more important to him. But I understood. Money changes people. Just like love changes people.

This whole mess was the fault of falling in love, and I would never allow it near me again. It hurt too much. I closed my eyes and lowered my chin to my chest.

"Bye, Jade," I breathed. "I hope you find your happiness."

The last thing I did was drop one of my favorite pens in the bag with the journals. I hung the bag on his door. I made it down the stairs and out into the pouring rain, running until I came to the small coffee house that was open all night. Once inside, I slowly typed out the words for a text to Maggie.

Most people think falling in love is a wonderful thing. It isn't. It fucking ruins everything.

I stared at it for a few seconds and pushed send. Her reply came within moments. It was good to hear her sweet voice.

"Oh my God, Rylan? Are you okay? Say something? It's all over the Internet."

"It's done, Maggie," I whimpered. "I want to come home."

It was raining when I boarded the plane in New York, and it was raining when the plane landed in Chicago. Everywhere I went I brought rain.

I was vaguely aware of the stares and whispers as I traipsed through the terminal. No one approached me for an autograph or photo, and for once I was incredibly thankful for social media. The breakup was all over the Internet. I'd gone online before I boarded the plane for Chicago and was inundated with RheartJ stuff. The heart between our initials was broken. It was the first time the RheartJ shippers and the rest of the fans united. No one wanted the band to break up. I turned Internet access off on my phone.

I sent a quick text to Maggie telling her my plane had landed. She told me she was waiting by our usual spot. I pulled my hat down lower and hurried toward the exit. It shouldn't have surprised me to see Mrs. Morgan standing beside Maggie. She patted my cheek and slipped her arm through mine. Maggie took my other hand and squeezed. I heard the familiar clicking of camera phones, but I didn't give a shit.

Maggie had parked illegally, slipping the parking lot attendant some extra cash, so the car was close to the door. I climbed in the backseat, thinking Mrs. Morgan would sit up front, but she slid in next to me and let me put my head on her shoulder. Maggie started the car and quickly turned off the radio. I was thankful for the silence.

The familiar landscape of Chicago was a welcome sight, and when Maggie turned down our street I went numb. It was nice that there weren't any reporters lurking, but maybe they hadn't gotten wind I was in Chicago.

The memory of the first time we met Jade flickered through my mind. But he wasn't here anymore and he wouldn't be here tomorrow or the next day or the next day. Tears streamed down my face and I leaped out of the car, raced into the house, and headed straight for my old bedroom.

The door was closed, and I came to a skidding halt. This wasn't my home anymore. I had no right to just barge in and think things were as I left them. I sank to the floor and buried my face in my hands.

"Rylan," Maggie said.

"I'm sorry. I didn't know where else to go." I choked the words out in between sobs.

She turned the knob and pushed the door open. It was still my room, and I threw myself into her arms. She helped me to the bed, and we lay down, spooning like we did the night I outed myself to my parents.

Mrs. Morgan put a blanket on us and told Maggie to call her later.

I STAYED in bed for three days. Maggie played my protector, answering my phone and shouting a lot. Several times I heard her crying, but most conversations ended quietly. When Maggie was fielding all my calls, Mrs. Morgan was sitting by my bedside trying to coax me to eat or at least drink something. Mrs. Morgan had also enlisted the aid of all the neighbors, telling them it was their job to protect one of their own. If they saw anyone who didn't belong in the neighborhood, they called the police.

On the fourth day, Maggie stomped into my room, ripped the shades open, and shouted at me. "Rylan, I know you're upset, but you stink. Go take a fucking shower and change clothes. You have five minutes, or I'm going to tie you to your bed and let Mrs. Morgan give you a sponge bath." Her evil laughter echoed through the entire house. I took a shower and put on clean clothes.

More days passed, and we fell into an odd routine. I'd get up and put on my running clothes. Maggie would grab her car keys. Mrs. Morgan would be waiting by the car wearing a brightly colored jogging suit and white tennis shoes, holding two cups of coffee.

The ladies would climb into the car and follow behind me while I ran. If we spotted any reporters, I'd jump in the car and we'd roar away and drive in circles until we lost the vultures and I could resume my run.

During the afternoon, Maggie would go to work and leave me with a detailed list of chores to keep me occupied. Thinking was dangerous. Remembering was worse. I stayed off the Internet. I didn't read the newspapers or any magazines. I barely spoke to anyone. Kelli called every day, but I couldn't carry on a conversation. Usually, I ended up apologizing for the hell I'd put her through. She always told me it had been her choice to play Jade's girlfriend. Most of the time I whimpered and listened to her talk. She put up with me, and I loved her even more.

As the days turned into weeks, Jade was becoming nothing more than an echo, and every day, more of him was fading. I wanted to hold on to him, but I knew that one day there would be nothing left to grab. It scared the shit out of me, but Maggie kept telling me it was how it should be. There were steps in the grieving process and I was getting close to acceptance. There was never any denial on my part that he was gone. Maggie kept telling me that I needed to start to live again. I didn't have the heart to tell her I didn't think it would ever be possible.

A day-to-day existence with small bits of happiness was probable, but never again would I offer my heart to anyone. I truly did not think I had a heart to offer anyway. Jade had ripped it out, and I'd watched it disintegrate the moment he told me he was agreeing with Andy and signing that new fucking contract.

"Rylan," Maggie said. She was leaning against the doorframe.

"Yeah," I said.

"Have you thought about what you're going to do now?" She spoke carefully and quietly. I knew she was afraid of upsetting me and sending me back into that black hole of despair.

"I think I may go back to school," I said. "Maybe I'll take a course or two online."

"You should," she said, smiling at me. "Mrs. Morgan made some lunch. It's a beautiful day, so we're eating on the deck."

"Give me a minute," I said.

She nodded and left my room. As I headed down the hall, my phone rang and Kelli's picture popped up on my screen. She usually didn't call me until the evening. I thought about letting the call go to voice mail, but it was time to get back into the real world. I should have ignored this one.

Maggie glanced at me when I walked into the kitchen. She was holding a large pitcher of lemonade. She took one look at me and knew there was something seriously wrong. There was always something wrong. I bet she was sorry she ever let me into her life.

"Rylan," she said.

"I need to go home for a few days," I muttered. "Kelli called and my dad is sick or something. She wouldn't talk about it over the phone."

"Do you want me to come along?"

"Thanks, but you have to work and other shit," I said. She'd put her life on for hold for me way too many times.

"I don't have anything going on that can't wait. I'm only working to stay busy," Maggie said. "You're more important than a silly job."

"I'll call if I need you."

She nodded and started to go outside with her lemonade.

"Maggie," I whispered.

She turned back and the pitcher dropped to the ground, shattering all over the floor. She sidestepped the mess and had her arms wrapped around me before the first tears spilled.

"I'm so sorry," I whispered into her neck. "I've never told you how much I appreciated everything you did for me. You stood by me through all the shit, my family, the fans, and Jade."

She tightened her grip and sucked in a huge breath. "I've said it before, Rylan, I will always stand by you. You're my friend, and I would do anything for you."

"I don't deserve you," I whispered.

She took my face in her hands and squeezed my cheeks. "Oh Rylan, you didn't deserve anything that happened."

"Thanks, Maggie." I hugged her again. "I better go. The taxi should be here shortly, and I still need to pack."

"Call me," Maggie said. "Okay? You don't get to plead the Fifth on this one." I nodded and sighed. As I turned to leave, she grabbed my arm. "Rylan, you are one of the best things in my life. Don't ever forget that."

"Thanks," I said. She still knew me, and it was comforting. I slowly walked to my room to drag out my suitcase.

CHAPTER ELEVEN

THE SQUEAK of my shoes on the tile floor made my skin crawl. The sight of my mother and brother leaning on each other in the family lounge made me want to turn and run. When Kelli spotted me, she dropped the magazine she was reading and rushed into my arms. Things were off. This was not a normal visit to see a sick person.

"What's going on?" I whispered into Kelli's hair.

"God, I'm sorry, Rylan," Kelli said. "I wanted to tell you, but Dad wouldn't let me."

My entire body went numb. I didn't want to feel the pain and sadness filling the room. It made me dizzy.

"Kelli," I said, holding her tighter. "What's going on?"

She sighed and went limp in my arms. "Dad is sick." I glanced at my mom and my brother again. The definition of sick hit me hard, and I had to sit down in the nearest chair. From the look on everyone's face, sick meant my dad was dying.

"He wants to talk to you," Kelli whispered.

My stomach dropped to my knees, and my heart thudded against my ribs.

"What is it?" I murmured as I stood up.

"Pancreatic cancer," Kelli said. "He…. I'll let him explain things to you."

"Jesus Christ," I murmured, and stumbled out of the lounge on shaky legs.

A nurse met me halfway down the hall and offered me her arm. "You must be Rylan," she said. I nodded and tried to swallow, but my mouth had gone dry. "I'm your dad's nurse, Serena. He talks about you a lot."

I furrowed my brow and thought maybe there had been some mistake and it wasn't my dad in the room. Why would he be talking about me? I had to be a gigantic embarrassment to him. I'd walked away from a ton of money and a career that from an outsider's point of view was phenomenal. My dad probably brought me here to laugh in my face and call me an idiot, but if he was dying, I suppose I could set it all aside and let him have the final say.

The nurse pointed to a closed door. "I'm glad you're here. He wants to see you, and he was petrified you wouldn't come." She patted me on the shoulder and then quickly whispered she absolutely adored my music and that I was one of the bravest people she had ever met.

I felt like I was in a dream, or maybe it was nightmare. I guess the only way to find out was to see what was behind door number one. I took a deep breath and pushed the door open. In the bed was a man who resembled my father, or what was left of my father.

"Serena, if you're here to give me another once-over, I may…. Rylan."

"Hi, Dad."

"You look like shit, son," my dad said. "Grab a chair and sit down before you end up in the bed next to me."

I stared at the man in front of me. I was pretty sure it was my dad, but I needed clarification.

"Why?" I asked.

My dad chuckled. "Sit down, kid. I want to talk to you before I take the final bus ride, so sit your ass down because it's more comfortable than standing. And if you don't, I'll come back and haunt you."

"How drugged up are you?" I asked. There had been tons of weird moments in my life the past year, but this one was quickly closing in on the top spot.

"Not enough," my dad said, groaning as he moved. "Please."

The last word was almost a whisper, but it sounded like an explosion in my head. My dad used the word please sparingly. It was usually reserved for my mom when she was beyond pissed at him. I immediately moved the chair next to the bed and sat down, staring at the man who was claiming to be my dad.

"How did this happen?" I asked.

"Damned if I know," he said. He frowned and shifted his body, gritting his teeth as he moved.

"Kelli said it's pancreatic cancer," I said quietly.

"Yeah, bitch of a disease," he said. "Look, it was my idea not to tell you, so don't be angry with her. I didn't want to add to your stress level."

"Dad," I said and leaned back, staring at the ceiling.

"Do you love him?"

"What?" I said. I almost slipped off my chair, and my flight mode kicked into high gear.

"We could sit here and beat around the bush, but I don't have the time to waste. It's a simple question, Rylan. Do you love Jade?"

"Dad, please, this is crazy. Why would you ask me that?" I sighed and ran my fingers through my hair. "Fuck."

"Fine, I'll answer the question for you. I saw it in every gesture, every touch, and every look. He's it for you, just like your mother is for me."

For a brief moment, I considered lying to my dad and painting a picture of a happy life without Jade, but I didn't have the strength. I was too tired to lie.

"He *was*, Dad. *Was*, not is."

"You're lying, kid. You never were good at it." My dad licked his dry, cracked lips and grimaced. "I need some water."

There was a pitcher sitting on the bedside table along with a glass. I poured the water and handed it to my dad, who took it with a shaking hand.

"You shouldn't give up on him."

"It wasn't my choice, Dad."

"Son—"

"Dad," I interrupted, throwing my hands up. "Why are we talking about this? You made it perfectly clear, several times in fact and rather loudly, that you didn't think my choices were right. We haven't even talked since Mom's birthday party, and now I find out you're dying."

My dad made to hand the water back to me, but he quickly set it on his tray and grabbed my wrist. For a dying man, he was still strong. "I made a mistake, Rylan. I was wrong. I let my pride cloud my mind. I worried about what other people would think of me. How your choices would affect me. Stupid, really.

"All I want for you in this life is to be happy. Don't waste time on what other people think is right. You never have before. You've always stood up for your beliefs. You know what's right, and Jade is it for you. Fight for him."

I pulled my hand away and let my head fall against the railing of my dad's bed. I hadn't been prepared for any of this, but I sure as hell didn't expect to be discussing my failed love life with my dad.

The idea that my father recognized the depths of my feelings for Jade was unnerving. I didn't want to think about him or the music or what my life had become.

The tears came before I could stop them, and I felt stiff fingers slide through my hair, gently stroking. A few minutes later, I heard something I hadn't heard in years. My father quietly singing. And it wasn't just any song, it was the first song Jade and I had written together. I didn't think he would be interested enough to know all the words to a song I'd written with my ex-lover.

"You're a good man, Rylan, and you deserve to be happy."

"It's not that simple," I said. "You're right. I do deserve to be happy, but it's not going to be with Jade. He chose money and fame over me. Sometimes, I don't think he ever loved me."

My dad raised his eyebrows. This was now the weirdest moment of my entire life.

"Give me that laptop," my dad said, pointing at a computer sitting on a chair by the window.

I had no idea my dad even knew how to operate a computer, but when I handed it to him, he started hammering on the keyboard.

"You sure about that?" my dad asked. I had no idea what the man was talking about. Clearly, he had ingested more drugs than he had admitted.

"Dad, this is crazy and weird. Why are we talking about this?"

"Because it's important, and I want you to know that I'm damn proud of you for standing up for what you believe is right. I don't think I would have had the balls to give up the money."

I rubbed my temples and sighed. "It wasn't easy. I just couldn't do it anymore. Maggie figured it was slowly killing me."

"She's a great friend. You should keep her."

"I plan to," I said.

"Move closer. Have you ever seen what happened the night of the final concert?"

I gaped at my dad. He had the computer open to YouTube and some fan-made video of RheartJ. The fandom must have imploded. The fractured heart between our initials was still by most of the stuff online.

"Did you know you blew up Twitter and Tumblr after the concert?"

"No," I said. "I stayed away from the media."

"This is your mother's favorite one," my dad mumbled and pushed play.

"Dad, please, I don't want to watch it," I said.

He placed his hand over mine and squeezed. When the familiar chords from the guitar started, my gaze was drawn to the screen. It was the first song I had ever heard Jade sing. I'd been hiding in the dark, crouching outside Mrs. Morgan's window like a common stalker when he had sung "Can't Help Falling in Love." It was a lifetime ago, and with each strum of the strings, it felt like someone was shoving a knife into my heart.

"Oh God," I cried when I saw the montage of touches, the smiles, and the heart eyes the fans always giggled about. The camera cut to shots of us with our fake girlfriends on staged dates. Jade always watched closely when Maggie and I would whisper or stand too close to each other. I told him we were talking about him.

We'd try so hard during our concerts to stay away from each other, but some mysterious force always seemed to be pulling us together. A hand on the shoulder, a shy smile, and tiny shake of the head drove the fans of RheartJ crazy. I didn't mean to let my love show, but it was unavoidable.

The last frame of the video was of me telling the audience at Madison Square Garden that this was my final performance. I'd never seen the video of the concert.

About a month ago, Maggie tried to get me to watch it, but I told her I didn't need to see it. I'd lived it. That was enough. The camera closed in on Jade's face when I set the microphone down. His brown eyes were swimming in tears, and he swayed when I turned from him and jumped off the stage. The camera stayed focused on him. He grabbed the microphone and shouted into it, but there was no sound. Andy rushed at him and grabbed him around the waist, signaling to a security guard for help. They dragged Jade off the stage, kicking and screaming. The camera cut back to the microphone and the stool. The spotlight was still shining brightly.

"Nice touch," my dad said, pointing at the microphone.

"Yeah, I figured I'd go out with a bang. Isn't that what you're supposed to do when you retire? I think I saw a hockey player leave his skates and stick in the middle of the ice after his last game."

"Have you talked to Jade?" my dad asked.

"No," I said. "Last I overheard, he was in the studio recording his solo album."

Dad punched more keys and brought up another video.

"I don't want to see anymore," I whined.

"This is a close-up of Jade yelling into the microphone. You know, you have some crazy fans."

The picture was really grainy from all the enlargements. I watched Jade's mouth move and he seemed to be screaming my name. The movement slowed more and the words slithered across the screen.

I love you. I love you. I love you.

My dad closed the computer, and we sat in silence. I didn't know what to do with this information. Jade could have been shouting fuck off, but it sure looked like he was yelling I love you.

"Are you going to hang around for a few days?" my dad asked. "I'm getting out of here and heading back to the farm."

He didn't need to elaborate. I knew he meant he was going home to die.

"Sure," I said. "Hey, Dad, can I call Maggie?"

"I think Kelli would like to see her, and I'd like to talk to her too." My dad sighed, and his face pinched with pain. "Can you get Serena and your mom for me?"

"Sure, Dad," I said.

I had my hand on the door when my dad whispered four words I never thought I would hear from him.

"I love you, Rylan."

The air left my lungs. "I love you too, Dad," I choked out, and shoved the door open, before I started bawling.

Serena was waiting right outside the door. "Are you okay, Rylan?"

"I don't know," I answered truthfully. "He wants you."

She brushed by me and disappeared into my dad's room. I stumbled blindly down the hall to find my mom.

"Mom," I said. "Dad needs you."

"Oh, Rylan, I'm so sorry for everything," she said, clutching me in a hug so tight she squeezed all the air out of my lungs.

"Mom," I gasped. "You're choking me."

She released me, and I panted for air. She looked torn, glancing down the hall and back at me. "Mom, go. I'm sticking around. Dad said I could call Maggie."

She nodded and smiled at me, before rushing down the hall.

"Lucas and a hospice nurse went home to get things ready for Dad. It's mainly about keeping his pain under control," Kelli said.

I sat down next to her and sighed, placing my head on her shoulders. "This has been one fucked-up year."

"Have you talked to him?"

"No. You?"

"No."

"I need to call Maggie."

"I already did. She'll be here tomorrow."

"Thank you," I said quietly.

IT WAS weird being back on the farm, but bearable with Maggie there. Once again, she put her life aside and came when I called.

Even though Dad was sick, life on the farm didn't stop. The crops were ready to be harvested, and Dad's friends and fellow farmers rallied around our family to help get the crops off the fields. I helped Lucas as best I could. Maggie learned how to drive the combine and stopped in the middle of the field to dance and pump her fists in the air. She was contagious, and her happiness spread like a virus.

My mother adored her and she won over my dad when she raved about his combine. She also made a mean chocolate chip cookie and could bring a smile to my face when all I wanted to do was frown.

"Why do you have so many tattoos?" my mom asked her one evening.

"They tell my story," Maggie said. "Some help me remember how far I've come. Some of them remind me to believe in myself when I don't think I have it in me to move forward. And some are just there because I needed them at the time."

"Did they hurt?" my mom asked.

"Some of them did," Maggie said. "In more ways than one."

My mom reached across the table and touched Maggie's wrist, tracing the words *I Regret Nothing* that adorned her skin.

"I think I'd like to get one," my mom said.

I coughed, and my brother looked like a dying fish gasping for air. My sister smiled, and my dad nodded.

"Then damn it, Kimberly, you should get one," my dad said.

"Will you help me pick something out, Davis?"

"Whatever you want, dear," my dad answered. "Rylan."

"Yeah, Dad?" I held my breath, wondering if he was going to ask me to take my mother to a tattoo parlor.

"I'd like to go for a ride out to the field."

"You do realize it's night," I said.

"Yep. It's a full moon, a harvest moon to be exact. I need to breathe the fresh air. It's getting a little stale in here."

I glanced at Serena, who was sitting in the corner reading a book. She looked up at me and nodded.

"Okay," I said, grabbing the keys.

"Not the pickup. Let's drive the tractor and bring that guitar of yours."

Serena quietly laid her book aside, gathered a few things, and pushed my dad outside. I had no idea how we were going to get him up into the cab. In the last few days, he'd gotten so weak he could barely walk more than two steps. But if Serena and my dad were determined, it would get done.

"Lovely evening," Serena said. We both silently agreed with her.

It was one of those summer nights that inspire poets to compose thousand word poems. People who lived in the city never saw the night sky filled with a million twinkling stars. The lights and pollution usually obscured the view. And honestly, most people never took the time to look. But out here, the details were on display and demanded to be seen.

The round moon hanging over the field cast its silver light over the land and lit up the swaying grass. The crickets sang and the occasional mournful howl of a coyote punctured the silence of the evening.

"I'll be right back," I said, heading to the shed to get the tractor. Serena nodded and kept walking toward the field. I paused for a few seconds, watching as they inched forward. My dad squeezed the arms of his wheelchair so hard his knuckles turned white. The pain gripped his body and wouldn't let go. I wanted to ease his suffering, but there was nothing I could do. It made my chest ache.

I sprinted across the yard, trying to outrun the sadness that hung in the air. In the darkness of the shed, I leaned against the tractor wheel for a few minutes to compose myself. My dad didn't need to see me fall apart, but it was hard watching a person fade away right in front of your face.

The roar of the tractor erased the quiet of the evening. The noise filled my head, temporarily drowning out the thoughts of death and sorrow.

"Do you want to drive?" I shouted at my dad over the rumble of the engine.

"No," my dad said. "You've got it."

It was a struggle for him to climb up the ladder, but we finally got him situated in the cab. Serena handed my dad a blanket and told him to put it over his legs.

"It's nice tonight," he said, scowling at her. They had a silent war of wills, but in the end, he did as he was told. Serena patted his knee and set a wire bound book down on his lap. We watched her jump down from the cab. Instead of walking back to the house, she collapsed in the wheelchair and stared across the field. She looked exhausted. The tractor rolled forward, and we were off.

"Do you hear it?" my dad asked.

"Yeah, Dad, I hear it," I answered. How could you not hear it? Tractors were loud.

My dad chuckled. "Not the tractor. Time."

"Time? Time makes a noise?"

"Before I got sick, I didn't notice it. The only moment we ever acknowledged the passage of time was when we celebrated a birthday, attended a New Year's Eve party, or some other day we set aside to remember the past.

"When I got the diagnosis, I started to pay attention to time. At first, it was a tiny ticking sound, barely audible, but as I got sicker and the diagnosis more dire, the sound got louder. Tonight, time sounds like a bell tolling."

I stopped the tractor in the middle of the field and stared at him. "Dad?"

"My time here is almost over, Rylan. I think the clock ticks louder the closer you are to death. I know it's a tired cliché, but time is a gift that we shouldn't waste. Don't waste your time being angry. There are so many things we can't control, and being angry isn't going to change anything."

"I'll try, Dad," I said. It was all I could give him, because I was angry with a lot of things. I was pissed that it took a fucking fatal illness to bring my dad and me together. I was angry with myself for believing in love and all that other shit. But now was not the time to dwell on my problems. This time was for my dad.

He leaned against the window and stared across the land. I'd never truly understood what my dad found so attractive about the whole farming thing, but tonight, as I watched him, his love for the land was etched in the lines of his face.

He asked me to drive around the field so he could memorize the feel of the tractor moving over the land he had tended for so many years.

We didn't talk much until the faint rays of light hit the horizon. I parked the tractor so we would have a great view of the sun kissing the land as it rose to signal the start of another day.

"You doing okay, Dad?" I asked.

He fiddled with the book for a few minutes and then handed it to me.

"I know I don't have the right to ask you," he said. "But since I'm dying, I'm bold. I would like to ask for your forgiveness."

Hearing him say the words out loud made my heart hurt.

"Open it," he said, gesturing to the book.

The first page had my full name written in silver script along with my birth date.

"Dad," I gasped as I flipped through the pages of the book. It was filled with pictures of me from an infant to toddler to brooding high school student. He ran his finger over a picture of me leaning against a fence. It was the day after Jesse had told me he didn't want to see me anymore. He couldn't risk people finding out about us. His image was more important to him than I was.

"I am your dad. I should have supported you and helped you cope with all the bullshit people threw at you."

I turned the page and saw more recent photos of me. Maggie must have given him some of her pictures. And then we moved to my music career. Pictures and articles and ticket stubs filled page after page.

"Where did you get these?" I asked. There were ten different ticket stubs from various cities and they all had been used.

"Your mother and I attended quite a few of your performances when we could get there."

"You hate the city," I said. "And crowds."

"But we wanted to see you, and it was the only way," my dad said. "Your mother and I knew you weren't ready to talk to us, and we didn't know how to ask for your forgiveness."

The idea that my parents had been in the audience watching me perform was overwhelming. I couldn't stop the tears that filled my eyes.

"Did you like the shows?" I choked.

My dad snorted. "We are so proud of you, and not because you're some famous pop star, but because you're a good person."

"I forgive you," I whimpered and reached across to hug the man.

"Thank you," he whispered into my hair. I felt a gigantic weight lift off my shoulders as I let go of years of anger. We couldn't change the past, but we could learn from our mistakes and let them go.

"Play for me," he whispered.

I played until the sun rose over the horizon and filled the dark sky with vibrant colors. When I stilled the strings of the guitar, the birds took over, filling the world with a happy song. A lone hawk circled the field, looking for breakfast. We watched the bird swoop down, skimming the land until it soared into the sky with a mouse clutched in its talons.

"The circle of life," my dad said. "Take me home, Rylan."

MY DAD died two days later.

CHAPTER TWELVE

FUNERALS IN my hometown were a huge deal. They were treated like social events where everyone cooked and baked enough food to feed half the county. My dad had been very clear with his funeral orders. A short church service, and after, everyone was to go to the farm and celebrate, not hole up in the basement of the church and sip lukewarm coffee. The food and drink would be served at the farm in the open air.

The church was filled to capacity, with more people milling around outside. My mother passed the word around town that if anyone approached me for an autograph or to say something vile, she would let Maggie take care of matters. When Dave and his family showed up, he volunteered to keep the crowds in order. He'd protected me for over a year; he wasn't about to stop now.

"You doing okay?" Dave asked.

I shrugged and let the man pull me into a bear hug. I wanted to ask if he still worked for Jade or if he knew anything about him, but I couldn't bring myself to ask. It would hurt too much if I knew he was doing well.

Most people were incredibly polite, offering condolences and then scurrying off to talk to other people. Maggie played her part wonderfully, chasing everyone away who lingered too long. Kelli and Lucas hovered nearby and watched my mother make her way through the crowds. Dave told me I was well protected.

There were generic comments about how lovely the service was and a lot of comments on the use of wheat instead of flowers to decorate the church. My dad was cremated, so we didn't have to form a line and stare at him in a casket. He said he wanted to be part of the land, not stuck in some fucking hole. His words, not mine.

After the service, we headed back to the farm to get ready for the celebration of my dad's life. I just wanted a fucking drink and some quiet for five minutes.

That stupid giant tent was set up in the backyard again. I found Lucas standing by the bar, staring into the bright blue sky. There was a small stage set up, and I wondered if someone was going to play or if a DJ was coming to entertain us.

"Hey," I said and patted Lucas on the back. "You doing okay?"

"Yeah. I'm fine. I'm sick of people telling me they're sorry for my loss and all the other awkward shit people say when someone dies. But, I'm good. What about you?"

Now that was the question of the moment. I had no idea. "Don't know?"

"What are you going to do?" Lucas asked.

I hadn't even asked myself that question. Before I got that phone call, I'd told Maggie I was going back to school, but now, I didn't know what the fuck was expected of me.

"I suppose I could hang out here for a while."

"Rylan," Lucas said. "It's not that I don't appreciate the help, but this isn't the life for you. You're meant for more."

"But…." Lucas didn't let me interrupt.

"You know, I actually like farming. I like the freedom of being my own boss, and the wide-open spaces of the country. The city makes me feel like I'm suffocating."

"That's what I feel like when I'm here," I admitted.

"Go back to Chicago or Los Angeles or New York or wherever it is you need to be happy," Lucas said. "I have Mom and Kate, and soon I'll have a son to drive me insane."

I smiled when I realized the boy I'd known as my brother no longer existed.

"Thanks, Lucas. And congratulations. You have a cool fiancé, and I'm sure you're going to be a great dad."

"You think so? I'm a little nervous about the whole dad thing," Lucas said.

"I know so," I said. "We better finish setting up before Mom comes out and shouts at us for messing around."

Lucas smiled and pulled me into a tight hug. "I love you, baby brother."

"Yeah, I love you too," I mumbled. This marked the first time Lucas had hugged me since I was seven years old and my favorite cat had died. I'd hid in the shed and Lucas found me crying my head off. He sat down and hugged me, telling me it was okay to feel bad, but it was her time to leave this earth. It was the way things were. Everything dies. It's how life works. I was thankful for his honesty, but it still hurt.

"Uh, Rylan," Lucas whispered. "Jesse Channing is headed our way. Do you want me to run interference?"

The fact that he said he would stand up for me was mind blowing. I stared at him and he nodded.

"How?" I asked.

"I put two and two together when Kelli told me about your reaction to him being at Mom's birthday party. And I heard him shouting at his wife about you."

"Oh," I answered.

"Rylan, I've always known, and I should have stood up for you. You were only a kid trying to figure out where you belonged, and we certainly made it clear that you didn't belong here. I'm so sorry."

"I forgive you," I said.

"You don't have to do that," Lucas said. "I don't deserve it."

"Yes, you do."

"Thank you," Lucas said, hugging me again. "Offer still stands."

"Thanks, but I'm okay," I said. "Could you stick close, though? Just in case."

He nodded and walked behind the bar, then moved the glasses around and inspected the labels of the liquor bottles.

I allowed myself to watch Jesse as he neared me. His cheeks were flushed, and his blue eyes were guarded. He kept fiddling with his dark hair, which if I remembered correctly, was a nervous habit.

He stopped a few feet away, unsure if he was allowed to come any closer.

I gave him a small nod, and he closed the gap.

"Hi, Rylan," Jesse said carefully.

"Hi, Jesse," I answered.

"I'm sorry about your dad." Jesse closed his eyes and sighed. "And... shit." He sighed. "I'm sorry for hurting you. It was a huge mistake to let you go, and I'll have to live with it for the rest of my life."

I touched his hand, and his eyes snapped open.

"You hurt me, Jesse, but it's in the past, and I'm tired of being mad at everyone. I forgive you," I said.

There was an awkward silence for a few seconds before I let him put his arms around me. Memories of tender touches and sweet teenage kisses floated through my head. When he let go of me, I could see tears dripping down his cheeks. I smiled, and he walked away from me.

"You okay?" Lucas asked.

"Sort of numb," I answered.

Lucas patted my back. "Here comes the inspector general."

I chuckled and watched as my mother approached us. She looked sad, but I was pretty sure she was going to be okay.

"Lucas," my mom said. "Kate is waiting for you in the house."

Lucas let go of me and walked away, leaving me alone with my mom.

"Come walk with me," she said. She took my hand, and we walked to the edge of the newly combined wheat field. The stalks crunched under our feet. "I'm going to miss your father."

"Me too," I said, and I meant it. Over the past few weeks, he had let me into his life, and I had shared mine with him.

She ruffled my hair. "You're a good man, Rylan, and I'm proud of you. We didn't say it enough when you were growing up, and I'm so sorry for not being available to you when things weren't good."

I placed my head on her shoulder and sighed. She dug in her jacket pocket and pulled out a slip of paper. She carefully unfolded it and smoothed out the wrinkles. I stared at the familiar scrawl of my dad's handwriting.

Don't hide from your talent. The world deserves to hear you.

"He's right, Rylan. I know it doesn't seem like it right now, but you need to find your place in the world, and hiding in this small town isn't for you." She took a deep breath. "You can talk to me about anything. I know you're hurt and sad and confused, and nothing I say will make it better."

"Mom," I said and leaned against her. She put her arms around me and held me, rubbing my back while I sobbed on her shoulder. "I hurt everywhere."

"I know," she said, and she did know. The haunted look I carried in my eyes was in hers as well. She'd lost her partner, her lover, her friend, just like I had lost mine. Only Dad was permanently gone; Jade was still wandering the earth.

Noise from across the field caught our attention. We heard car doors slamming and low murmurs of conversation drifted through the air. People were mingling around the yard. "You ready?" my mom asked as she laced her fingers with mine.

I wasn't anywhere near ready, but I nodded. I'd become an expert at lying.

As we got closer to the tent, my mom stopped. "Would you sing for me?"

"Right now?"

"Yes," she said.

"I might need a drink to get through it," I said.

My mom nodded, and we went over to the bar. I was surprised at the amount of people who were gathering near the stage. I caught a glimpse of brown sun-kissed hair and frowned. It was nothing new. I thought I saw him everywhere. Maggie and I had started calling my random sightings echoes.

People cleared a path so we were able to get to the bar. Lucas was standing there with his very pregnant wife. My mom waved at Kelli and Maggie to come over.

"Tequila," she said to my brother. He put up four shot glasses and poured the liquor.

"Do you want lime and salt?" my brother asked.

My mom shook her head. "I'm doing the first shot alone," she said. She took her glass and stared at it for a few seconds. I saw her lips move, silently telling Dad she loved him. She tossed her head back and sucked the drink down, then slammed the empty glass on the bar for my brother to refill.

"To Dad," I said. Kelli and Lucas repeated my words, and we drank. I set the glass down and looked at my mom.

"To family," she said and drank her second shot.

"Hit me again," I said to Lucas. "And fill another glass."

Maggie had backed away from us, but I waved her over and handed her a shot glass. Her eyes were swimming with tears. "Without you," I said, staring straight at her, "I don't think I would have survived this past year. To you, my friend."

"To you, Rylan," Maggie whispered.

"To us," I said.

"To us," she repeated. We clinked glasses and drank.

"My mom wants me to sing," I said. "Will you come up with me? I don't think I can be up there alone. There's always been someone with me."

She put her arm around me. "I'll be there for you."

I reached for Kelli and both women walked with me to the small stage. Someone had set up a microphone, along with a keyboard. There was also a guitar leaning against a chair. Kelli and Maggie wrapped me in their arms.

"I don't know if I can do this," I murmured. I hadn't played any music since Madison Square Garden. The only thing I'd done was write "Echoes of Us," and I didn't know if I could sing that song. It might destroy me.

My mom was standing up at the microphone, and the crowd quieted.

"I am humbled by the outpouring of support for me and my family. Davis would think you were all crazy for shutting down harvest today, but I'm glad you did," she said. The audience laughed. "My son, Rylan, is going to grace us with some music."

"You'll be fine," Maggie said. "Go." She gave me a push toward my mother and her outstretched arms.

Mom walked me over to the keyboard and kissed me on the cheek. I bit my lip and stared at the guitar.

"Uh," I said into the microphone. "Thanks for coming. My dad is the only person who's ever heard this song. He insisted I share it with you. You're going to have to bear with me, though, because I'm not really a solo act. I've always had someone up here with me, but I guess it's time to learn to stand on my own.

"This is called 'Echoes of Us.'"

I poked at the keys, playing a few notes. I had to start over three times before I could get the first line out of my mouth. It made my entire body ache.

Standing here all alone
In a place we used to share
You are everywhere, everywhere
Your voice fills my head
But it's fading fast
Slipping through my outstretched hands
Like an echo dying
Echoes of us, Echoes of us

I frowned and stopped playing, lowering my head. Tears dripped on the keys. "I can't do this. I'm sorry. I'm not a solo act. I never wanted to let him go, but I had no choice."

There was a loud gasp from the audience, and I felt a warm hand on my shoulder. "I'm sorry," I choked.

"Me too," the voice whispered.

The whisper wrapped around my heart, and I was scared to turn around. It was possible I'd finally stepped off the deep end.

I squeezed my eyes shut and bit my lip, willing myself to turn around. He looked real. His hair was slightly darker and a little longer. Those beautiful brown eyes stared back at me with an intensity that made my toes curl.

"Jade," I whispered.

"Rylan," he said. He reached out and moved my hair away from my eyes.

"What are you doing here?"

"I'm hoping it's where I belong," he said.

"Kiss the boy," someone yelled. It sounded like Mrs. Morgan. "I didn't come all this way for a sad ending. I demand my happily ever after."

"Is that Mrs. Morgan?" I asked.

"I went home and you weren't there," Jade said. "Mrs. Morgan hollered at me for about forty-five minutes before she told me what happened."

"You deserved to be shouted at," I said.

"I'll never let you go again. Not for anyone or anything," Jade said.

"You promise," I whispered.

"Always," he said. He touched my wrist, then dug into the pocket of his jeans and pulled out my infinity bracelet. "I had it fixed."

I let him put it on my wrist.

"That was a beautiful song you were singing," Jade said.

"I wrote it for you," I said.

"I don't want to be an echo anymore," Jade said.

I turned away from him and stared at the bright blue sky. It reminded me of the day my dad died. There wasn't a cloud in the sky, and you could see for miles in all directions. Sometimes I wished I could see my life as clearly as I could see the land in front of me. My gaze settled on Jade, and my dad's words came back.

He is it for you, like your mother is for me.

"I won't be your dirty secret anymore," I whispered.

"Does that mean you want to try?" His voice trembled, and I could see his hand shaking.

"I'm scared," I said truthfully.

Jade took a step closer to me. I resisted the urge to put up my walls, and held my ground. He slowly raised his hand, letting his fingers graze my cheek, trailing down my jaw until he traced my lips.

"Can I show you something?" Jade asked.

I nodded, and he rolled up his sleeve, revealing his tribal tattoo circling his bicep. In the middle of his arm, dripping off the tattoo, was the heart. Only now, there were two letters surrounding the heart. JheartR.

I bit my lip and raised my shirt, exposing my heart tattoo. It was now RheartJ with the infinity symbol embracing the initials.

"Nice," Jade said, tracing the infinity symbol. His touch sent shocks racing through my body.

"I went to the tattoo parlor with my mom after Dad died. I had this added while she got her own tattoo."

"Rylan," Jade said.

"Hmmm," I said.

"I never stopped loving you," he said.

"I tried to stop," I said. "It wasn't good, Jade."

"I would like to kiss you," he said. "I mean, if you'll let me. I mean, you know, Mrs. Morgan deserves a happy ending. It was a long fucking drive."

"Shut up, Jade," I muttered and pressed my lips against him.

I was home.

The crowd roared, and Mrs. Morgan wolf whistled. When I opened my eyes, members of our band were filing up to the stage. Ella waved and blew me a kiss. Ms. Diaz was talking to my mom and Serena. She had on a gold sparkly hat with a silver blouse and gold billowing skirt. She glowed in the sunshine.

Trevor jumped on the stage and bear-hugged me. "Great to see you, man," he said. "After the party, I want to talk to you and Jade about signing with me."

"With you?"

"Yeah, I'm breaking out on my own, and I would like to sign you two," he said, grinning at me. "The real you."

I grabbed him and gave him a real hug. I felt more people hugging me and turned around to see Ethan, Jens, and Brody grinning at me.

"God, I've missed you guys," I said.

It was the best group hug I'd ever received.

There was noise up on the stage. Brent and Dave were helping some other guys set up equipment.

"Shall we jam?" Ethan asked.

"I'd fucking love to," I shouted and grabbed Jade, dragging him to the microphone. "This is Jade, and I'm Rylan. Hang around and we'll blow your panties off."

Mrs. Morgan pumped her fist in the air. My mother put her fingers in her mouth and whistled. Mrs. Morgan knuckle bumped her.

We played until the sun touched the ground and set the sky on fire. When everyone had finally cleared out and it was just my friends and family, I stood next to Jade and watched as the darkness settled and the stars slowly came to life.

I smiled at my sister and brother. Kelli dropped to her knees and lay back on the ground. Lucas followed suit, pulling his very pregnant wife with him.

I smiled at Mrs. Morgan, who grinned at my mother. Soon everyone was flat on their backs, staring up at the sky. Jade laced his fingers with mine and we joined everyone.

"This is magnificent," Mrs. Morgan said.

A star shot across the sky. "Make a wish," Jade whispered.

"Don't have to," I said. "It already came true."

TEEGAN LOY began writing a long time ago. Notebooks filled with ideas were stacked around the house. One day, she sat down with renewed ambition and something fantastic happened: she completed a story. Now most of her time is spent writing, but she takes an occasional break to go to the movies, where she imagines her stories on the big screen. She also enjoys watching hockey, filling her iPod with music, and driving her daughter around town to various activities.

You can find Teegan at the following:

Twitter: @TeeganLoy

Facebook: https://www.facebook.com/teegan.loy

Her blog: http://teeganloy.wordpress.com

Or you can e-mail her at teeganloy@gmail.com.

CPSIA information can be obtained at www.ICGtesting.com
Printed in the USA
LVOW11s1951091113

360664LV00001B/20/P